A SURPRISING DEVELOPMENT

"I heard my mother visited you yesterday," Jordan said, turning her toward him and pulling his coat more securely around her.

So this was why he wanted them to be alone, thought Nicole. He would, no doubt, ring a peal over her head for speaking to his mother as she had. But why take her on a picnic? Why be so courteous and complimentary, if his intent was to chastise her? Nicole did not know the answers, but she was determined not to be intimidated.

"She did, but it wasn't by invitation," she said deliberately.

An unexpected smile curved his lips. "I never thought it was." He ran his hands up the lapels of the coat and over her shoulders, letting them rest on her upper arms.

"I practically threw her out."

"She probably deserved it," he said, still smiling.

"She called me a lightskirt and a witch."

"I know you're not the one, but I'm uncertain about the other," he remarked in an amused tone. He placed a finger under her chin and tilted her head upward until she met his gaze. He touched his lips to her forehead, then the tip of her nose, and finally her lips, leaving them there long enough to remind her of what they had once shared.

Nicole almost purred beneath his touch. Her defenses were falling, and she was glad he wasn't the mind reader in the family.

DANGEROUS GAMES   (0-7860-0270-0, $4.99)
by Amanda Scott

When Nicholas Barrington, eldest son of the Earl of Ul-
combe, first met Melissa Seacort, the desperation he
sensed beneath her well-bred beauty haunted him. He
didn't realize how desperate Melissa really was . . . until
he found her again at a Newmarket gambling club—being auctioned off by her father to the highest bidder. So,
Nick bought himself a wife. With a villain hot on their
heels, and a fortune and their lives at stake, they would
gamble everything on the most dangerous game of all:
love.

A TOUCH OF PARADISE   (0-7860-0271-9, $4.99)
by Alexa Smart

As a confidence man and scam runner in 1880s America,
Malcolm Northrup has amassed a fortune. Now, posing
as the eminent Sir John Abbot—scholar, and possible
discoverer of the lost continent of Atlantis—he's taking
his act on the road with a lecture tour, seeking funds for
a scientific experiment he has no intention of making.
But scholar Halia Davenport is determined to accompany
Malcolm on his "expedition" . . . even if she must kidnap
him!

*Available wherever paperbacks are sold, or order direct from the
Publisher. Send cover price plus 50¢ per copy for mailing and
handling to Kensington Publishing Corp., Consumer Orders,
or call (toll free) 888-345-BOOK, to place your order using
Mastercard or Visa. Residents of New York and Tennessee
must include sales tax. DO NOT SEND CASH.*

The Willful Wife

Alana Clayton

Zebra Books
Kensington Publishing Corp.
http://www.zebrabooks.com

ZEBRA BOOKS are published by

Kensington Publishing Corp.
850 Third Avenue
New York, NY 10022

First Printing: March, 1998
10 9 8 7 6 5 4 3 2 1

Printed in the United States of America

For my absolutely wonderful
brother-in-law
JOHN BREADEN
who has always galloped to my rescue.

*A village on the road
from London to Dover*

The rapid tattoo of hoofbeats reverberated in her mind. He was getting closer and she yearned to do as she had done for the past seven years: pack her belongings and travel as far and as fast as she could.

Instead, she forced herself to remain seated. It was time to stop running, time to face him and their past so that she could live her life in a normal manner once again.

It would be good to hear her real name spoken, good to see her old friends. She hoped they had not forgotten her during her absence.

A horse snorted, saddle leather creaked, and bits jangled, interrupting her thoughts. She closed her eyes and concentrated; the horses were carrying him and his friend nearer. His presence was much stronger; she could almost feel his heart beat, just as it had once beat against hers. She remembered, all too well, the scent and feel of him, how she reveled in their intimacies. But, little by little, the closeness that made them one had been destroyed by forces she had not fully understood, and had been too innocent to cope with.

The situation would be different now, she vowed. She had matured during their years of separation, and she would not be easily intimidated by him or those around him.

She took several deep breaths to compose herself, brushing aside the bit of last minute self-doubt.

The hoofbeats were louder now. Squeezing her eyes tightly

closed, she saw two men on horseback enter the village. They stopped to speak to an old man enjoying the warmth of the sun, then turned their horses in her direction. She watched as they approached and dismounted in front of her house. It was too late to reconsider; a knock sounded at the door and she opened her eyes—he was here.

One

"I always considered you a reasonable man, Drew."

"Like to think I am."

"Then why are we on our way to see a . . . a fortune-teller?"

"Mrs. Leighton's not exactly a fortune-teller, Jordan. Not like a gypsy, if that's what you mean."

"Then what exactly is she?"

"Don't know how to explain it. She just knows things. Have a friend, Quinton Courtney, who married Claire Kingsley, a woman with the same ability. Little off-putting at first, wondering if she knew what I was thinking, but she assured me she didn't intrude unless asked."

Jordan looked at his friend as if he had two heads. But he still looked the same. His unruly sandy hair verged on red, and light freckles scattered across a slightly crooked nose that had been broken more than once. As usual, his face wore a good-natured smile, which had caused many men to underestimate the intelligence it hid. And, at present, Jordan wondered whether he should also question Drew's intellect.

"You mean you actually believe this nonsense?"

"Believe what I see with my own eyes. If one woman has the power to see what I can't, stands to reason there might be others. Heard from reliable sources Mrs. Leighton's one of them."

"So we're to visit a miserable, dark hovel and talk to a woman who, no doubt, consults a crystal ball." Jordan made a sound of disgust. "First she'll take your money, then she'll spout a bunch of nonsense, and you'll be no closer to finding your jewelry."

"Perhaps not. Perhaps we'll both be surprised," Drew responded calmly.

The house, when they found it, was not the hovel Jordan had predicted. It was of moderate size and well-kept, with a garden of riotous blooms surrounding it.

A maid, with a white apron covering her gray dress, took Drew's card and left them standing on the step while she determined whether her mistress was at home. She soon returned and they followed her into the house.

The woman was standing and staring out one of the tall windows when they entered the parlor.

"Mrs. Leighton?" said Drew.

She turned, and light streamed in around her, leaving her face in relative shadow. "Yes."

"I'm Andrew, Viscount Stanford, madam. You were recommended by several friends who said you might be able to help me find something that's gone missing."

She took a few steps forward and Jordan's breath caught in his throat at the sight of her face. His heart beat rapidly, there was a roaring in his ears and, for the first time in his life, he thought he might swoon.

"It's true, I've been able to assist some people, my lord. But you must understand, I can't promise success."

"Understand completely, Mrs. Leighton, but would still like to try if you're willing."

"As long as you don't expect miracles, my lord. Shall we be seated, gentlemen?"

"My apologies, madam. Forgot my manners. May I present Mr. Jordan Worth, friend of mine."

Mrs. Leighton's gaze met his. Jordan expected a spark of recognition to widen her dark brown eyes, and perhaps an exclamation of surprise to fall from her lips. But not the slightest trace of astonishment crossed her face.

"Mr. Worth," she acknowledged with a cool nod of her head before settling herself in a chair.

He was wrong, thought Jordan, drowning in indecision. Surely, if this were Nicole, she would not be able to address him with such composure. Perhaps, he thought as he indulged in fancy, she was a twin he had never heard of. Or she truly was Nicole, but had suffered an accident which left her with no memory of him. Bah! He was beginning to think like someone in one of those lurid novels that young girls read. This woman merely strongly resembled Nicole, he reasoned, and he had been unfortunate enough to stumble upon her. Yes, that had to be it.

"Would you care for refreshments?" Mrs. Leighton asked once they were seated.

Jordan had been grateful to get off his shaky legs, and had yet to find his tongue after the shock of seeing such a near likeness of Nicole.

"No, thank you," replied Drew. "Don't want to keep you long."

"Then, tell me what it is you're searching for," Mrs. Leighton said.

"There was a burglary at my home a fortnight ago," began Drew. "Took some of the family jewels. Like to have them all back, of course, but there's one piece—a ruby and diamond ring—that is especially important."

"It's the family betrothal ring, and there's a certain young lady you'd like to offer it to," added Nicole.

Andrew blushed slightly. "That's true. Do you think you can help?"

"I'll certainly try, my lord. Let's go into another room where I can concentrate better," she suggested, rising. "I hope you will excuse us, Mr. Worth."

Jordan nodded, his hands clenched tightly on the chair arms, and watched closely as she moved gracefully out of the room. When Mrs. Leighton had turned to him a moment before, he had been able to see the right side of her face. At the corner of her lips was a small black dot which he had always called a beauty mark. Nicole claimed that every woman in her family who had the gift of second sight also bore the mark.

Mrs. Leighton was not the widow she claimed to be. She was his wife, Nicole, who had been missing nearly seven years.

But if she was Nicole, why had she not been shocked at his sudden appearance on her doorstep? After all, she had left him, slipping out while he was away from home. She had changed her name and hidden from him for the past seven years, so she should have been the one to grow faint at their meeting.

But she had been as cool as a professional gambler holding a winning hand. There had not been the slightest bit of recognition in her dark eyes, nor the faintest blush of pink on her cheeks to indicate they were more than strangers meeting for the first time.

Nicole had blushed often when they first met, he remembered. She had just made her come-out and was unaccustomed to attention from a gentleman. They had fallen in love and married quickly, unwilling to endure a long betrothal with the passion that blazed between them each time they were together.

Then, suddenly, she was gone and, despite their problems, he had missed her more than he thought possible. For the first few weeks, he had been a madman—scouring London and riding over the countryside, night and day, searching relentlessly and futilely for his wife. But Nicole had disappeared completely.

After a time, his frantic state of mind turned to one of sheer determination. For the next four years he had searched diligently, employing Bow Street runners and others renowned for their skill at finding missing persons. He offered rewards and followed every lead, but by the time he reached the vicinity where a woman answering Nicole's description had been reported, she was gone.

After four years, he had given up and accepted the fact that Nicole had either left the country or was dead. He hoped that she had gone to America or Canada, for he would hate to think she was lying in a grave somewhere with no one to mourn for her.

The door opened, pulling Jordan from his reverie. Mrs. Leighton and Drew entered. From the look on his friend's face, Jordan concluded the meeting had not been successful.

"Mrs. Leighton is unable to tell me where the jewelry is or who took it," he informed Jordan.

"I'm sorry to disappoint you," she said. "Perhaps if I had been able to visit the room where the theft occurred I could tell you more, but, even then, I might see nothing. I warned you that this is an unpredictable talent."

"To be sure, madam. Not blaming you in the least. Would like to invite you to my home. My aunt's in residence. Look at the room, stay and enjoy town life for a time, no matter what the outcome."

"How generous, Viscount Stanford," she said sincerely. "I don't know whether I'll be able to do that, but I'll give it some thought."

"We're traveling to the coast. Will be back this way in a fortnight or so. Will stop for your reply, if you have no objection."

"I have no objection at all," replied Mrs. Leighton, smiling fondly at Drew.

Jordan stepped forward. "I wonder if I might have a private word with you, madam. You see, I've also lost something and wonder if you might help me find it."

She hesitated a moment. Her answer would determine the rest of her life.

"It's been some time ago," he continued, his eyes daring her to accept his challenge. "Just two months short of seven years, to be exact. I don't know if your powers are strong enough to see back that far."

"Why don't we find out, Mr. Worth," she replied coolly, and led the way out of the room, her back stiff and her shoulders squared.

When they were alone, Jordan stared at her, the silence lengthening far beyond what society would call polite.

Nicole stood her ground without flinching. When they were first married, one of his looks could easily reduce her to tears. Now she returned his gaze with aplomb, without a trace of a tremble.

Jordan still could not believe his eyes. The woman standing before him was more slender than Nicole had been when he had last seen her, and she carried herself with a great deal more confidence. Her face was slimmer, her cheekbones more prominent, and her dark eyes even more arresting than they were in her youth. Her hair, dark and gleaming, was drawn back, displaying her aristocratic bone structure to best advantage. Jordan was forced to admit that she was a lovely woman, no matter what her real identity.

"I am almost certain, but I must ask. Are you Nicole?"

Her pause tested Jordan's control, but he finally heard the truth.

"Yes." The reply was succinct, and given with no explanation.

Her calmness mocked his chaotic thoughts, and Jordan fought to subdue the anger and relief that flooded him. "Then there is nothing wrong with your mind," he stated.

"My mind is in perfect order, Jordan. It always has been, despite what you believed during our marriage."

"I never accused you of having lost your wits," he barked.

"But you thought it," she shot back.

He ignored her accusation. There were things he needed to know and he would not be caught up in petty bickering.

"Do you realize what you have put me through?" he asked between clenched teeth.

"I have a vague idea."

"Your disappearance nearly drove me mad. I searched for four years without finding a trace of you. I didn't know whether you were living or dead."

She remained collected in the face of his anger. "I've been quite well."

"Dammit! I can see that. What I want to know is why? Why did you leave without saying where you were going? My God,

Nicole! If you had wanted to get away, you could have gone to the country estate. I wouldn't have bothered you if that was what you wished."

"I doubt that, Jordan. It isn't in your nature to leave me alone or you would have already walked out the door."

"I'm curious, as any man would be whose wife has left him without cause."

"Without cause in your mind perhaps, but not in mine," she corrected. "And, if you will remember, I left you a message."

"Gammon! Some drivel about both of us being miserable."

"It was the truth. Admit it, Jordan, I was an embarrassment to you. Ask your mother if you don't believe me. She was the one who said she could no longer appear in public because of my strange behavior." Nicole paused, and her voice softened. "I was ruining our marriage, and I couldn't bear to see you come to hate me."

"You could have changed," he replied petulantly. "That is what I expected when we spoke of your . . . our problem."

"I tried, Jordan, but I can't reject something that is such a part of me. I attempted to warn you about my ability to see things before we married, but you chose to ignore it. If I remember correctly, you told me that marriage and a babe would cure me of childish games."

"And well it would have if you had but given it a chance."

Nicole shook her head, a sad smile on her face. "No, it wouldn't, Jordan. Nothing but death will change me. I can't give up my gift—it's not a game that I play on a whim, but what I am. You didn't understand that before, and perhaps I didn't either, or I wouldn't have married you in the first place. But now I do, and I won't betray myself again."

She paused, waiting for a reply, but none came. Jordan only stared at her and she realized he still could not accept what she was. Seeing that, she moved toward the door. "Now, you must excuse me," she said briskly. "I have an appointment I must keep."

Jordan's mouth fell open. He could not believe she was dismissing him so casually. "What do you mean? You've answered nothing. There are many things we need to discuss."

"But not today, Jordan. It will take far too long, and I simply do not have the time."

"But I'm your husband. I haven't seen you for seven years," he exclaimed.

"Then it won't matter if we wait a little longer for this conversation, will it?" She smiled and walked through the door into the parlor.

"Look forward to seeing you in a fortnight," said Drew, bowing over her hand.

"It will be a pleasure, Viscount Stanford," she replied pleasantly.

"How do I know you won't vanish again now that I've found you?" asked Jordan, after Drew had disappeared through the door.

Nicole laughed out loud. "You did not find me, Jordan. I allowed you to discover my whereabouts."

It was Jordan's turn to laugh, but it was a short, bitter sound.

Nicole waited until he was sober again. "How do you think I've avoided you all these years?" she asked, her head tilted inquiringly. "I knew each time you drew near. I've been able to elude you, and the other men you sent, quite easily. But I'm tired of running, Jordan. I've decided there is no need for me to suffer for your inability to accept me as I am. I am no longer content to cower in the shadows, to hide my real identity as if I'm a criminal. I want my life back, and I mean to have it. It is you who will need to adjust, not I.

"So, you see, my days of running are over. You will be able to find me anytime you please."

Before Jordan knew it he was in front of the house, the door closed firmly behind him.

Nicole breathed a sigh of relief when the stout barrier of wood separated her from Jordan. It had not been easy to face him again even though she had had ample time to fortify herself.

She had changed considerably in the past six years. She had matured, grown comfortable with her unusual ability, and had sworn she would never again be bullied into being something other than what she was. But, despite all this, her heart had beat a little faster when she first saw Jordan.

He cut an even more imposing figure than he had when she had last seen him. His jacket stretched across broad shoulders that were much more substantial than they had been seven years ago. And she could not help but notice the creaseless riding breeches which covered well-muscled thighs.

The contours of his face were more sharply defined, which Nicole found even more arresting than the youthful curves she remembered. Not a trace of gray showed in his nearly black hair which had curled around her fingers many times in the past. His brows were still a dark slash above gray eyes that had shown not a spark of warmth when they met hers.

Remembering the coldness of Jordan's gaze, Nicole examined the decision she had made to see her husband. It was more than just a desire to use her real name again. It would soon be seven years that she had been missing, enough time to enable Jordan to legally remarry.

Jordan had always wanted a family; it was something they had often discussed during their time together. He would marry for children, if not for love, and that she could not permit.

Nicole rang for the maid. "Betsy, I want you to begin packing. We are going to London."

"For how long, ma'am?"

"For good. We're going to live there."

"Me, too?"

"If you wish."

"Oh, I do, ma'am, I do," the maid said fervently.

"Then hurry on. I'll be up to help you soon. I want to be gone before the week is out." Before Jordan returns, she thought, a secret smile curving her lips.

She wondered what his solution to an unwanted wife would be. Would he endeavor to send her abroad? Give her money and ask her to disappear? At all events, she would probably never know, because she wouldn't be here to listen to his suggestions, and by the time he found her it would be too late.

Two

Jordan was dusty, tired, and angry. Nicole's note had rekindled the outrage he had felt after being so quickly and unceremoniously ushered out of her house.

Her reassurance that she had no intention of running away had meant nothing. When he returned, the house had been as empty as last night's bottle of wine, and Nicole was nowhere to be found. Oh, she had left a message all right, but it said nothing more than that she was returning to London and would contact him there.

Jordan was furious with himself for being so easily duped. He had thought himself over Nicole, but the sight of her had affected his senses, and he had believed her promise. While her maturity had made her more beautiful than he remembered, she still could not be trusted.

Jordan was only a short distance from his London town house, and he sighed with relief that his journey was almost at an end. If only he had not found Nicole again. In just a few months, he would have been returning to a much different welcome than the empty house and lonely dinner he now faced.

When he had started the journey with Drew, his plans had been to marry Melanie Grayson in two months' time, and put Nicole behind him for good. Melanie had turned down offers from several reputable gentlemen while they waited for the seven years to be over. Now he must tell her he already had a wife, one that was very much alive and determined to rejoin society.

Jordan considered Melanie's blond beauty, and his anger increased. For the want of a few months, he would be deprived of a loving wife and family, for he could not foresee being able to reconcile with Nicole in order to have children. He had no grounds for an annulment and, while he was rich enough to afford a divorce, it would put him beyond the pale socially.

The idea of keeping Nicole a secret and sending her out of the country with a generous sum of money passed through his mind. With her beauty, she would soon find someone willing to marry her and he could continue his life as he had planned. He shook his head and muttered to himself, drawing a few curious stares from passersby. No, it was far too late for that. If Nicole's note was reliable, she was already here in London, most probably ruining the rest of his life.

Jordan's brows rose in surprise when he saw the welcoming light falling from the windows of his town house. The door was opened by the butler, and he stepped into a hall scented with the delicious aroma of beef and fresh-baked bread.

"How did you know to expect me this evening?" Jordan asked, handing Harrison his hat and gloves.

"Madam advised the staff that you would be here, and she was right almost to the minute."

"Madam?" he repeated, bewildered by Harrison's answer.

"You see, there are advantages to my talent, Jordan."

The voice came from behind him, and Jordan whirled around to see Nicole descending the stairs to the front hall.

"What the devil are you doing here?" he burst out.

"At one time, this was my home. And since you voiced such concern about my whereabouts the last time we spoke, I thought you would be pleased to have me here."

Jordan's face darkened with rage. Nicole noticed the interested look on Harrison's face, and quickly moved to her husband's side.

"Why don't we go into the drawing room? I've just ordered a bath drawn, and you can have a glass of sherry while it's being made ready." She turned and stepped through the doors before he could refuse.

While Nicole busied herself pouring his drink, Jordan had time to collect himself. The first flush of anger receded, and an unanticipated feeling of relief permeated his body. He had not lost her again; he would not need to wait until she contacted him to find out whether she was real.

"How long have you been here?" he asked, his question sounding more like a demand.

She crossed the room and handed him a glass of amber liquid. "I arrived not long after I saw you."

"You did not convey any such intention."

"It was a sudden decision. I told you I wanted to return to my life again, and our meeting made me realize there was no reason to delay any longer. The Season has already begun so there could be no better time. I came back to this house because I thought it would be more convenient while we straighten out matters between us."

He took a long drink from the liquor in the glass, hoping it would numb the frayed endings of his nerves. "There would be nothing to straighten out if you had stayed missing a few months longer."

"I realize this is awkward for you," she said, sounding softly sympathetic. "And I'll leave immediately if you still feel the same after our discussion."

"I can't imagine what could change my mind. I'll make sure you have money enough . . ."

"Jordan, please," she interrupted. "Finish your drink, then change for dinner. Cook has your favorite meal waiting. After that, we'll talk."

Jordan distrusted her soothing voice and reasonable suggestions; however, he downed his sherry and went upstairs to give himself over to the services of his valet.

Several hours later, Jordan was again in the drawing room with a glass in his hand. He felt considerably better after cleaning off the dust of his furious journey, and enjoying a better meal than he had eaten in weeks. Swirling the brandy in his glass, he thought he would be content if only Melanie, with her blond hair, blue eyes, and frivolous chatter, had been at his side. Instead, he raised his gaze from his glass to encounter the mysterious darkness of Nicole's eyes watching him cautiously.

Jordan took a long swallow of brandy. "I suppose we should discuss our situation," he began. "I was going to offer you the country estate with my promise not to intrude. But since you've made it plain you intend to enter society again, I assume that you won't be satisfied rusticating."

"I've been rusticating for seven years. That's long enough to revive the most jaded member of the *ton,*" she mocked.

He ignored her wry remark. "I'm sure this house doesn't hold any fond memories for you, so I'm willing to purchase a separate residence for you here in town."

"Jordan, there's something—"

"Please, Nicole, let me finish." He took another swallow of brandy, then began again. "Such an arrangement will be a nine days' wonder, as you well know, but eventually the gossip will die. I'll set up your establishment and furnish an adequate allowance. Further, I will not object to any . . . any acquaintances you make with other gentlemen as long as you are discreet. I will promise the same." Jordan was surprised at the sharp twinge of pain that shot through him with this last stipulation.

"May I speak now?" Nicole asked.

Jordan nodded, quickly drained the last of his brandy, and reached for the bottle again.

"Please, Jordan." Nicole's hand blocked his. "Wait until we're finished. I want you clear-headed for what I have to say."

Jordan set his glass on the table and settled back in his chair. "Go ahead."

"I appreciate your generous offer, but there's something you need to know before we make any decision about our living arrangements."

"I can't think of anything you could say to make me change my mind."

She stood and rang the bellpull. "Perhaps I should have said there is someone I want you to meet," she explained. A light tap sounded at the door before it opened.

Jordan recognized the maid as being the same one who had been at Nicole's house in the village. She was holding the hand of a young boy, who quickly shook free of her restraint and ran to Nicole's side.

The boy's hair was as dark as Nicole's, but as she led him toward Jordan, he stared into eyes the exact shade of his own. Jordan was shocked into silence and immobility. Nicole's voice came to him from a far distance.

"Jordan, this is your son, Philip. He's six years old, and has been asking about his father."

"Hello, Philip," Jordan said unsteadily.

"Hello," Philip said and smiled shyly. "Are you really my papa?"

Jordan glanced up at Nicole. "That's what your mother says, and she's always right, isn't she?"

Philip nodded.

"Would you like to sit on my knee?"

Philip looked up at his mother; Nicole nodded encouragingly.

"All right," he said, and climbed trustingly onto Jordan's lap. He was a curious little boy, and was soon chattering away. "Mama says you're a he-ro. She says you did brave things, and the prince gave you a medal. Is this it?" he asked, touching the fob Jordan wore.

"No, but I'll show it to you tomorrow. Will that be soon enough?"

"Yes," agreed Philip. He smiled happily and leaned back against his father.

Jordan blinked the moisture from his eyes. He held the miracle that was his son, the son he feared he might not ever have, and listened to his chatter until Nicole's voice interrupted.

"It's past time Philip was in bed," she reminded them gently.

"Oh, no," said both man and boy.

"Oh, yes," Nicole replied, laughing. "You promised if I let you stay up to meet your father, you'd go to bed without a fuss, didn't you?"

"Yes," Philip agreed, pouting.

"Then be a good boy and go along with Betsy."

"Will you be here tomorrow?" asked Philip, looking up at Jordan with hope in his eyes.

Jordan gave him a tender hug. "I promise," was all he could manage to get past the lump in his throat. He watched as the child kissed his mother, then took Betsy's hand and skipped from the room.

As soon as the door closed, Jordan lunged to his feet, towering over Nicole. Waves of anger flowed from him, and it took all of Nicole's courage not to flee.

"Why in God's name didn't you tell me? I had a right to know!" Jordan reached out to grab her, then pulled back and slammed his fist down on the nearest table.

In all of their time together, Nicole had never seen him this angry. This was what his enemies saw; this had won him his medal. Somehow, she held her ground, but wondered whether she had pushed him too far.

"You're lucky you're the mother of my son, or I couldn't answer to what I might do at this moment," he raged, striding around the room.

"Jordan, I—"

"No. Don't say a word. I don't think I can tolerate any more of your excuses. I must breathe some fresh air before I can discuss this with you."

Nicole listened as he crossed the hall and slammed the outer door behind him. Had she waited too long? Had she lost the chance for her son to know his father? She had done what she thought was right. Living with Jordan had been smothering her spirit little by little. If he had known they had a son, he would have taken the child, whether she had come back to him or not. She could not lose Philip, and she could not return to the life she had led. She had made the only choice possible, and she did not regret it, no matter how angry Jordan was at the moment.

It was hours later when Jordan returned, his footsteps echoing in the early morning stillness. Nicole sat in the drawing room, a piece of embroidery on her lap. When she heard him approach the door, she picked it up and pretended to be busy with her needle.

"What a lovely scene," Jordan said, his words slightly slurred. "My devoted wife, the mother of my son, waiting patiently for her husband's return." He stumbled once crossing the room, and threw himself into a chair opposite hers.

"I was just getting ready to retire," said Nicole. "If you will excuse me," she added and began to rise.

"Oh, no, madam wife. We have matters to discuss, if you will remember. I am sufficiently relaxed . . ."

"You mean drunk," interjected Nicole.

". . . So that you need not fear my reaction, no matter what unsavory details you reveal."

"There are none."

"No? Then, tell me, how have you lived these past years? Surely not by fortune-telling."

"If you will remember, I had a fund from my parents. I invested it, and have been able to live quite comfortably on the income."

"And I suppose this ability to see things we mere mortals cannot allows you to know where to put your money."

"It has helped at times."

"Hah! Do you truly expect me to believe this foolishness?"

"No more than you did when we were married, sir."

"I remind you that, much to my distress, we are still married, madam."

"And it is our marriage that we should be discussing, not how I have made my living these past years."

"There seems to be little left to discuss. I have a son to consider now."

"We have a son," she corrected him.

A particularly nasty smile tugged at the corners of his lips. "That remains to be seen," he said.

A cold shaft of fear shot through Nicole. "What do you mean?"

"I mean that the boy remains with me, no matter where you choose to live."

"And you mean for me to live elsewhere," she stated flatly, disappointment replacing fear. Nicole squared her shoulders. She knew as well as anyone that, under law, Jordan had control over his son's life, but she would not give up so easily. "Well, I won't be separated from Philip. I'm his mother. I've raised him, not you."

"Only because you chose to keep him from me," he shot back.

"If you had known I was increasing, your reaction would have been the same and I would have been trapped with a man who belittled me and a mother-in-law who hated the sight of me."

"That isn't true. I didn't belittle you—it was your behavior I thought unbecoming."

"By 'behavior' I assume you mean my second sight. Don't you realize by now that it's part of me? That there is no way to separate it from me?"

Jordan waved a negligent hand as if swatting a pesky fly, and ignored her comments. "As far as my mother is concerned, she was only worried about the consequences to our family."

"Cut line!" she barked out, causing Jordan to jerk upright in his chair.

"Your mother was against us from the start. I don't know why, but she did everything she could to prevent our marriage. When that failed, she set her sights on turning you against me, and she finally succeeded."

Jordan rubbed his forehead with his hand. The long day with all its conflicting emotions was catching up with him. He yearned to stretch out and let sleep swallow his troubles for a few hours.

Jordan spoke slowly and carefully. "I've had enough arguing. I don't care what the devil you do. I'll support your household whether you go to the country or stay here in London, but Philip remains with me."

Nicole stared directly into his eyes, her gaze defiant. "Then so do I," she replied just as deliberately.

The next morning Jordan sat on the edge of his bed, holding his head and moaning. The liquor had given him a few hours of blessed oblivion, but he doubted the aftereffects were worth it.

As he got himself ready to face the day, the evening came back to him in its entirety. It was odd to know that he was not alone in the house, that his wife and child were but a few rooms away. He attempted to imagine his future. If Nicole meant what she said, and he had no reason to doubt it, she would not be parted from Philip. Her decision insured that he would be locked into a loveless marriage for the rest of his days.

After a solitary breakfast, Jordan spent time with Philip. His son was a bright little boy, and Jordan was thankful for him, since his future no longer included the hope of a large family.

That perturbing thought reminded him of other pressing obligations, and he bid his son goodbye. He had several unpleasant tasks to perform and there was no sense putting them off.

* * *

Agatha Worth had just finished a late breakfast when Jordan arrived. She was a forceful-looking woman, with an aggressive manner that allowed her to ride roughshod over nearly everyone around her.

Her hair was more gray than black, and pulled away from a face that was too round for the severe style. After thirty-two years, she still wore black in deference to a husband whom she had never loved.

Mrs. Worth lived with Robert, Duke of Weston, who was Jordan's first cousin. The two men were only a few weeks apart in age, and had been raised as brothers. The late duke and duchess, and Agatha's husband, Richard, had all perished in a fire when Robert and Jordan were less than a year old. Soon thereafter, Agatha had moved to the ducal mansion with the two babies, and had remained there since.

After so many years in residence, she considered the house her home, and would not hear of living with Jordan or setting up her own establishment. Robert was agreeable. His aunt played a doting grandmother to his children, since she had none of her own.

Although she hadn't seen her son for some weeks, Mrs. Worth did not demonstrate any great joy when he arrived. Jordan had often wondered at her lack of maternal feelings, and was suddenly grateful that Philip had a mother who loved him, and did not hesitate to show it.

"I can't offer you refreshments, Jordan, for I'm on my way to make calls."

"I will only stay a minute then. There's something I want to tell you before you hear it elsewhere." Jordan hesitated, uncertain of how to proceed.

"Well, don't dawdle, get on with it," Mrs. Worth demanded, several frown lines creasing her forehead.

Jordan had suffered too many shocks over the past twenty-four hours, and his thinly-held patience snapped. "Nicole is back," he announced baldly, pleased to see that he had stunned his mother into momentary silence.

"You can't mean it!" she replied in disbelief.

"But I do."

"I cannot credit it. Where is she?"

"I saw her on my trip to Dover with Drew a fortnight or so ago. When I returned to London, she greeted me at the door as if she had never been gone."

"You cannot allow this."

"She is still my wife—there's nothing I can do."

"Send her away. Our lives have been normal since she's been gone. I won't suffer the embarrassment of her fortune-telling, or visions, or whatever it is she claims to do."

"I'm afraid she still professes to have second sight," said Jordan. Mrs. Worth groaned. "I'm also afraid she refuses to leave."

"Offer her money. Give her anything she wants, but get rid of her," she ordered.

Even though she was his mother, Jordan did not care for her dictatorial attitude. "I've done my best, but she's decided to stay where she is, and she has good reason."

"What reason could there be to ruin our lives?"

"I have a son, ma'am. His name is Philip. I only met him last night. I've told Nicole that I won't let him go, that he will remain with me no matter what she decides."

"A child?" Mrs. Worth laughed. "So she's brought back a bastard for you to raise and you've accepted him as your own," she sneered. "You're a fool, Jordan."

Jordan kept a firm grip on his temper. "Nicole didn't know she was increasing when she left. He's the right age—a little over six years old. When you see him, you'll know he's mine. I can't deny it, and I don't wish to. Philip is my son, and Nicole's made it plain that she won't leave the boy."

"And you didn't insist, did you? You've always been besotted with that creature. Whenever she was around, you never thought with your head. I don't know why I expected you to change."

"My personal feelings toward Nicole do not enter into it. She doesn't want to be separated from Philip, and I respect that."

"And she will soon have you jumping at her every wish," charged Mrs. Worth.

Jordan had taken enough. "And if I am, it will be my own business. I thought I was doing the right thing coming here to tell you about Nicole, but I can see now that I shouldn't have wasted my time." He gave a slight bow and turned toward the door.

"If you had told me she was never coming back, then the news would have been welcome," Mrs. Worth retorted, always determined to get the last word.

Jordan did not answer as he made his way to the front door. Melanie was next on his list and, as he drew on his gloves, he shuddered to think of how she would accept the news.

Melanie was in a small sitting room with her mother when Jordan arrived. After all the proper greetings had been made, Mrs. Grayson excused herself. She had letters to answer, she said, with an arch glance.

Now that he was alone with Melanie, Jordan did not know how to begin. Perhaps it would be best to be direct.

"Melanie, there's something I must tell you." He spoke gently, taking her small hand in his.

"Jordan, you sound so serious. Whatever is it?"

"I . . . that is . . ."

"Don't tell me you cannot escort me to the Havershams' ball tonight." She sounded close to tears.

If Melanie was upset over such a trivial matter, Jordan wondered, what would she do when she heard his news?

"No, it isn't that." Jordan reconsidered his statement. He was a married man again, and no longer free to escort her to the ball. "I mean it is, but . . ."

"Oh, Jordan, you promised," she cried.

"I know, I know," he soothed. "But something's happened that has changed everything."

"What could possibly be more important than the ball? It's said to be the event of the Season. Everyone who's anyone will be there. Perhaps even Prinny himself."

"Melanie, listen to me," Jordan said patiently, clasping her hand between both of his and leaning forward until he had her full attention. "I don't know how to tell you this. I know we've made plans . . . I mean, we both expected . . . Dammit, Melanie!" he said, frustration overcoming patience, "Nicole is back."

Melanie's eyes widened and her mouth gaped from shock. "Nicole?" she whispered. "Your wife?"

He nodded, wishing there had been a gentler way of telling her. "I met her by accident when Drew and I travelled to Dover. When I returned home, she was already there." Jordan was beginning to tire of repeating the story, and belatedly thought he should have called everyone together and gotten it over with all at once.

"You mean you're living with her? Oh, Jordan, how could you?" she wailed, pulling from his grasp and dropping her face into her hands, sobbing.

"I'm not living with her, Melanie. At least, not the way you mean. We are both living under the same roof, but that's all. We're not . . ." He stopped abruptly, remembering he was talking to an innocent young woman.

Melanie only cried harder. "I can't believe it," she said between sobs. "She's ruined everything! Make her go away again," she pleaded.

"I can't do that, my dear. You see, I have a son I didn't know about, and I won't turn him away. Nicole insists on staying with him. Even if she left, we'd still be married. I'm afraid there's nothing I can do, except to say I'm sorry."

"Sorry!" Melanie repeated, raising her tear-stained face to glare at him. "Sorry! Do you realize the time I've wasted? I'm nearly on the shelf! I've turned down offers from men of exceptional standing to marry you, and now you tell me you're *sorry?*"

Strands of blond hair had come undone, and her eyes had the look of a crazed animal. "Well, it just won't do. I won't allow her to ruin my life. You must send her away. No one will know, and we can go ahead with our plans as if nothing has happened."

He captured her hands again. "I can't do that, Melanie. Everything has changed now that Philip is involved."

"She's fooling you, Jordan. The child is someone else's and she's been deserted. That woman is using you to raise her illegitimate offspring," Melanie charged, a snarl twisting her dainty lips.

Jordan wondered at the similarity of Melanie's and his mother's reaction.

"This was all Viscount Stanford's doing, wasn't it?" Melanie continued. "He knew where she was and took you to her. He's never liked me, and he did this to keep us apart," she charged.

"That's foolish, Melanie. Drew and I weren't even acquainted when Nicole and I wed. He knew nothing about her until we saw her—"

"That's what he'd like you to believe. Someone must have told him about it, and where to find her. I tell you, he did it to spite me, but I'll have the last laugh. He won't get away with this, and neither will that . . . that woman who calls herself your wife."

Jordan was exhausted when he climbed into his curricle a short time later. Too much liquor and a sleepless night, combined with telling his mother and Melanie the bad news, had taken its toll.

He was sorry to be at odds with his mother again, and he sorely regretted the loss of Melanie; but Philip and his welfare came first now. The boy had been without a father for the entirety of his short life, and Jordan meant to make up for that.

How he and Nicole could get along together living under the same roof was another question. She had changed since he had last seen her, and he wasn't altogether sure that her transformation was for the best.

Three

"You look wonderful," sighed Betsy, adjusting a fold of Nicole's gown.

Nicole examined her figure in the mirror. "Thank you, Betsy. I've never considered myself vain, but I must admit I've never been in better looks."

It had been years since Nicole had been able to patronize a London seamstress, and the results were far superior to the village women who had made her clothes.

She had forced herself to exercise restraint, restricting her activities until her gowns had been delivered. She did not want to appear in society looking countrified. So she had spent her time indoors, and taking short strolls in the small garden behind the town house. It had been confining, but well worth the effort, thought Nicole as she stared into the mirror.

In a strange but welcome reaction, as soon as Nicole's presence in London was known, invitations began pouring in. The Season had been a dull one so far, and all the hostesses were vying to be the first to boast of having the runaway wife as a guest.

"Bring my cloak, Betsy. I feel ready to step into the lion's den."

Jordan stared out over the ballroom floor, wondering if Melanie would attend. He hadn't contacted her since he had advised her of Nicole's return. Perhaps it wasn't honorable, but he wanted to see her again, hold her in his arms as they waltzed, and whisper that he couldn't bear to think of her with anyone else.

He didn't need to be reminded that he was a married man. That was burned into him each time he saw Nicole.

For the first few days after his wife's return, Jordan had seldom dined at home. However, the few times he did, he found the meal delicious and, where he had anticipated hostile silence, the conversation that had passed between them had been engaging. Jordan learned that his wife had many interests, and had not rusticated even while living a quiet life in the country. She discussed politics and investments as proficiently as the Regent's latest folly.

But no matter how entertaining their time together, he did not accept it as adequate to make up for what he had lost. He clung stubbornly to his resentment over Nicole's return, examining it daily in order to keep his bitterness fresh.

Philip was the only good thing that had come out of his ill-fated marriage. He doted on the boy, and they spent a great deal of time together. Nicole seemed pleased that he took such an interest in Philip, and never intruded when he and his son were together.

If truth be told, Jordan did not find his new life uncomfortable. In fact, if his stubbornness would allow him to admit he might be wrong about his future being ruined, he would have liked to have spent more time at home. He was even beginning to think his avoidance of Nicole was unwarranted. She made no demands on him, nor did she question him no matter how late he arrived home. She gave no indication that she was even interested in how he spent his time, but he had to admit he was beginning to wonder how she spent hers.

There was a stir at the door of the ballroom which drew him back to the present. He craned his neck to see what was causing the commotion.

"Anyone interesting?" asked Drew, appearing at his side.

"Can't tell yet," replied Jordan, losing interest and searching the room again for Melanie's golden curls.

"Might want to look again," suggested Drew.

The crowd parted before Nicole as she strolled into the room as casually as if she were in Hyde Park. Jordan's breath caught at the brazenness of her entrance. After all she had done, she should be ashamed to show her face. But here she was, decked out in a gown as fine as any in the room, smiling and nodding as if it was only last night that she had attended a ball with the present company.

Uttering an oath, Jordan made his way through the group that surrounded Nicole until he reached her side.

"I believe I shall claim the first dance," he said smoothly, taking Nicole's hand and leading her onto the dance floor. He was surprised at her complacent attitude as they began the steps. He had expected her to pull away, and had been prepared to escort her from the ball when she made a scene.

"I'm amazed at your forwardness," he said, forcing a smile. The condemnation in his voice was in direct contrast to his pleasant expression.

"I wouldn't call attending a ball being forward," Nicole replied calmly. "After all, I was invited."

"Surely you know that Lady Trent only invited you for the sensation you would cause."

Nicole met his gaze, allowing a slight touch of humor to show in her expression. "No matter how low your opinion of me, please give me the benefit of some sense. I've had invitations flowing in every day since I've returned. And, yes, I'm quite aware of why I'm receiving them."

"Then why . . . ?"

"Why am I here? Why did I choose tonight to embarrass you? Come now, Jordan. It's time you stopped seeing everything I do as an affront to you. It may jar your consequence, but I gave you not one thought when I selected an invitation to accept."

Nicole paused in her speech to nod and smile charmingly to

a couple warily circling them, then returned her attention to Jordan, still maintaining her pleasant demeanor. "I told you when we first met that I was determined to return to society and reclaim my life. Well, I am doing just that."

Her bluntness kept him silent for a moment. "Then why did you wait?"

Nicole smiled. "Why for what other reason than clothes? I couldn't face the *ton* without being dressed to the nines, could I?"

Now that Jordan's initial anger had passed, he was able to observe Nicole's appearance. She wore a silver dress which clung precariously to her shoulders, and flowed gracefully to her silver slippers. Her hair was a mass of shining curls, and what looked suspiciously like real diamonds dangled from her ears.

"And I suppose I should expect to receive the bills for all your frippery?" he growled.

Nicole laughed out loud. "Don't tell me you resent buying your wife's clothing," she teased. "Think of how much more embarrassing it would be if I wore rags."

"And what of these?" he said, flipping a diamond earring with his finger.

"You won't receive an enormous bill," she assured him. "There are other ways to acquire jewels than from a husband."

Jordan was jolted by her answer. All the while he had been angry with Nicole, he had never thought of her with another man. He should not have been so witless. He couldn't deny that she was a beautiful woman, and would attract men wherever she went. How could he have expected her to spend seven years without a man in her life?

"Well, that's one relief," he said, attempting a nonchalance he didn't feel.

The dance ended and he stood holding her in his arms, experiencing a strange unwillingness to let her go.

Nicole made no effort to free herself from his embrace. "I

think you had better brace yourself for some unpleasantness," she said.

"Did your second sight tell you that?" he asked contemptuously.

"No, just ordinary observation," she replied, glancing over his shoulder.

Jordan turned and came face-to-face with Melanie. She was leaving the floor with her partner, a young man Jordan did not know. Whether their encounter was accidental or planned, Jordan couldn't judge, but it was enough to shake his composure.

This was the woman he had expected to marry, to bear his children, and with whom he would spend the rest of his days. Now all their plans were shattered thanks to the woman who stood on his other side. He turned, angry enough to tell Nicole what she had done in spite of the audience avidly looking on, but she was gone. He turned back to Melanie, wondering what words of consolation he could offer, but he only caught a glimpse of her back as she, too, disappeared into the crowd.

Jordan stood alone on the dance floor, feeling more solitary— and more foolish—than he had in many a day.

"Would like to introduce a friend," said Drew as Nicole stood fanning herself in the overcrowded room.

"I would be delighted," replied Nicole, studying the petite young woman with honey-hued hair and hazel eyes standing by his side.

Drew urged the woman forward. "My friend, Lady Alura Courtney. Mrs. Worth," he said briefly.

"I believe my new sister-in-law is a distant cousin of yours," said Alura after the initial greetings were over.

Nicole paused a moment to review her vast array of kin. "I'm afraid I haven't kept up with the doings of my relatives recently."

"Claire Kingsley is her name," offered Alura.

"Oh, yes," acknowledged Nicole, her eyes lighting in fond

remembrance. "I haven't seen Claire since we were children. How is she?"

"On a trip to the Continent with my brother, Quinton, Marquess of Ransley. They were married just a short time ago. They don't expect to return to London until the Little Season."

"It sounds very romantic. I'm happy for Claire."

"Should be happy for Quinton," offered Drew. "He's a lucky scoundrel to have found her. Saved his life and his daughter's."

"It's true," confirmed Alura. "Juliana, Quinton's daughter, hadn't spoken for over a year when Claire met her. Now she's a normal little girl, and we owe it all to Claire."

"It sounds as if my cousin wrought a miracle," replied Nicole.

"Oh, she did," agreed Alura. "And that's one reason I wanted to meet you." She looked a little embarrassed, a slight flush rising to her cheeks. "I hope you don't think it forward, but I wanted to reassure you."

"About what?" asked Nicole, clearly intrigued.

"Alura doesn't explain well," volunteered Drew.

"I do too," exclaimed Alura, swatting his sleeve with her fan. "Just give me time."

Nicole hid a smile. Alura and Drew were evidently friends of long standing, and the young woman had no inhibitions about allowing her true feelings to show.

"Drew told me about your special . . . talent. Well, Claire has the same gift. She suffered quite a bit of disbelief and ridicule from people until the facts proved her correct. I wanted you to know . . . well, I know that being special—like you and Claire—isn't easy." She paused for a moment, searching for words. "I wanted you to know that I believe in your gift and I'd like to be your friend," she finished in a rush.

Nicole blinked rapidly. Alura's refreshing forthrightness and offer of friendship touched her. "I must admit my first days back in London have been more solitary than I would have liked. I accept with thanks," she said.

"Since we are related by marriage, you must call me Alura," said the young woman, showing a captivating smile.

"And I am Nicole." She offered her hand and received a warm clasp in return. Drew looked on, a satisfied smile on his face.

"Now, we shall do something about your solitary existence, won't we, Drew?"

"Of course," Drew replied, staring at Alura, his heart in his eyes.

Jordan was not enjoying the evening nearly as much as his wife. He had tracked Melanie down, and managed to get the promise of a dance from her. He waited at the edge of the floor and claimed her hand before the last notes died away.

"Don't pull at me so," she complained as Jordan made his way toward the French doors. "And why are we going this way? We should be dancing."

"I'm in no mood to dance and pretend that everything is normal between us. I want to talk to you." He led her through the doors onto the terrace.

"This isn't proper, Jordan," she scolded peevishly.

"Before I left London on that damnable trip, it was proper," he complained.

"Yes, but now you have a wife."

"You just danced with a man who has a wife."

"But I wasn't expecting to marry him," she argued.

"Please, Melanie. Let's not waste time quarreling. I want to know if you're all right. I don't want you to suffer because of my situation."

"Suffer? You don't want me to suffer?" she repeated in disbelief, her voice rising. "You should have thought about that before you found your wife and brought her back to live with you."

"I told you I had nothing to do with that. I was not even

searching for her when we met, and she came to town on her own."

Melanie sniffed. "The result is still the same. We cannot marry as long as she is here. Mama and Papa have both advised me to find a husband as soon as possible. They said I've waited for you too long, that I'm practically an antidote, and no one will want me now."

"Fustian! You're a beautiful, entrancing woman, Melanie. Any man would be proud to have you at his side."

Even under the strained circumstances, Melanie preened at his compliments. "Perhaps they did exaggerate a bit," she conceded, "but the fact remains that you are no longer free to marry me, and I must look elsewhere."

"Oh, Melanie," groaned Jordan. "How I hate to hear you say that. If there was anything I could do to change it, I would. You must know that."

"Then get rid of her," she hissed. "You're an intelligent man—think of something."

Jordan was taken aback by her malevolence. "You're forgetting, I have a son to consider," he reminded her.

"Keep your son, but get rid of that woman. I can't imagine she had the nerve to come here tonight. Doesn't she know everyone is talking about her?"

"If she can do what she says she can, I'm sure she's aware of every word that's being said about her," Jordan commented wryly.

"I've heard the gossip about her fortune-telling," Melanie said contemptuously. "It's only more reason for ridicule. How can you have anything to do with a woman like that?"

"I can't very well throw my son's mother into the streets," he snapped, smarting under Melanie's criticism. "Besides, it's my understanding that she has the means to set herself up and live quite well without my support."

An expression of disdain curled Melanie's lips. "You seem determined to keep her with you," she charged. "You have made your decision. Now, I must go—I've stayed too long as it is.

Let me know if you change your mind. In the meantime, I wish
you luck with your wife," she sneered. Spinning away from
him, she flounced across the terrace and disappeared through
the French doors without a backward glance.

Jordan leaned against the stone parapet, wondering what he
had done to deserve the muddle in which he found himself.
Even though he knew it was necessary, it was hard to forget
Melanie. She had been the woman who would right all the
wrongs, the woman of his dreams, and now those dreams were
reduced to ashes.

Was there some way to rid himself of Nicole without ruining
his own life? If so, he didn't know what it was. Short of murder,
he was stuck with her.

Then there was Philip to think about. His son had changed
his life in the few days he had known about him. Jordan awoke
each morning thinking of things he wanted to share with Philip,
places he wanted to go, stories he wanted to tell. He couldn't
let go of Philip, and Nicole wouldn't leave without her son.

There was no end to the circle, no way out. He must accept
what life had dealt him, and manage it the best he could.

Two days later, Drew and Alura were taking tea with Nicole
in the drawing room

"Still nothing new on the jewel thief," Drew commented.
"He's robbed four other houses since mine."

"And no one's seen anyone?" questioned Nicole. "The servants haven't heard anything?"

"Not a thing," confirmed Drew. "The man comes and goes
in the night, even though everything's always locked up right
and tight."

"It's certainly a puzzle," agreed Nicole.

"Oh, go ahead and ask her," urged Alura.

Nicole smiled at her impulsiveness. "Ask me what?" she said
to Drew.

"Um. Well. Wondered if you'd take a look around at my

house. See if you can . . . ah . . . see anything about the robberies."

"Of course I will. I promised. I just didn't know if you still wanted me to do so since you've found out I'm Jordan's wife."

"Makes no difference. Jewelry's still missing."

"Good," said Alura, almost bouncing on the settee. "Then you'll come."

Nicole laughed. "Yes, I'll come."

"Tomorrow?" asked Alura.

"If that's what you want, then, yes. Tomorrow."

Andrew, Viscount Stanford, lived in a town house not far from the Worths' home. Nicole wandered through the ground floor with Drew and Alura trailing in her wake.

She felt nothing out of the ordinary until she reached the library.

"This is where the burglar entered," she said, looking at the tall windows that covered one wall.

"Evidently," confirmed Drew. "Found one of the windows slightly open the morning after the jewels went missing. 'Course, all the servants denied any knowledge of it."

Nicole stared silently at the window for a few moments. "As well they should," she finally answered. "The servants had nothing to do with it. A man entered by himself," she continued, her voice taking on an almost singsong rhythm. "He's very confident. He knows he won't be interrupted."

"I was out that evening," murmured Drew.

"It's late," Nicole said, her eyes shifting to the clock on the mantel. "Nearly two o'clock in the morning. He lights a candle and goes to the desk." Nicole moved a few steps forward. Drew's gaze sharpened as she knelt down. "He pulls back the corner of the rug," she continued, suiting her action to the words. "And lifts the door." Nicole slipped her fingers into a slight indentation and raised a small, hinged section of the floor.

Alura's gasp was quite audible in the stillness. She glanced up at Drew and saw that Nicole held his full attention. Nicole reached into the dark space. "There is a box holding your jewelry. The man removes it and leaves the way he entered. It takes only a few minutes."

Nicole stopped speaking. After a few moments more, she looked up at them, blinking a few times to clear her vision. "That's all," she said, rising to her feet.

"Did you recognize him?" asked Drew.

"No, I'm sorry. He wore a hat, and his face was covered with some kind of large handkerchief. He was dressed all in black, so there's nothing to distinguish him. "I'm sorry," she said again, sincerely contrite about not being able to tell him more.

Drew waved his hand. "It's more than I knew before. Clears the servants, and that's comforting." His brow furrowed as he gave some thought to his predicament. "If I made arrangements, would you visit the other homes that were robbed?"

Nicole hesitated. Regardless of what Jordan thought, she did not enjoy the notoriety that usually went along with her gift. But, on the other hand, she had promised Drew she would help him if she could. And since she was certain that it was Alura who was the object of Drew's affection, she wanted him to retrieve the betrothal ring to slip on the young woman's finger.

"Can we do it discreetly?" she asked. "I would rather not feed the gossip mongers so soon after I have returned to society."

"Of course," Drew assured her. "Will make secrecy a requirement. The families are anxious to find their treasures, so they'll agree to almost anything."

"With that stipulation met, I'll be happy to do what I can."

"Good. Will let you know as soon as I can set up another visit."

* * *

It was three days later that Jordan found out about the activity in which his wife and friends were involved. A flash of anger made his vision blur for a moment and his hands clench at his side. Nicole had barely settled in and was already making trouble for him. If his mother heard about this nonsense she would be complaining that Nicole was making a laughingstock out of them again, and she would be right. This time he meant to see that the foolishness stopped before it began.

He arrived home in a flurry, tossing his hat and gloves carelessly at Harrison.

"Where's Mrs. Worth?" he demanded, pausing momentarily to hear the answer.

"In her sitting room, sir."

"We are not to be disturbed," he ordered brusquely, striding down the hall toward the back of the house.

Nicole was at her desk when Jordan burst into her room. He stood, legs apart, hands on hips, observing her in stony silence while she finished her letter and laid aside her pen.

"Just what do you think you are doing, madam?"

"Answering letters," she said, purposefully misunderstanding his question.

"You know very well that isn't what I mean," he replied, advancing toward her.

The room seemed to shrink as he invaded her private sanctuary. His large body and his outrage absorbed space until Nicole thought surely the walls would bow outward from the pressure. Concealing her inner trepidation, Nicole faced Jordan with a calm front. She rose unhurriedly from her chair at the desk and moved to the settee near the fireplace. She seated herself and motioned to a chair nearby.

"Won't you be seated, Jordan? Then tell me what has upset you so."

"Upset? Madam, you would be extremely lucky if I were only upset. I've just left Drew. He told me about what you've been up to, so there's no need to deny it."

A frown of concentration settled on Nicole's face. "We have

agreed to go our own separate ways, so there's no reason to either confirm or deny anything to you. But tell me what is so dreadful that it has put you in such a taking."

"Don't act the innocent. You know very well what I'm referring to—your part in this ridiculous scheme to find the thief who's been making off with half the *ton's* jewelry."

"Oh, that." Nicole shrugged. "I'm simply keeping my promise to Drew. If you remember, before I came to town I said I would visit his home to see if I could find out anything more about the robbery."

"And the other three houses you've visited?"

"Why, they've also been robbed. Drew asked me to look at the rooms where the robberies occurred. We had the permission of the owners. They're desperate to get their jewels back."

"They must be, to allow you to traipse through their homes in order to see some vision about a crime that happened weeks ago."

"Jordan, if you don't believe in my gift, why not just ignore it? All this stomping about and yelling can't be good for your constitution."

Jordan drew a deep breath and stared at his wife. She did not seem a bit upset that he was angry. When they first married, she would have been in tears, begging his forgiveness and promising never to do such an addlebrained thing again.

Perhaps a successful application of common sense to the problem she was trying to solve would show her the folly of her ways. Jordan knew of only one way to achieve that end.

He forced himself to speak calmly. "Drew says you haven't been able to see the face of the man who's been stealing the jewels."

If Nicole was surprised by his change in manner, she did not show it.

"That's true. I can see him committing the crime, but his face is always too well covered for me to distinguish his features. He dresses in black, so his clothing is no help either."

"I will make you a wager," Jordan said, lowering himself into the chair Nicole had offered him when he first entered.

"A wager, sir? With a lady? How very unconventional of you," she said, eyes wide.

Jordan almost smiled at her teasing, but caught himself in time. "It's plain you believe in what you call your gift. So I suggest we put it to the test. I will also attempt to solve the string of recent robberies. Whichever one of us reveals the identity of the jewel thief first wins the bet."

"And what will be the prize?" Nicole asked.

"If I win, you will give up this foolishness of being able to see things beyond the human eye. If you win, I will accept your gift, and will no longer plague you about it."

Nicole was surprised that Jordan would make such a concession; he must be sure of himself. However, she was not so confident. Her gift was not completely reliable. She was not always right, nor could she consistently see what she wanted. If this was one of those times, she risked the possibility of returning to the life from which she had escaped. Even as a young, inexperienced woman, she had found it a miserable existence. Now that she had lived independently for so many years, she feared it would be nearly impossible for her to suppress part of her character.

If she lost the wager, she would be forced to make another crucial decision: whether to remain with Jordan or desert her husband again. If she stayed and kept her part of the bargain, her life would be a silk-lined prison, for denying her gift was denying an integral part of herself. She would shrivel like an unwatered plant, turn brown and crumble into dust.

But if she decided to flee, she could not abandon Philip. And if she took him, she knew that England would be too small to hide her, for Jordan would never quit searching until he found his son.

No, it would be necessary to leave England for the Continent, or perhaps Canada or America. If that were the case, she would be repudiating Philip's right to his inheritance, and to his father's guidance and love.

Nicole was backed into a corner and she could tell by the smirk on Jordan's face that he knew it, had planned it. If she declined, he would never let her forget, or take her seriously. If she agreed and lost, he would also have what he wanted: his son and a complacent wife. There was only one solution. She must win the bet. Failure would lead only to despair.

"I will accept your wager," she said, taking pleasure in his surprise.

"You will?" he asked in a disbelieving voice, cautious now that he believed success was within his grasp and a dilemma which had been ruining his life was nearly resolved.

"Of course. I'm looking forward to silencing your disbelief once and for all." She smiled confidently.

For a moment, just for a very slight moment, Jordan felt a qualm of uncertainty. If she won—as she seemed to think she could—he would have no recourse other than to allow her full freedom with her claims of visions. The resulting humiliation could drive him out of society and ruin his son's future.

But she would not be victorious. Her claims were just products of a fanciful mind. He would win his wager and insist she honor the terms. He smiled confidently. When this was over, he might not have a wife who would share all the intimacies of life, but he would certainly have an obedient one.

A short time later Jordan stood in the hall outside Nicole's sitting room, feeling inordinately pleased with himself. He was well on the way to getting control of his willful wife. He would be the last one to admit that he was jealous of Nicole, but he felt her success with the *ton* was unwarranted. She had done nothing to deserve to be feted as she was.

She should have been ashamed of what she had done, and hidden away from the public humiliation that would normally follow on the heels of her story when it became known.

However, an unusual situation was developing. Instead of being shunned, she was sought out, and her calendar was filled with events. It was true that she had her fair share of gentlemen admirers, but she had also attracted a large group of women. He could only wonder what respectable ladies saw to admire in a wife who had deserted her husband merely because he had ordered her to give up a ridiculous belief.

Jordan put his thoughts aside. He did not want to remember Nicole's disappearance and the years that followed. He meant to rebuild his life, and the first item of business was winning the bet with Nicole. He felt he had handled the situation extremely well. He had not made the same mistake twice; he had not ordered her to forget her visions and act in a normal manner. Instead, he had suggested a perfectly reasonable measure to set the matter at rest for all time. He would quickly rid London of a thieving scoundrel while insuring that his life would be as unexceptional as any man's. What a difference in thinking seven years had made, he thought smugly.

Accepting his gloves and hat from Harrison, Jordan strode out into the bright afternoon light, the very picture of a victorious gentleman.

"You're risking a great deal on this bet," said Alura later that afternoon.

"I had no choice," replied Nicole. Alura had stopped by to invite her for a drive in the park, and Nicole could not help but take advantage of a sympathetic ear. She hadn't known the young woman long, but she felt comfortable with her; Alura was, after all, a relative by marriage.

"Can you be certain of your success in this instance?" questioned Alura.

"Not entirely. My gift works in different ways. Sometimes I see scenes in their entirety—those are the easy ones. Others come in flashes, and some are merely feelings that I must work out in my mind. And then there are times when I see nothing at all."

"What causes it to fail?" asked Alura, clearly fascinated.

"First, you must understand that I don't walk around listening to everyone's thoughts. You can't imagine the emotions seething inside most people. To allow those into my mind would invite madness. So I've learned to erect my own defenses to block those thoughts out until I want to listen to them."

"Does it work?"

"Most of the time. However, if a person is experiencing intense emotions, they can be strong enough to break into my thoughts. At first, it was distracting to be walking through a crowd and be almost knocked off my feet by feelings of rage or love. Now, it's something I've grown accustomed to, and have learned to clear it from my mind immediately. Unless I want to know who is loved that strongly," she teased, a smile curling her lips.

Alura blushed, wondering whether anyone would ever love her that much.

"But I haven't answered your question yet, have I?"

"I've forgotten what it was," replied Alura, laughing.

"You wanted to know why there are times I can see nothing at all," Nicole reminded her. "There are people," she said slowly, seriously considering her answer, "who are capable of blocking me out as surely as I can them. They are usually very strongwilled individuals, or people who have learned to cope with emotions by locking them away and not thinking about them."

"But what do you do when you need to see what they are thinking?"

"It's possible to break through by surprising them with a revelation of some sort. If the news is shocking enough, their guard usually drops adequately for me to use my second sight. Sickness or a physical injury can also weaken their resistance, though I must admit there are those hardened enough to remain in control of their thoughts through most adversity."

"What if the thief is one of those people? You may never be able to find him. Then you would lose the wager, then you would . . ."

"Don't remind me," broke in Nicole. "I won't allow myself to think about defeat. Instead, we are going to go driving in the park and enjoy the lovely sunshine."

Four

Melanie Grayson had often been favorably compared to an angel, with eyes so blue as to challenge the celestial heavens on a perfect day, hair more golden than any treasure, and a smile sweet enough to charm the most callous individual.

But Melanie's many admirers would be hard put to recognize her as she drove toward the Duke of Weston's residence to call on Agatha Worth. The innocent blue of her eyes was lost between lids narrowed in fury and her mouth was set in a hard, thin line; the gold of her hair dulled in the face of such malevolent intent.

Her demeanor did not soften as she stepped from the carriage and walked stiffly across the cobblestones to the Duke's front door. She had arrived with a purpose in mind, and was determined to remain until she had come to an agreement with Mrs. Worth. This was her last chance to win Jordan, and she did not mean to fail.

Agatha Worth received Melanie in a small sitting room given over to her use. It was furnished in an overabundance of pinks and greens which had a stupefying effect on any mind in its presence for a short time.

She did not rise or offer a warm welcome as Melanie entered the room and advanced across the carpet toward her. From their first meeting, Agatha had recognized Melanie as being as coldly calculating as herself, and knew that the outward amenities would be wasted on her.

"I assume this isn't merely a social call," she said as Melanie settled on a pink velvet settee across from her.

"Not in the least," replied Melanie, unable to pretend otherwise. "It's business, pure and simple. I want to marry Jordan, and I need your help," she stated bluntly.

Mrs. Worth was not at all surprised at Melanie's appearance on her doorstep. In fact, she had been expecting it since Jordan had advised her of Nicole's return. However, she could not suppress the gratification of seeing the haughty Miss Grayson tumbled from her lofty perch, begging for a favor.

"Surely you know by now that Jordan's wife has returned?" Agatha asked, unable to resist taking her down another peg.

"I would not be here otherwise."

"Then I can't see that there's anything more to discuss."

"That woman was gone for almost seven years," said Melanie, too infuriated even to utter Nicole's name. "Then she pops up from out of nowhere and expects to take her place again as if nothing had ever happened."

"And doing a good job of it, I would say," responded Agatha.

Melanie's face twisted with the hatred she could no longer suppress. "Well, I won't stand for it," she spat out. "Jordan is mine. Another two months and we would have been married. I won't give him up to some grasping female with a mewling bastard dragging at her skirts."

"It seems the decision has already been made. Nicole is living in Jordan's house while, if rumor has it right, he has broken with you."

"That will not be the situation for long," snapped Melanie. She rose from the settee and began pacing the small room in short, quick steps.

Mrs. Jordan watched Melanie's frantic movements and smiled in satisfaction. It was well known that Melanie needed to marry money—and a great deal of it—to pay off her father's gambling debts. And while her beauty was admired, her family was not high enough placed, nor did she have sufficient dowry, to attract a titled husband. Jordan was a wealthy man who had accepted Melanie without either asset. Their marriage would have saved the Grayson family from ruin.

Although she did not allow it to show, Agatha was as anxious to get rid of Nicole as Melanie, perhaps even more so. Mrs. Worth had successfully plotted her son's life for over thirty years, and she would not allow such an insufferable bit of baggage as Nicole to ruin her plans at this late date. While Agatha outwardly scoffed at the idea that the chit had second sight, she shuddered at the thought that there might be some truth to the rattlebrained nonsense. She had certain secrets that must not be revealed.

The best thing would be for Nicole to disappear again. This time for good. Agatha had already been scheming a way to get rid of her unwanted daughter-in-law. Now, here was Melanie walking right into her web—a perfect scapegoat if something went wrong.

"And just how do you plan to dispose of Jordan's wife?" asked Mrs. Worth.

"Don't call her that," hissed Melanie, turning on the older woman, her hands balled into small fists at her side. "She is not his wife, and never will be if I have my way."

"They are legally married—nothing can undo that. I cannot imagine Jordan agreeing to seek a divorce, and I have heard of no grounds for an annulment."

"Perhaps we could drive her away," suggested Melanie, returning to the settee and taking a seat.

"And if we are successful, will you wait another seven years before she is declared dead? And what if Jordan doesn't want to marry you then? By that time, your childbearing years would be over, and Jordan wants a family. I assume that the son Nicole claims is his is the main reason she's presently living under his roof."

"The child is a bastard," Melanie stated unequivocally. "She was probably having an affair with someone seven years ago. It would be understandable that when she began increasing she ran off with her lover. Now she's been deserted and has come running back to Jordan."

"You will never be able to convince Jordan of that. He's positive the child is his, and will never let him go. Even if he married you, he wouldn't give up his first-born."

"Jordan can keep the brat," said Melanie, dismissing the problem with a flick of her hand. "He can always be sent off to school. It's that woman I want to be rid of."

"It might be necessary to do some unpleasant things," warned Agatha.

"I would do anything," Melanie said eagerly. "Do you mean you will help me?"

"I will give it some thought," mused Mrs. Worth.

"Don't take too long," begged Melanie. "I don't want Jordan to accept her back in his life."

"Then it will be up to you to prevent that. Keep his resentment high by reminding him what he is missing because of Nicole's return. Paint a pretty picture of a loving wife and a flock of children gathered around his knee." Mrs. Worth smiled at Melanie's look of distaste.

"Mention his cold wife, and an only child that might not be his," continued Mrs. Worth. "It shouldn't be hard to keep them estranged."

"I'll do my best," promised Melanie, "but we must come up with something permanent."

Mrs. Worth's mind was already working furiously to adapt her schemes to include Melanie. "I'm sure that we'll arrive at a plan that will meet our needs," she replied. "Now go along and make yourself irresistible for Jordan. We'll meet in a day or two and discuss the possibilities."

"Maude, I'll take tea," Mrs. Worth said as soon as the door closed behind Melanie. The maid arose from the corner where she had been sitting sewing, and left the room. Maude had been with Mrs. Worth since the birth of her son. She knew all there was to know about her mistress, and Mrs. Worth trusted her implicitly.

"I had thought our problems were over," Agatha said as Maude placed the tea tray in front of her. "But it seems we have one more task to finish before we'll be truly safe."

The women looked at one another and smiled in complete harmony.

"Is there nothing more that you can remember about the robbery?" asked Jordan, staring about Drew's library.

"Nothing to remember. Everything was as it should be. Nothing out of place except the open window."

"No muddy footprints?"

"Hadn't rained for a week," replied Drew economically.

"No monogrammed handkerchief or calling card dropped conveniently on the floor?" Jordan said wryly.

Drew answered with a short bark of laughter.

Jordan was disappointed. The criminal evidently knew what he wanted and where it was located. He was in and out quickly and without mistake.

"The only thing we can assume is that the man is accepted into society, or knows someone who is and who passes along the information he needs."

"Seems a reasonable assumption," agreed Drew.

"But that doesn't narrow the field or give us much to go on," reflected Jordan. "Do you know of anyone who's deeply in debt?"

"Half the young blades in town, and many of their fathers," responded Drew. "New gambling hell opened at the beginning of the Season last year. Holds vowels that could bankrupt more than one family."

"Who owns it?" asked Jordan, his attention briefly drawn away from the burglaries.

Drew shrugged. "If anyone knows, they're not saying."

"Well, there's nothing here to see. We'll visit the clubs next, and attempt to verify whether anyone is sporting more blunt than he should be."

Drew eyed his friend, and decided to chance giving him some advice. "This wager could be a huge mistake," he said.

"You only think that because you believe in Nicole's flummery."

"She is an intelligent woman," pressed Drew. "Not taken to flights of fancy."

"What do you call being able to see things that have already happened or things that are yet to be? If those aren't flights of fancy I don't know what is."

"It's reality for a woman like Nicole," argued Drew.

Jordan gave a snort of disbelief, but Drew doggedly continued.

"Told you before. Claire's cousin married my best friend. She was able to see what caused his child to be unable to speak, and cured her. She helped expose a spy who was dealing secrets to Napoleon and, most importantly, she foresaw Waterloo."

"If these women are so exceptional, why don't we put them in charge of the country and live in paradise?"

"Doesn't work that way and you know it," Drew replied mildly. "Wouldn't be accepted so openly. They must work behind the scenes to achieve anything with their talent."

Jordan sighed, controlling his impatience at Drew's acceptance of such rot. Where had his common sense gone?

Remembering his own past with Nicole was something Jordan avoided, but if telling Drew about it would help his friend regain his good judgement, Jordan would break his rule.

"You should have known Nicole before she became convinced her daydreams were true," Jordan said, steeling himself to speak of the memories that had haunted him for seven years. "She was a beautiful bride." He stared off into space, and while he did not admit he loved his wife, the depth of his feelings was obvious to Drew.

"During our betrothal I thought her visions were just entertaining parlor games. It wasn't until after our wedding that I realized what I thought of as a game was serious to Nicole. To be fair, she tried to explain that the women in her family could see things, but I paid no attention, thinking it was just a woman's passing fancy."

"Should never have done that," interjected Drew.

"Too bad you weren't around to give me advice. I could have used it. I thought I knew everything about women—that they were all the same—but Nicole proved me wrong.

"After we married, I realized that seeing things was a way of life for Nicole. Some of the visions she claimed to see came true, and when I attributed her success to lucky guesses she became irritated with me."

Drew looked at Jordan in astonishment. "You invest, don't you?"

"Of course."

"Investment is guessing what will happen in the future. Anyone ridicule you for that?"

"That's altogether different."

"You're attempting to see into the future," insisted Drew.

"We're talking about Nicole, not me," said Jordan, ignoring Drew's argument and resuming his narration. "Every successful guess made me feel increasingly uncomfortable around her. At one point, I found myself wondering if there was a possibility she was telling the truth and could see into my mind," he admitted uneasily.

"Had the same feelings when I first met Claire Kingsley, but she set me straight. People with the gift don't peer into your mind unless asked," announced Drew. Meeting Jordan's astonished look, he said, "Code of honor, I suppose."

Jordan shook his head in disbelief before continuing. "Then my mother called one day. She complained Nicole was making a laughingstock of the Worth name, and demanded I have her stop claiming to see visions. I'm ashamed to admit it, but I was relieved. Her accusations shifted the burden of guilt for a short time, and allowed me to talk to Nicole with all the zealousness and purity of a man who only wants the best for the honor of his family.

"For several weeks afterward, I was pleased with the results.

It's true Nicole was more silent than usual, perhaps even withdrawn. But not once did she mention visions, and I felt it was just a matter of time before she forgave me and life would return to normal."

"Life's never normal with women like Nicole," said Drew.

"I found that out the hard way," muttered Jordan. "A fortnight later I returned from a visit to my country estate and she had disappeared. The next time I saw her was when we stopped at her house on the way to Dover."

"Must have been a shock."

"Definitely," Jordan replied shortly. "What I'm trying to prove with this long and boring recital of my life with Nicole is that she isn't a witch, or a wizard, or a fortune-teller. She's merely a woman with an outlandish imagination and the ability to convince a few others that the nonsense she spouts is truth."

"What about those times when she's right?"

"As I said, good guesses," Jordan replied in a hard, clipped voice. "Nothing more to say?" he asked after a short silence.

"Not until you're ready to face the truth," said Drew calmly. "And that may not be until you've lost the wager."

"I suppose I'll become bored with this one day," said Alura, looking around the crowded ballroom in delight. "But I still find it exciting."

"I felt the same way when I first came out," replied Nicole, smiling at her young companion.

"And did you tire of it?" Alura asked.

"I didn't have time. I met Jordan and we married quickly."

"And you ran away soon after," said Alura. "Oh, my goodness," she burst out, covering her mouth with her gloved hand. "I didn't mean to say that—it just slipped out. Please forgive me for bringing up such unpleasantness."

Nicole chuckled softly. "There's no need for apology. It is something long past and does not disturb me any longer. I left voluntarily and, although there were things I had to give up, I still believe I made the right decision."

"It must have taken a great deal of courage to leave your home and husband, particularly when you were increasing."

"I had no idea I was going to have a child when I left," said Nicole. "It was a lonely and frightening experience giving birth without family or friends around. Something I wouldn't want to do again," she confessed.

"I can imagine—" began Alura, before a voice from behind them interrupted their discussion.

"Two beautiful ladies all alone. Luck must be with me tonight." The voice was smooth as silk, but in a practiced manner that suggested hours of repetition to get just the right intonation.

Nicole immediately recognized the man behind the voice and forced a smile. "Why, Mr. Fitzpatrick, what a lovely compliment."

"And most sincerely deserved, Mrs. Worth," replied John Fitzpatrick, bowing to the women.

Fitzpatrick was a man who looked as if God had run out of dust when it was his turn to be formed. He was shorter and slighter than most men; even his hands and feet were small and delicate, more suited to a woman than a man. His features were bland enough to be entirely forgotten as soon as he was out of sight. As if realizing how the world would perceive him, Fitzpatrick was flawlessly turned out. Every perfectly tousled hair was in place, and his black evening clothes were expertly tailored. Still, with all his perfection and politeness, there was something about the man that Nicole could not like.

Nicole wondered why Alura remained silent. Usually, the girl bubbled over. "Are you enjoying yourself, Mr. Fitzpatrick?" she asked for want of something else to say.

"I always enjoy myself, ma'am. I was out of the country for a while and missed the society. However, now that I'm back, I intend to make up for lost time."

"Nicole," said Alura, tugging at her sleeve to gain her attention. "If you remember, we are promised for supper. It is almost time."

"Of course. You'll excuse us, Mr. Fitzpatrick?"

"Reluctantly, Mrs. Worth," he replied, bowing, "and with envy for the lucky gentlemen."

The women moved away, but Nicole felt Fitzpatrick's eyes watching them until they were swallowed up in the crowd.

"What is this about being promised?" asked Nicole as soon as they were out of earshot.

"I couldn't stand him any longer," replied Alura with a shudder. "And I didn't want to spend supper with him."

"So, there is no one waiting for us," stated Nicole.

Alura smiled impishly. "Drew is always waiting for me," she said. "And if I'm not mistaken, that's your husband with him." She nodded toward the door where the two men stood on the edge of the throng.

Nicole hid her uneasiness as they approached the men. She purposefully avoided Jordan in public except for polite exchanges when necessary. But she could not refuse to accompany Alura without arousing suspicion as to the actual nature of her and Jordan's relationship. Despite the independence and confidence that she had acquired over the years, she did not want to embarrass either one of them in front of the *ton*.

"We are looking for supper partners," said Alura, smiling up at Drew.

"Couldn't find anyone in a crowd this large?" he teased.

Alura rapped him lightly on the arm with her ivory and silk fan. "None that suited," she replied. "At least not until we saw you two handsome gentlemen, and wondered whether you were free for the next hour or so."

Alura and Drew's familiar banter made Nicole yearn for such ease between herself and Jordan. But she knew, with all that had passed between them, it would never be.

"Would be pleased to escort you," said Drew. "That is, if you promise to behave."

Alura giggled. "And if I break my promise?"

"Will turn you over my knee," said Drew, looking as fierce as his genial face would allow. "What do you say, Jordan? Should we take a chance with this hoyden in our company?"

Jordan grinned at Alura. "I suppose so. We can always put her behind a potted palm if she misbehaves."

"You wouldn't!" Alura cried in feigned indignation.

"Only way you'll know is to try," replied Drew, offering her his arm.

Nicole felt awkward as the couple moved away. She had taken meticulous precautions not to force herself on Jordan either in private or public. She realized that red-hot anger simmered just below the surface of his controlled demeanor, and she did not want to ignite it.

Years ago, Nicole had accepted that their marriage had been a mistake, that neither of them had been mature enough to save it. But Jordan had not had time to adjust to the situation. He had thought her dead until a few weeks ago, and had not had any reason to sort out the problems that had plagued their short union. He was still living in the past, while she had moved on to the future. But she could not blame him.

"I'm sorry," she apologized, meeting Jordan's gray eyes. "Alura doesn't know our true relationship."

He stared at her until she felt heat rise to her cheeks. "Neither do I," he said abruptly.

She did not know exactly what he meant or how to answer. "I . . . that is, tell them I am plagued with a headache and have gone home."

"Is your distaste so strong, you cannot dine at the same table with me in public?"

"No. No, of course not. I just thought . . . I don't want to embarrass you or force myself on you. After all, Alura gave you no choice in the matter."

"I'm perfectly capable of removing myself from unwanted situations when necessary," he replied, taking her hand and placing it on his arm. "Seeing us together may halt the endless speculation about the true circumstances of our marriage."

"Our true situation is simple," she said, still confused by his manner.

"Is it? Perhaps you would explain your view then."

"Jordan, this is not the place to discuss our private lives," she said in a whisper.

"You're right," he agreed. "And supper awaits us." He led her into the dining room, where she lost herself in Alura's endless chatter.

"Why were you so silent with Mr. Fitzpatrick?" she asked Alura the next afternoon as they enjoyed tea in Nicole's drawing room.

"I cannot like the man," Alura replied shortly.

"Is there a reason?"

"Yes," she said, small white teeth nibbling at her lower lip, while she wondered whether to confess the reason for her distaste. "He did the most despicable thing to friends of mine," she suddenly burst out, unable to restrain her hostility any longer. "When their father died, he took everything and turned them out of their home."

"How could he do that?"

"By some trickery. Although neither Caroline nor Charles can prove it."

"Would you break a confidence if you told me about it?"

"Oh, Nicole, I've been wanting to say something for the longest time. My first thought was that you might be able to help them, but I didn't want you to think I had befriended you merely to impose on your gift."

"I don't think that at all," Nicole reassured her. "If I can help your friends, I will be happy to. Now you say Fitzpatrick took their home. Was there nothing they could do?"

"Oh, they tried, but they had no proof. Here I am starting at the end. Perhaps I should begin at the beginning."

Nicole smiled. "A good idea."

"Caroline and Charles's father was the Honorable Nevil

Hardesty, the second son of the Earl of Westchester. Their father died nearly a year ago. The day before his death, Caroline said he was particularly jubilant. He called Caroline and Charles into the library that afternoon and said that some months earlier he had made a terrible mistake. He had been gambling and had lost everything to a man called John Fitzpatrick."

Nicole suddenly saw Fitzpatrick's delicate hands, dealing cards from the bottom of the deck. She shook her head, clearing the vision from sight.

"He said he had been saved by a friend who was with him," continued Alura, unaware that anything had broken Nicole's attention. "Realizing that Hardesty was in his cups, but unable to dissuade him from the bet, his friend insisted upon a period of three months for Hardesty to pay the bet, rather than immediately forfeiting his home and possessions, if he lost.

"As you can imagine, Mr. Hardesty lost. But he did manage to acquire the money to pay off the debt, and had just done so that morning. He waved a paper at Caroline and Charles, telling them it was the receipt that proved the debt was paid. He said he felt better than he had in months and meant to celebrate that evening.

"That was the last time they saw him alive. The next morning a servant found him sprawled across his desk. He had been killed by a blow to the head. The intruder had entered the library through the French doors. The room was torn apart, but nothing noticeable had been taken."

"I think I can see where this is going," said Nicole.

Alura nodded. "Before Mr. Hardesty was in his grave, Fitzpatrick was on the doorstep demanding that Caroline and Charles leave the house immediately. He had their father's gambling vowels, which he said had never been paid, and he claimed that the estate was his."

"If Mr. Hardesty had paid the debt, why did Fitzpatrick still have the vowels?" asked Nicole. "They should have been destroyed, or Mr. Hardesty should have taken them when he paid Fitzpatrick."

"And that's what would have happened in the normal course of events. But Charles said Fitzpatrick claimed he could not find the vowels when Mr. Hardesty paid him. Fitzpatrick attempted to persuade Mr. Hardesty that he could take his word as a gentleman that the debt was paid, and that if he ever located the vowels he would destroy them."

"I assume Mr. Hardesty was not so green as to fall for that," commented Nicole.

"No, indeed. He insisted upon Fitzpatrick writing out a paid receipt," replied Alura.

"And when Fitzpatrick appeared after Mr. Hardesty's death, Caroline and Charles could not find the receipt, I suppose?"

"They searched the house from top to bottom, but couldn't find it. They were certain their father had paid Fitzpatrick. Why else would he even tell them about the debt?" reasoned Alura. "But eventually they were forced to turn over the estate to Fitzpatrick. They're living in rented rooms now, still hoping that a miracle will restore their home to them.

"I thought . . ." said Alura, looking at Nicole. "I had hoped you would agree to speak with them." Her cheeks turned pink with embarrassment. "I know that I'm imposing, but I feel so very sorry for them."

Nicole reached over and patted her hand. "I shall be happy to talk with the Hardestys, but don't get their hopes up. These things do not always work out. Remember, I haven't been able to help Drew yet."

"I know, but they have nowhere else to go."

"I'll do my best," promised Nicole. "Shall we invite them to tea tomorrow?"

"Could we?" Alura smiled broadly and clapped her hands together. "That would be wonderful."

Nicole finished her tea and looked out the window. "It's such a beautiful day—would you like to join the parade in Hyde Park this afternoon?"

"I would enjoy it immensely," said Alura.

"Then I will order the carriage round and we shall be off."

* * *

When Nicole returned from Hyde Park, she was welcomed by a loud barrage of discordant notes pouring from the pianoforte in the drawing room out into the hall.

"What is going on?" she asked Harrison in a loud voice. "Did the pianoforte need tuning?"

"I believe Master Philip indicated an interest in playing the instrument, madam. And Mr. Worth is giving him his first lesson."

"But Mr. Worth cannot play a note," said Nicole.

"Just so," replied Harrison, his face expressionless.

Nicole stepped to the drawing room door. Philip was sitting on Jordan's lap at the pianoforte, banging on the keys, and laughing hilariously. Jordan occasionally joined in by striking keys that Philip's short arms could not reach.

Nicole's heart melted. She had ached for her son to know his father, and now her desire was being fulfilled.

Philip looked up and saw her at the door. "Mama. Listen, I am playing a song." He banged a few more times on the keys.

"That's wonderful, darling. Where did you learn such a wonderful tune?"

"Papa taught it to me."

"He has a little left to learn," admitted Jordan. "But I believe he shows great promise."

"I can only hope his interest is fleeting or that he improves quickly. Else all the servants will be driven from the house."

"That will be fine, won't it, Philip?" said Jordan, looking down at his son. "We will have full run of the house without anyone interfering. We can slide down banisters, and roll around on the drawing room floor, and . . ."

"Don't give him any ideas," pleaded Nicole. "He dreams up enough mischief on his own."

"Then if you will excuse us, Mrs. Worth. Master Philip must learn this arrangement by tonight. He's scheduled to play it for Prinny at this evening's soiree."

The banging followed her up the stairs, and was still faintly discernible after she had closed her door. But she never had one serious thought about complaining.

Five

Nicole was surprised to find Jordan still at the breakfast table the next morning. Usually he had already left the house for his ride in the park before she came down. It was one of those unspoken agreements that had developed during her first days back. Nicole stayed in her room longer than she normally would have if still living in the village, and Jordan left early, even on days when he might ordinarily have lingered had she not been in the house.

He looked up from the post when she paused in the doorway. "I'm sorry—I didn't realize you were still here," she said.

"Don't let me keep you from breakfast," he replied cordially. "I'm afraid I was late in rising this morning."

"I don't want to interrupt," she said, still not moving farther into the room.

"You aren't." He frowned. "But perhaps you'd rather have breakfast alone."

"It's nothing of the sort," she protested, quickly crossing the room and filling her plate.

Jordan had gone back to opening letters and intently scrutinizing their contents. Too intently, if Nicole was any judge. He was ill at ease even though he had hastened to insist she join him, and was attempting to immerse himself in the post to avoid conversation.

A lump suddenly formed in Nicole's throat. She remembered the mornings when they first married. Still warmed from a long night of lovemaking, they had spent breakfast making plans for the day, reaching out to touch one another, thinking of the night to come. Nicole toyed with her buttered eggs, hoping he would not notice her lack of appetite.

Jordan cleared his throat and laid down the letter he had been reading for the third time. "Nicole . . ."

She waited, her fork suspended above her plate, frozen in place.

"Nicole . . ." he began again.

She wished he would speak his mind and be done with it. She would take breakfast in her room every morning to avoid this embarrassment.

"The other evening. When we had supper together at the ball . . . His voice trailed off and he seemed to be searching for words.

"Yes," she said encouragingly, wondering where the conversation was leading. Would he tell her he did not want to be caught in such a predicament again?

"It wasn't unpleasant, was it?"

The question was not what she expected. "No, not at all. At least, I didn't think so," she amended.

"Neither did I," he said, meeting her gaze for the first time.

"The conversation was engaging. You enjoy Alura and Drew, don't you?"

"I consider them good friends." Nicole was confused by his questions and wondered what they meant.

Jordan dropped his gaze to the table for such a long time that Nicole bit her tongue to keep from telling him to get on with it. Her nerves were strained by the interminable waiting to hear what he would say next. Did he disapprove of her friendship with Alura and Drew? Would he demand she no longer see them? If that were the case, Nicole did not know whether she could follow his dictates, even for the sake of providing a father for Philip.

"I think it would be good for us to be seen together more often," Jordan finally said. "It would be better for Philip if we could eliminate some of the gossip by presenting a united front. Don't you think?"

Nicole was momentarily at a loss for words. Of all the things he could have said, this was what she least expected. Jordan was actually suggesting they spend time together. Her pulse quickened as she envisioned a life with him: being held tightly in his arms as they circled a dance floor; a picnic beside a lovely solitary lake; an outing to see the latest art exhibit. But the visions, and the brief flash of hope, died quickly as she grasped the substance of his suggestion. Jordan was doing it for Philip. He was concerned the child might meet with ridicule as he grew older if his parents were openly at odds with one another.

"Nicole?"

"I'm sorry," she apologized, forcing her thoughts into some pretense of logical order. "I do agree," she said shortly, unable to conjure up anything more eloquent from her confusion.

"Then shall we arrange to attend some entertainments together?" he asked.

"Of course," she agreed passively.

Jordan took her indifference to mean she was less than enthusiastic about the idea. "Are you sure about this?" he questioned, watching her intently.

Nicole heard the doubt in his voice and forced a smile to her lips. "I'm sure. I was just mulling over the invitations we've received, wondering which ones would be best."

"I have a suggestion for this evening," he said.

"What is that?"

"I've promised Philip a visit to Astley's. I thought you might like to accompany us."

Nicole had never visited Astley's Royal Amphitheatre, although she was aware of its reputation. Astley's offered a hodgepodge of events to delight children of every age. On any given night, the audience would be entertained with a wide array of performances including equestrian acts, jugglers, and pantomimes, to name a few.

Philip had never seen its like and Nicole yearned to be there to watch his reaction.

"I would like it above all things if you're certain I wouldn't be intruding."

"We have just decided to be seen together," he replied. "I can't think of a more lively place to begin our new agreement than Astley's. The performance begins at half-past five."

"Philip and I will be ready," she said. Even though Nicole knew this was for Philip's benefit, she experienced a moment of joy when she thought of the three of them attending Astley's as a family.

"I'll leave the other invitations to you. Whatever you decide to accept will be fine with me." He glanced at his watch. "I'm afraid I must go—I have an appointment."

"Go ahead," she urged him. "We can discuss this later if need be."

Nodding, Jordan gathered his letters and left the room. After placing the post in the library, he was on his way out of the house when Harrison opened the door to a short, rotund man, who peered at him through spectacles perched precariously on the end of his nose.

"You must be Mr. Worth," he said while handing his hat to the butler.

"I am," confirmed Jordan, baffled at who he might be.

"I'm Horace Grenville, Mrs. Worth's man of business," he revealed, handing Jordan a card.

Jordan was surprised that Nicole had a man of business. He remembered she had mentioned managing the funds her parents had left her, but he had not put much stock in it.

"You should be proud of your wife, sir," continued Mr. Grenville, unaware that Jordan had no knowledge of Nicole's business ventures. "She's an excellent judge of investments—you'd do well to follow her lead. Why, she is far more successful than any gentleman I represent. She seems to have a great knack at choosing investments whose returns are most favorable, most favorable indeed," he said, rubbing his hands together.

Nicole had heard his voice and hurried out of the breakfast room. "Mr. Grenville," she said, interrupting the conversation. "How good to see you."

Jordan was holding Grenville's card and staring at the shorter man with a puzzled expression on his face.

Nicole saw no reason for Jordan to be drawn into her financial affairs. "Shall we go into my sitting room where we can be more comfortable?" she said, guiding Mr. Grenville down the hall.

"A pleasure to meet you, Mr. Worth," said Grenville over his shoulder before returning his attention to Nicole.

Jordan watched the two until they disappeared through the door at the end of the hall. Horace Grenville seemed convinced that Nicole was quite a success, but Jordan wondered whether his words were nothing more than mere flattery, voiced to please a husband who might direct some business his way.

Jordan shrugged. If Nicole wished to play at being a businessman, or woman, it was her money she would lose. The idea that she used her visions to choose investments, and succeed, was too ridiculous to seriously consider. The diamonds she had worn to the ball momentarily flashed before his eyes, but he blinked them away. He did not want to think of the alternative, if she had not been successful enough to buy them for herself.

Accepting his hat and gloves from Harrison, Jordan stepped through the door to greet the morning. He was a little less pleased than he had been before Horace Grenville had appeared on his doorstep, reminding him of how little he knew about his wife.

Memories of the evening at Astley's were still fresh in Nicole's mind the next day. It was an outing they had all enjoyed tremendously.

Jordan had obtained a box in the first of the three tiers. Philip had hung over the edge of the box, unable to take his eyes from the sawdust ring where ponies raced as fast as their short legs would carry them.

The huge, fifty-lamp chandelier shone down on acrobats and clowns and magicians, all vying for the audience's approval. Several times during the evening, Jordan's and Nicole's eyes had met. At those times, all the animosity was gone; they were merely two parents, sharing the happiness that Philip was deriving from the performances. How she wished they could always be in such accord.

Now, it was nearly twenty-four hours later, and Alura's friends demanded Nicole's attention. She glanced at the people gathered around her tea table that afternoon. Caroline and Charles Hardesty were pleasant-looking people. They both had brown hair with a reddish cast, and brown eyes. Charles was taller than Caroline, but they were both slim and carried themselves with assurance.

Alura was there, sitting on the edge of her chair in anticipation of what the afternoon would bring.

"Thank you for seeing us," said Charles Hardesty.

"We certainly appreciate it," agreed Caroline. "Alura is convinced that you can help us. It would be wonderful if you could—nothing we've tried so far has worked."

"I'll be happy to do what I can, but I want you to know that what I do is generally not well thought of. If it becomes known that I'm helping, you could be ridiculed."

"Our situation could not become any worse than it is," replied Caroline, her eyes filling with unshed tears. "Oh, I don't want to become a watering pot, but the loss of our father and everything dear to us has been overwhelming."

"I understand," commiserated Nicole. "I, too, once lost everything dear to me. I shall do all I can to help you regain your possessions, but if I fail you must realize that you have the courage within you to continue."

Caroline nodded and gave her a watery smile.

"We don't expect miracles, Mrs. Worth," replied Charles seriously. "Your willingness to attempt to help is more than most people have offered. It's amazing how friends disappear when ill fortune strikes," he commented cynically.

"Yes, it is," she agreed. "Now, let's get busy and see if we can reverse your fortune. Tell me everything you can remember about what led up to Mr. Fitzpatrick taking your home."

Nicole had already heard the story from Alura, but the Hardestys told it in more detail. When they had finished, Nicole leaned back in her chair and thought for a moment.

"The paid receipt for your father's debt could be done away with by now," she mused. "However, I have a strong feeling that it's hidden somewhere. I must get into your family home to see if it's there."

"But we looked everywhere before we were forced to leave," said Caroline.

"I know, but perhaps you missed something. A secret place that no one knew of except your father."

"Or Fitzpatrick could have found it," suggested Charles.

"It's possible that Fitzpatrick saved the receipt to gloat over his victory. However, it would be risky."

"But how can you get into the house to search without rousing Fitzpatrick's suspicions?" asked Alura.

Nicole frowned in concentration. "Does the house have a ballroom?"

"Yes," said Caroline. "We usually gave a ball sometime during the season."

"All the better. If I'm any judge of character, Fitzpatrick is attempting to be accepted into the *ton*. He has the means, and now he has a house and furnishings, all in the best of taste. He must be reminded that in order to succeed, he will be expected to entertain the people he intends to impress."

"And who will suggest that to him?" asked Charles.

"Why, I will," replied Nicole, fluttering her lashes as coyly as any flirt, causing the three young people to break into laughter.

Nicole waited until the merriment had died down. "You mustn't worry if it takes a little time," she cautioned. "I'll need to cultivate Mr. Fitzpatrick so it won't seem odd when I suggest he host a ball. Trust me that it will eventually work out."

"We'll do our best," said Caroline. "But I'll be on pins and needles until then."

"If there's anything we can do . . ." said Charles.

"I'll let you know," said Nicole. "In the meantime, merely continue as you are."

"Thank you so much," said Alura, after Nicole had shown the Hardestys out.

"There's nothing to thank me for yet," replied Nicole. "And there may never be."

"They've felt alone for so long, that merely your willingness to try means a lot."

"We'll see," murmured Nicole. "Now I must plan my assault on Mr. Fitzpatrick's pride."

"You chose well if you meant everyone to see us together," said Jordan, guiding Nicole into the ballroom.

The crush at the Pattersons' ball indicated it was a huge success. They had been through the receiving line and endured the curious inspections of their host and hostess. Now Nicole steeled herself for the evening ahead.

She forced a smile and looked up at Jordan. "That's what you wanted, wasn't it?"

"Yes, it was. And I meant it as a compliment, not a complaint." He returned her smile and, feeling a shiver run through her, slipped his arm around her slim waist, drawing her closer. Nicole had not displayed any anxiety when he had mentioned his plan, but perhaps she was better at hiding her emotions than she used to be. Since he had suggested they attend together, she deserved all the support he could offer.

Nicole felt the warmth of Jordan's hand through the thin material of her dress. His touch revived sensations she had thought buried long ago. Her mouth turned dry as cotton, and she stared sightless over the crowd until she was able to fashion words into a semblance of sense.

"Perhaps we should circulate," she suggested.

Jordan chuckled. "It looks impossible, but if you're brave enough to risk your life, I must uphold the courage of all gentlemen."

"Look, there are Robert and Elizabeth," Nicole exclaimed, her voice filled with delight. "They haven't changed at all," she said impulsively, then glanced quickly at Jordan, wondering if the remark would remind him of her desertion.

"They might not agree with you," he replied, his countenance remaining amiable. "Shall we attempt to make our way over to them?"

"No. I don't think they would want to renew their acquaintance with me. After all, Robert is a duke and must protect his position."

Suddenly, Nicole was overwhelmed by the obstacles between her and a return to a normal existence. She had been foolish to think she could simply take up her life where she had left off. People had been hurt when she had disappeared. Some had grieved when they thought her dead, others had written her off as a selfish woman who had run away with her lover.

In any case, too much time had elapsed; other lives had continued, while she had waited in a strange netherworld of solitude to protect herself and Philip. Her confidence faded completely as she contemplated the pain of being ignored by Robert and Elizabeth.

"Don't turn missish on me now," Jordan said. "Robert's my cousin—he would support me even if he didn't approve. But let me set your mind to rest. I saw Robert a few days ago, and he immediately asked about your well-being. They were late coming to town because the children came down with the measles, so they didn't know you had . . . had returned. He asked us to dine with them, but I made an excuse. I didn't know if you wanted to see them."

"Of course I do," replied Nicole softly. Her vision blurred

with unshed tears. A soft white handkerchief appeared in her hand and she dabbed at her eyes. "Thank you," she said, handing it back to Jordan, wondering whether he would take her tears as a sign of weakness.

Jordan was surprised at Nicole's obvious distress. She had remained absolutely stoic since her return, and he had often wondered whether she was as cold as she appeared. Despite reminding himself that he was only with Nicole for the good of Philip, his feelings toward his wife warmed a little.

"Are you ready to see Robert and Elizabeth?" Jordan whispered in her ear.

His warm breath curled around the shell of her ear, increasing the turmoil in her breast. Unable to speak, Nicole nodded, and they made their way across the floor.

The Duke and Duchess of Weston did not concern themselves about creating a public spectacle when they greeted Nicole. Robert gave her a warm hug and kissed her on each cheek, as did Elizabeth. Their obvious joy at seeing Nicole, would go a long way toward reestablishing her in society. They moved a few steps to a small windowed embrasure, effectively isolating themselves from the crowded room.

"Your grace, I'm so happy to see you again," said Nicole, smiling.

"Such formality, my dear. I liked it much better when I was just plain Robert. Could I be that again?"

"I didn't know . . . I mean after what happened . . ."

"That's all in the past," said Elizabeth. "Why not put it behind us, and begin again?"

"I would like that," said Nicole, wondering whether she would need Jordan's handkerchief again.

"Good, then it's settled," said Robert, patting her hand. "Now shall we celebrate this reunion by granting me the honor of this next dance?"

"Well, I . . ."

"That is, unless you'd rather spend it with your husband," he said, a humorous glint in his eye.

"Yes . . . no . . . I mean," she stuttered to a halt, glancing up at Jordan. His evident concern, followed quickly by Robert and Elizabeth's enthusiastic welcome, had completely upended her composure.

Robert burst out laughing.

"Surely you remember how Robert enjoyed teasing you," said Elizabeth. "He'll behave himself as soon as he's on the dance floor, because then he must concentrate on his steps."

"I dance as well as any man here, and I'll prove it," replied Robert, offering his arm to Nicole. "That is, if you don't mind," he said, looking toward Jordan.

After the closeness he had shared with Nicole earlier, Jordan had looked forward to holding her in his arms on the dance floor. "Not at all," he said, unwilling to allow anyone to detect his newly discovered feelings. He watched Nicole's expression closely, hoping for some sign that she was as disappointed as he. However, she accompanied Robert onto the floor without a backward glance.

"She's more beautiful than ever," remarked Elizabeth, breaking into his reverie.

"Yes, she is," agreed Jordan. "And more independent than I ever thought she could be."

"Nicole was a child when you married. She's a mature woman now, accustomed to living on her own. You should expect nothing less."

"I know. And I'm attempting to adjust. We have agreed to give Philip as near a normal home as possible, but we may end up ruining one another's life completely."

"Surely it can't be all that bad. Remember, it took time to arrive at this impasse—it will take time to resolve the problem."

"Not another seven years, I hope," replied Jordan wryly.

Elizabeth laughed and took his arm. "I don't think it will be that long. Now, I must show Robert I can still attract men. Let's dance."

"I trust I'm not being lured into a duel," replied Jordan, leading her onto the floor.

* * *

Jordan had returned to the small embrasure, hoping that Nicole would be there. He had caught only brief glimpses of her since she had disappeared with Robert. While they had not agreed to live in one another's pocket during the evening, he had expected them to be together more than they had. But Nicole had moved from dance to dance, with one man then another, without returning to him. To his surprise, Jordan felt a flare of jealousy.

He watched as she circled the floor with Fitzpatrick and wondered what she saw in the man. He had returned several years ago from the Continent, where he boasted he had been highly successful in various ventures, but never explaining what they were.

A year or so ago, Fitzpatrick had come into possession of Nevil Hardesty's estate. Many said by pure thievery, but it could not be proven. Now, he assumed a mantle of respectability which was thin enough to read through. Jordan did not trust the man, and he did not like his wife becoming friendly with him.

His wife. A few days ago, Jordan would not have thought of Nicole as his wife. Something imperceptible had changed between them, and he was not sure he liked it at all. He had always thought he had a strength of purpose that could not be easily breached, but tonight was proving him wrong.

His opinion of Nicole had shifted. First, several evenings ago when they had joined Drew and Alura for supper, and he had seen Nicole laugh and talk like the woman he had fallen in love with so many years ago. Then, tonight, when tears had glittered in her eyes, revealing a vulnerability which he thought had disappeared with the young girl he had married.

"I was beginning to think you weren't here."

Jordan started slightly, looking down into Melanie's wide blue eyes. He had been unaware of her approach, which was peculiar in itself. Usually he would scour the room for a glimpse of her golden curls as soon as he entered, but she had not once invaded his thoughts this evening.

"I haven't been here long," he lied, feeling guilty at forgetting her.

"I've missed you," she said softly, pressing seductively against his side, allowing her body to curve against his.

This was what Jordan yearned for, what he was so angry about losing. He should not feel as uncomfortable as he did with Melanie beside him. Dammit! It was Nicole. He had allowed her to slip beneath his defenses, find a soft spot, and dig in before he could remind himself of her deception.

"If everything was as before, we would be man and wife by now. We would go home together, and never be parted again," she said, pressing even closer as he turned toward her.

The embrasure and a strategically located potted palm offered them a modicum of privacy, and Jordan took full advantage of it. His arms went around Melanie, his hands tracing the softness of her shoulders down to her tiny waist and to the flare of her hips.

She was right. If it were not for Nicole, he would not need to hide in a corner with Melanie. They would be married and he could take her home to a bed that had been solitary since Nicole's disappearance.

His anger flared, all gentle thoughts of Nicole fleeing before it. "I'm sorry, Melanie. If I could change the situation, I would."

"Is there nothing you can do?" she asked, her eyes wide and innocent, a hint of moisture gathering.

"Nothing that I've thought of yet," he replied, determined to ignore his temporary weakness for Nicole. She was shrewd, and he had no doubt she had planned every heartwarming moment that had occurred this evening. Well, he would not allow her to play on his emotions any longer. He had wasted years worrying about her well-being while she deliberately avoided him, playing cat and mouse around the countryside. She would not find him so easy to reach again. He would concentrate on the angel he held in his arms.

"I must go," said Melanie. "I'm risking my reputation by being here with you."

"How can this be wrong?" he said, dropping a kiss on her forehead. "You were my affianced."

"That was before *she* returned," said Melanie, still unable to utter Nicole's name. "Now, I must accept that we will never be together." She gave Jordan a small, brave smile, which tore at his heart.

"Do not lose hope, my dear. I haven't," he murmured, wiping a tear from her cheek.

"I fear it's too late. Papa insists I quit moping about and concentrate on finding an eligible gentleman. I suppose I must do as he says." She stepped away from Jordan and straightened her gown.

Jordan couldn't bear the thought of someone else touching this woman who reminded him of all he had lost. "Put your father off, Melanie. Give me a little more time to see whether I can find a way to escape this coil."

"I'll do what I can, Jordan, but I don't think he'll be patient much longer. After all, we waited years for you to be free, only to have all our plans come to nothing."

If I paid his debts I imagine he'd be willing to wait, thought Jordan, uncharitably. Instead he said, "Be brave, my darling, and have faith."

Melanie dashed away another tear and stepped out of the embrasure.

Jordan remained in the shadows, attempting to regain control of his anger and frustration. The music and laughter seemed to mock him with their gaiety. His life was a shambles, while a few feet away people danced the evening away.

All the good will he had been building with Nicole had been stripped away by seeing Melanie. He was ashamed he had been gulled so easily. He didn't deserve someone as good and true as his angel, but he meant to try his best to find a way they could be together.

Just as Jordan stepped from the alcove, Nicole circled the

floor, laughing up at her partner. Her hair gleamed beneath the chandeliers, and the small, dark beauty mark drew his eyes to the corner of her lips. His hands closed into fists by his side. How could someone so lovely bring such chaos to his life? He would allow it no longer. He would honor his promise to Melanie, and find a way to escape Nicole's clutches.

Suddenly a wave of passion struck Nicole, causing her to sway beneath its force. Its strength had broken through the barrier she always erected to protect herself from picking up unwanted revelations. She looked around to find the source, and her eyes met those of Jordan's. He was standing on the edge of the dance floor, fists clenched, eyes intently following her movements.

Nicole's heart plummeted to the bottom of her stomach. It was clear that something had happened, and whatever it was, it had caused all Jordan's resentment to surface again. Their short truce was over.

Six

"There's been another one," exclaimed Alura, rushing into Nicole's sitting room in a flurry of blue ruffled skirts.

Nicole looked up from her embroidery, amused at the young woman's excitement. "Another what?" she inquired.

"Another robbery," replied Drew, following closely in Alura's wake. "At the Goodcastle home. Lady Goodcastle insisted you be called in. Lord Goodcastle asked if I would approach you. Thought you might want to visit the house as soon as possible."

"Of course," replied Nicole, carelessly tossing aside her sewing and rising. "When can we go?"

"Now, if you want," said Drew. "They're anxious to act quickly."

"I'll be ready in a moment." Nicole was at the door before the words were barely out of her mouth. She had donned her bonnet and spencer, and was pulling on her gloves when Jordan arrived home.

"Where are you off to?" he asked, scanning their faces.

"There's been another robbery," repeated Drew for Jordan's benefit.

"And you're going to investigate?"

Alura nodded.

"Without me?" Jordan couldn't believe that Drew would ignore him when he knew the importance of the wager in which he and Nicole were involved.

"Harrison said you were out," responded Drew, looking a little ashamed. "Thought we'd leave a message."

"Are you committed to contacting Jordan before you tell me about the robberies?" asked Nicole. She fought down a wave of rising anger. She had begun this search as a favor for Drew before Jordan had turned it into a personal contest between them. Now she found out that Jordan was using his friendship with Drew as a wedge to get the upper hand.

Drew did not like the uncomfortable feeling of being caught between the two. "No," he replied, staring at the floor.

Jordan opened his mouth, then closed it without speaking.

"Not committed to seeing either of you before the other," continued Drew, raising his gaze to meet both of theirs. "Am committed to finding the thief. Both of you can help. Shouldn't need to worry about hurting feelings in a situation such as this. Should all be working toward the same goal."

"You're right, of course," agreed Nicole, though she still felt a shaft of resentment against Jordan.

"Sorry," said Jordan.

Drew waved aside their apologies. "Enough room for all of us in the carriage," he said.

"If there's no objection . . ." murmured Jordan.

"None at all," said Nicole. "Let's just be on our way," she remarked, moving impatiently toward the door. Harrison jumped to open it as she swept through, leading the way down the shallow steps to the carriage waiting in front of the house.

Nicole and Jordan shared a seat, facing Alura and Drew. Jordan's close proximity reminded her of the brief intimacy they had shared at the ball. She did not know what had happened to shatter that fleeting moment, but since that night he had treated her with the politeness of a stranger.

The uneasy silence in the carriage had gone on far too long for comfort, thought Nicole as she searched for a neutral subject. "What was taken?" she belatedly asked as the coach carried them through the crowded London streets.

"A chest full of jewels, if you take Lord Goodcastle seriously," said Alura.

"They returned home around three this morning," added Drew, relieved to have something to say. "Lady Goodcastle was wearing the family emeralds. Old settings, but large, good quality stones. Worth a fortune. Didn't lock them up. Though probably wouldn't have done any good."

"You mean she just left them lying about?" asked Nicole.

"On her dressing table," confirmed Drew.

"And the man entered her rooms?"

Drew nodded. "Must have been as quiet as a mouse. No one heard a thing. This morning the emeralds were gone."

"What about Lady Goodcastle's maid?" asked Jordan. "It seems she would have the ideal opportunity to rob her mistress."

"First person they questioned. Woman says she went directly to her room after Lady Goodcastle dismissed her. Been with the household for years. They tend to believe her."

Jordan looked skeptical, but said nothing as the carriage drew up before the Goodcastle house.

The group was greeted by William, Earl of Goodcastle, a genial man who seemed sincerely baffled that anyone would steal from him.

Lord Goodcastle ran a hand over his balding head. "It came as a shock, I'll say that. We searched the house, all the servants' quarters, and found nothing. That's when my wife insisted we call on you," he said to Nicole. "Seems she has heard of your . . . er . . . your ability to see things."

"I have more than just *heard* of Mrs. Worth," said Lady Goodcastle, coming down the stairs to join them. "I am a believer in what you can do, my dear," said the older woman.

"Thank you, my lady," replied Nicole, pleased that the countess would openly support her.

This was the first that Jordan had heard about Nicole being invited by the Goodcastles, and he was not pleased that people so high in the instep were encouraging his wife in her foolish ideas.

"Were there any broken windows or doors?" asked Jordan, attempting to draw attention away from Nicole.

"None broken," Goodcastle replied, "but a window was found open. The butler swears he inspected every door and window before he retired, but no one will admit to unlocking it."

"Mind showing us around?" asked Drew.

"Anything that might help," said Goodcastle. "The window that was unlocked is in here." He began to open a door on the left side of the hall.

"I'd like to see the kitchen door," said Nicole, staring down the hall.

Goodcastle looked at Jordan, but before the two men could decide whether to grant Nicole's request, Lady Goodcastle spoke.

"You may see anything you wish, Mrs. Worth. We've asked for your help and we'll do whatever we can."

Lord Goodcastle shrugged and turned to follow his wife and Nicole toward the back of the house.

There was nothing unusual about the door. It was stout and plainly made. Jordan wondered why they were here when it was obvious the thief entered through a window. He bent over the lock, looking for evidence that it had been forced open, but could see no fresh scratches. Straightening, he moved back in the narrow passageway to give Nicole an opportunity to examine the door.

Nicole placed her palm flat against the wood and closed her eyes, concentrating intently. This was important; she must not fail.

"He came in this entrance," she affirmed.

"But how . . ." began Goodcastle.

Lady Goodcastle motioned for him to remain silent.

Nicole turned, her eyes not seeing any of the people in the hallway. "He went this way," she said, moving down the hall, the others trailing along like ducklings behind their mother.

She paused in front of double mahogany doors. Opening them, she stepped into the library. "He stops here first. He has a candle, a white one. He lights it and looks around the room."

A white candle indeed, thought Jordan. He wanted to shake his wife. She was leading them on a merry chase, and everyone but himself seemed to be mesmerized by her performance. And what a performance it was! That singsong quality of voice, the way she moved in such a light, airy manner; no wonder the others could not see through her charade.

Nicole stopped in front of a portrait of a woman hanging behind the desk. She pulled on one side of the frame. There was a faint click and the painting swung away from the wall. Nicole opened a panel in the wall behind the picture, revealing a small safe.

"He looks here first," she said. "He's searching for emeralds. He's seen Lady Goodcastle wearing them, and knows the stones are worth a fortune."

"Someone we know?" said Goodcastle, before his wife shushed him again.

"He's angry when he doesn't find what he wants," continued Nicole, "but he isn't going to waste his evening. There's a diamond necklace and earrings which he takes. He leaves the topaz set. He doesn't admire them, and they aren't worth the trouble. There's money; he doesn't count it, so I can't tell how much. Then he finds the set of sapphires. He's pleased with those."

"Should be—I paid enough for them," muttered Goodcastle.

Nicole turned, facing the room. "He starts to leave. He's still angry because the emeralds aren't in the safe, but he's a stubborn man. He decides the emeralds must be in Lady Goodcastle's room, and he's determined to have them." Nicole walked out into the hall and began climbing the front stairs.

Jordan craved to yell at her to stop the nonsense, but the others were following her, soaking up her every word and move. He stalked along behind, keeping a tight lid on his anger.

Without the slightest hesitation, Nicole turned down the hall and went directly to the third room on the right. "He stops here and listens." She put her ear to the door. "He hears nothing and eases the door open a little at a time."

They entered the room behind her. It was Lady Goodcastle's sitting room. Through a door to the left was a bedroom and a dressing room.

"There's nothing in this room, and he goes to the bedroom door."

Lady Goodcastle gasped. "So close," she murmured.

"By God! The nerve of him," burst out Goodcastle, his face turning red.

"He sees Lady Goodcastle is sound asleep. He's gone too far to turn back now. He makes his way carefully across the bedroom to the dressing room." Nicole stood in the small room, the others clustered around the door. "The emeralds are in plain sight on the dressing table," she continued. "He smiles in satisfaction, picks them up, and puts them in his pocket."

The group made their way back to the ground floor, and followed Nicole toward the kitchen door. As she neared the entrance, she hesitated, then stopped completely.

"He hears something," she said in a hushed voice. "He's taken too long. Someone is already in the kitchen. His way is blocked."

Nicole turned and retraced her steps down the hall toward the front of the house. She hesitated at the library doors. "He considers going in here again," she said. "But then he decides to try the drawing room. He thinks there might be French doors there. It would be easier to get out." She entered the room and moved across to the long windows set into one wall.

"He realizes he has no choice but to escape this way. He goes out through the window." She stood for a long moment, staring at the window. She breathed a deep sigh and turned toward the people gathered around her. "That's all."

"But who was it?" asked Goodcastle.

"I don't know. As usual, he was dressed in black. He wore

a hat and the bottom part of his face was covered with something dark—perhaps a scarf."

Goodcastle made a sound of disgust.

"I'm sorry, my lord. Even though there's only a small chance he might be seen, he's very careful."

"There's no need to apologize," said Lady Goodcastle, giving her husband a cross look.

"Not your fault," agreed Goodcastle quickly. "I just wish you could have seen him."

"So do I," replied Nicole, exasperated that she could not identify the man.

"We know more than we did before," said the countess. "The man is someone we probably know, who perhaps was also at the ball we attended last night. I wonder if it would do any good to get a copy of the guest list."

"Many people come without an invitation," contributed Drew.

"True," agreed Lord Goodcastle. "And it could have been someone in the crowd outside." His face grew gloomy at the thought.

"There's one thing wrong with the story," said Jordan, disgusted with the instant acceptance of Nicole's rendering of the robbery. "It was the window that was unlocked, not the door."

"I wondered if anyone would ask," Nicole said with a smug smile. "It was simple for him to enter the back door—he had a key."

"He couldn't have," objected Goodcastle.

"I suggest you check the key that's kept in the pantry and see if it's still there."

Lord Goodcastle did not stop to question her knowledge of where the key was kept, but hurried out of the room.

"Is that all?" asked Drew.

Nicole glanced at Jordan. "I'm afraid it is."

"It still doesn't help us identify the man. If he'd only leave off his hat and scarf," complained Alura.

"That would be helpful," agreed Nicole, wryly. "But he's

been cautious so far. We can only hope that he'll soon make a mistake that will reveal his identity."

"That means more robberies," said Drew.

"I suppose it does," Nicole admitted. "But there's nothing else I can do at the present."

"Don't mean to accuse you of neglect," apologized Drew.

"Of course not," said Lady Goodcastle. "As I said, at least we know something, and that's better than being left completely in the dark."

"You were right. The key's gone," burst out Lord Goodcastle as he rushed into the room. "I don't know how he could have gotten it."

"Do you mind if I talk to your servants?" asked Jordan, judging it was time he took an active part in the investigation.

"Do whatever you like, if you feel it might do some good," said the earl, his face red with indignation.

Some two hours later, Jordan and Nicole again faced Drew and Alura in the carriage as it rattled over the cobblestones.

"They all swore they hadn't given the key to anyone," grumbled Jordan.

"Wouldn't admit to it anyway," added Drew.

"Perhaps they didn't," remarked Nicole. "It could have been stolen."

"How could our thief have managed that? There's nearly always someone in the kitchen. The staff has been with Goodcastle for some time and seem to be a loyal bunch. But I suppose one could have been bought off," Jordan speculated.

"I talked to Lady Goodcastle while you were interviewing the servants," revealed Nicole. "She told me about the ball they had given just last week. I remember receiving an invitation, but we were engaged elsewhere." Her mind briefly skipped back to that night when they had shared a short time of respite from the animosity that simmered between them. "She said it was quite the crush."

"I'm glad you enjoyed socializing," remarked Jordan, a sharp edge to his voice.

Nicole ignored him. "She hired extra servants to help her staff. There were deliveries being made for several days, and the house was full of guests, probably both invited and uninvited."

"But any one of them could have taken the key," said Alura, her eyes wide at the implication.

The muscles in Jordan's jaw jerked as he clenched his teeth. "Why didn't you mention this earlier?"

"I was too busy socializing," she said sweetly. "Besides, our agreement did not include sharing of information. I'm doing this merely to prove that I'm playing more than fair."

Alura looked back and forth between them uncomprehendingly, Drew cleared his throat, and Jordan gave an ungentlemanly snort of disbelief.

Nicole and Jordan entered the house and handed their outerwear to Harrison. Jordan opened the drawing room door and motioned Nicole in. Lifting a questioning brow, she stepped past him into the room and settled herself in a wingback chair.

"What is it you're holding back?" he asked abruptly.

"I don't understand what you mean."

"You understand perfectly well. You didn't tell everything you saw at the Goodcastle house."

"It shouldn't matter to you what I saw, since you don't believe in my ability."

A flush began creeping out of Jordan's collar, staining his neck a deep red. "I didn't say I believed it. I've told you before, you're good at guessing. But you thought you saw something you're not revealing."

"And if I did?" said Nicole, tilting her head inquisitively. "We have a wager riding on which of us can identify the thief first. Why should I help you?"

"Dammit, Nicole! I'm not asking for your help. Your meddling could get you into trouble. Now tell me what you think you saw," he demanded.

Nicole's laugh was like a match to tinder. He grabbed her by the shoulders, pulling her out of the chair to stand before him, his fingers cutting into the softness of her arms.

"It's nothing to laugh about," he gritted out between clenched teeth.

"Let go of me, Jordan."

He glared down at her.

"I said, let go of me."

Her deliberately spaced words broke the tension that held him. His fingers slowly loosened on her arms until his hands fell to his sides. He closed his eyes a moment, and when he opened them the fury was gone.

"I'm sorry. I've never done anything like that before to a woman." He turned away from her and walked to the window, staring out.

He was right; there had been something more, admitted Nicole silently. She had detected a faint, unfamiliar scent as she had followed in the thief's footsteps at the Goodcastle home. It could have been a perfume or pomade, or perhaps even a strongly scented soap. But it was not one of the common scents that currently pervaded the parlors and ballrooms. It would be a simple scent to recognize if she encountered it again, solely because of its uniqueness.

But there was no reason to tell Jordan about it. He would only ridicule her again. Even if he believed her, she could not explain the scent to him so that he could identify it.

And that wasn't all. Something else nibbled at the edge of her mind, something she had missed that morning at the Goodcastle house. She tried, but could not concentrate with the emotions Jordan stirred up in her. She would need to wait until she was alone to consider what it was.

"Jordan?"

He turned toward her, his face a weary mask.

Nicole did not know why she felt the need to console him. "I saw nothing more that could help you win."

"It wasn't winning I was thinking of." He rubbed a hand across his face. "I am concerned about your welfare."

Nicole could not believe what she had heard. Was there a chance for them after all?

Jordan looked directly at her. The loneliness reflected in his face pierced her heart.

"You and Philip love one another. You have cared for him his entire life. I'd wager that you always kissed the hurt away, sat with him in illness, have been his playmate when there was no one else. I don't want him to lose that no matter how we feel about one another."

Nicole wondered whether he was speaking from the experience of his own childhood. She could not imagine Agatha Worth in the role of a loving mother.

"A child needs his mother," said Jordan, breaking into her thoughts.

"And his father," Nicole added softly.

Jordan searched her face, and understanding suddenly washed over him. "That's why you came back, isn't it? Philip was at an age where he needed a father. Someone to guide him, and to look up to."

Nicole's gaze dropped to the floor.

Since Nicole had returned, Jordan had felt he had the upper hand. Whether she had allowed him to find her or not, she had voluntarily come back to their home. He had felt a certain smugness, even though he swore to himself he did not love her any longer.

But all along he had been playing the fool. By her own admission, Nicole had purposely met him. No doubt she had a list of requirements for a father.

"If I had not passed your scrutiny, would you have run away again without telling me about Philip?" Her silence gave him his answer.

"What did I do to make you hate me so?" he asked, all emotion drained from his voice.

"I don't hate you," objected Nicole. "I've never hated you."

"You must, to have kept my son from me."

"You didn't know you had a son, so you couldn't have experienced pain over Philip's loss," she reasoned. "And while we may have had a . . . an enjoyable physical relationship . . . I don't believe we ever truly knew one another. If we had, you wouldn't have turned against me so quickly."

"You knew I wanted a family," he accused. "Don't you think I suffered not only from losing you, but when I realized I might never have children of my own? I thought I did understand you. That we had a marriage that would last. And if you will remember, I didn't turn against you—your visions came between us."

"It wasn't my visions, it was your mother," argued Nicole. "She was the one who convinced you that I was an embarrassment to your family. She was the one who urged you to put me in my place."

"And you were the one who chose to leave before we could even discuss the problem."

"Discuss? You didn't even know the meaning of the word. You ordered—I was to obey. You didn't understand then, and you still don't. I am not playing at seeing visions. My second sight is a part of me, a part of my family down through generations. Drew and Alura have told you of my cousin and what she accomplished with her gift. But you will not believe any of us, will you? You go blindly on your way, certain that what you believe is just and right."

"And you alone determined what was right for our son. Am I so different from you?" he asked, catching her off guard.

"I . . . I don't know," she replied honestly. "Perhaps I do believe I know what's best for Philip. I suppose every mother thinks she knows what is best for her child. But I came back when I could have hidden from you for as long as I wished.

You would have never known about Philip if I had decided differently."

"So I should thank you for giving me my own son? I should be grateful that you allowed me to miss the first six years of his life?"

"I did what I thought was right, Jordan."

"For yourself," he roared, then took several deep breaths to regain his composure.

"And what was right for my baby," she insisted. "Do you think it was easy? When I found I was increasing, I wanted to come back. I was frightened. I was a young girl who knew nothing about having babies and raising them. Then I remembered your demands. I was to be no more than a puppet with you and your mother pulling the strings. I did not want it for myself and I certainly did not want it for my baby."

"Surely, I was not that bad."

"In my eyes you were," she replied sadly, but honestly.

Nicole felt a great sorrow well up in her. They had been two innocent people caught up in circumstances that had brought them to this end.

Jordan heaved a great sigh. "For the moment, Nicole, forget the past. Forget that I don't believe in your visions, or that I doubt your reasoning that everything you've done has been for our good. Try, if you can, to ignore your dislike for my mother. But most of all, let us put aside this foolish wager. I suggested it because I thought it might be an expedient way to . . ."

"To bend me to your will," interrupted Nicole.

"To end our differences," said Jordan. "However, I was wrong. Whatever you might think, I don't want you hurt. I don't want Philip to lose his mother."

Nicole remained silent. Why was she disappointed that his concern was for Philip? She could expect nothing more.

"Do we both agree that the bet is off?" Jordan asked.

"If that is what you wish," she answered woodenly.

"I'll admit I'm relieved you won't be traipsing all over town investigating the robberies. If the man were cornered, he could prove to be dangerous."

"I think you misunderstood," said Nicole, rising from her seat. She walked to the door, then turned to face him. "I only agreed to abandon the wager, not the investigation. I fully intend to keep my promise to Drew and the other people who have been robbed. I'm going to do my best to find the thief. Now, if you will excuse me." Without another word, she disappeared through the doors, leaving him staring after her.

Seven

"You're slighting your task," commented Mrs. Worth, nodding toward the door.

The ballroom was crowded, but Melanie could see Nicole and Jordan standing at the entrance. "I've not had the opportunity, but I'll take advantage of this evening," she vowed.

"You must make your opportunities," replied Mrs. Worth evenly. "Or else neither of us will get what we want."

"You've never told me what you hope to accomplish by helping me get rid of that woman."

"Let's just say I would be happy to see the last of Nicole and her meddlesome nature. But that won't happen if you don't follow my instructions."

"Don't ring a peal over my head," complained Melanie. "You promised you'd have a plan by now, but I've heard nothing."

"It's taking longer than I thought—we must be circumspect. In the meantime, it is up to you to keep Jordan distracted."

"I'll do my best," promised Melanie. She forced a smile to her lips and began making her way across the room.

Jordan observed the throng in the stuffy ballroom. "It's uncanny how you can pick the events that are going to be absolute crushes. You must have some sort of a . . ." He left the sentence unfinished, cursing himself for speaking before thinking.

"Some sort of second sight?" asked Nicole, vastly amused at his slip.

Jordan did not enjoy being the target of Nicole's goading. "I was going to say, *intuition*," he replied pompously.

"Nearly the same thing."

"I know I agreed to this," he said, ignoring her comment. "But could you choose something a little less crowded the next time?"

"You did say the idea was to be seen together, so I thought the more people the better. After we establish that there's nothing worth gossiping about in our lives, we need not be together so often." She wanted to be rid of his company as much as he did hers. She did not like the feelings that had begun surfacing, keeping her awake at night, obliging her to listen for his return more often than she liked.

"That's true," he grumbled, wondering why he wasn't relieved at the thought of their enforced closeness coming to an end.

"Why, Jordan, I haven't seen you in the longest time."

Jordan turned and was face-to-face with Melanie. She was looking more like an angel than ever in her white dress trimmed in blue.

His admiration lasted a shade too long for Nicole. "Jordan, do introduce me to your friend," she trilled sweetly.

"Ah, yes. Miss Grayson, may I introduce Mrs. Worth," Jordan said shortly.

Nicole studied the woman who had enthralled her husband. Outwardly, she was a fetching little thing, and Nicole could see why a man would be attracted. This was the kind of fragile-looking woman who appeared to need protecting from the harshness of life. But Nicole caught a glimpse of hardness in Melanie's blue eyes and knew that it would be dangerous to underestimate the woman.

"Good evening, Miss Grayson. It's a pleasure meeting you," she said smoothly, as if she sincerely meant it.

"I've heard a great deal about you," replied Melanie, barely concealing her smirk.

"I'm sure you have." Nicole couldn't help herself. Connect-

ing with Melanie's thoughts was extremely easy; she did nothing to conceal them. Nicole was immediately pulled into a vor-
tex of hate more intense than she had ever felt, and it was all
directed toward her. She quickly pulled free, forcing herself to
remain expressionless and polite to Melanie.

Jordan was extremely uncomfortable caught between the two
women. The undercurrents swirled around them, threatening to
break into the open. He must separate them before they drew
the very sort of attention he strove to avoid.

John Fitzpatrick approached and although Jordan did not like
the man, at that moment he almost felt grateful for his company.

"Ladies. Worth. Pleasure seeing you," said Fitzpatrick. "Miss
Grayson, I wonder if you have the next dance free?"

"I'm sorry, but I'm already promised," Melanie said. With a
girlish giggle she clutched Jordan's arm, looking up at him
through thick lashes.

Jordan could say nothing. To deny it would hurt Melanie, to
agree that he had arranged to dance with Melanie might set
Nicole off, and either would feed the *ton's* speculation.

"My apologies," said Fitzpatrick. "I naturally assumed . . ."
his voice trailed off as he looked from Jordan to Nicole.

"That's perfectly all right," replied Melanie. "Jordan asked
me days ago, or otherwise I would be pleased. Perhaps later."

"Delighted."

"Come, Jordan," said Melanie, tugging at his arm. "The mu-
sicians are ready to begin."

Jordan cast a dark look at Fitzpatrick and Nicole, but followed Melanie onto the floor.

"Mrs. Worth, would you care to dance?"

Nicole did not want to dance with Fitzpatrick. However, she
did need to become more familiar with him, or she could never
hope to suggest he hold a ball at his house.

"Not at the moment, Mr. Fitzpatrick, but I would enjoy your
company if you're not otherwise engaged."

"If I were not free, I would make myself so to enjoy your
company."

Fitzpatrick's flattery was too patently false to impress Nicole, but she smiled as if she believed every word.

Jordan swore under his breath as he guided Melanie around the floor. "Why did you say we had arranged this dance?" he asked, carefully controlling his temper so he would not upset her.

"Oh, I don't know, Jordan." She pouted prettily, long enough to allow him to admire the effect. "I have lost you and it's all her fault," she complained. "It was beneath me, I know, but I just couldn't stop myself. Please don't be mad," she begged. "It's only because I . . ." She stopped for a moment, her eyes filling with unshed tears. ". . . Because I care so much," she finished in an anguished whisper.

"Melanie, my dear, please don't punish both of us this way. You know my feelings. I'm trying to think of some way to escape this trap, but as yet I've found nothing."

Melanie wanted to fall on the floor, kicking and screaming in sheer frustration. Neither Mrs. Worth nor Jordan had come up with an expedient way to be rid of his wife. If they did not suggest something soon, she would find a way herself.

"I'm not blaming you, Jordan. But if it weren't for her, we would be married now," she reminded him. "If she would only go away and leave us to fulfill our happiness. I didn't tell you before," she said, lowering her gaze, "but I had made such a lovely baby dress, embroidered with tiny blue flowers." Melanie did not flinch at the lie she told so convincingly. "I took it out today and it caused me such pain, I've sworn to give it away."

"My dear," murmured Jordan, thinking of the child who would never wear the tiny dress. "You must stop torturing yourself."

"I can't help it, Jordan. You were my world, and now I'm so alone."

Jordan was afraid Melanie would burst into tears on the dance floor. "Shall we get a breath of fresh air?" he asked, guiding her toward French doors that opened onto a terrace.

"That would be wonderful," she replied, smiling bravely up at him.

Nicole watched Jordan disappear onto the terrace with Melanie. He was a fool. All their efforts to appear a normal couple could be ruined by his indiscretion.

She would not worry about it. Going about together had been his idea; she had been doing quite well without him. She would continue her undertakings and ignore her husband, who was being led around like some caper-witted green-head by a scheming opportunist.

"Shall we stroll out into the hall?" asked Fitzpatrick. "I believe the crowd is thinner there."

"It is quite the crush, isn't it?"

"A success in the eyes of the *ton*," he agreed.

"It's such a beautiful house," said Nicole, admiring the portraits on the wall. "But you are probably not that impressed, living as you do."

"My home is not all that grand," he replied modestly.

"You live in the former Hardesty house, do you not?"

"You know it?"

"Who does not?" she replied, observing the expression of satisfaction cross his face. "Why, I remember the Hardestys throwing such wonderful balls. They were the talk of the Season. The ballroom is of such a spacious proportion, and the decorative details are magnificent. In all my years away from London, those were some of my most cherished memories," said Nicole, hoping she was not doing it up a bit too brown.

"Yes, I suppose it is rather fine," conceded Fitzpatrick, preening a bit.

"It's a shame you haven't planned a ball," she mused. "It would be the most sought-after invitation in town."

"Would it? I mean, it would, wouldn't it? Perhaps I should consider it." He stood, finger tapping his chin, deep in thought.

"That would be marvelous, Mr. Fitzpatrick," praised Nicole,

as if the decision were already made. "I hope you will not forget me, for all the *ton* will be clamoring for an invitation."

"You shall be first on my list, madam. If it had not been for you, I would not have considered it."

"Thank you, Mister Fitzpatrick. I look forward to it with great anticipation."

Fitzpatrick raised her hand to his lips, a distinctly amorous light in his eye. It was definitely time to draw their *tête-à-tête* to an end, thought Nicole. She had achieved her goal; Fitzpatrick would have a ball, and she would be invited. It would be the perfect opportunity to search for the receipt which would allow the Hardestys to reclaim their home. Well worth the time spent with Fitzpatrick.

"I think I hear a waltz being played, Mr. Fitzpatrick. It's my favorite—may I accept your kind invitation to dance?"

"A pleasure, madam," he said, offering his arm.

Jordan was unable to guide Melanie's attention to anything other than how they could manage to be together. Listening to her made him face the truth of the matter. There was no legal way to be rid of Nicole. Barring her death, they would remain married and there was nothing he could do to change the situation.

He felt guilty because he had kept Melanie's hope alive. It was time to confess his helplessness and allow her to find another man who could give her a home and family.

"Melanie, my dear?"

"Yes, Jordan." She snuggled close to him, resting her head on his chest.

"Ah, Melanie. I have something to say to you. It isn't pleasant, and you're going to be upset, but it must be said."

"Nothing could be worse than what I've already endured," she said. "The only thing that holds me together is knowing that someday we'll be together."

Jordan's heart sank. This was going to be worse than he thought. "That's what I want to talk with you about, Melanie."

Alana Clayton

He took her hands and held them against his chest, looking down into her eyes.

"I've given our situation considerable thought. I've consulted everyone I know and the answers are all the same. There is no way we can be married as long as Nicole is alive."

Melanie was outraged. "Divorce her," she demanded.

"I can't. The process would take quite some time, and there is no guarantee that a divorce would be granted. If it was, we would be beyond the social pale and we could not live in such isolation no matter how strong our love. And before you ask, annulment is not an option either. I'm sorry, Melanie, there is no way."

"And just what am I to do?" she insisted.

"You must find someone who will love you and marry you. Someone who will provide a home and take joy in raising a family with you."

"That is easy for you to say. You are a man who may pick and choose where you please. I must flirt and cajole and hope that a man I admire will offer for me. If not, I must take what I can and be thankful."

"That's not true, Melanie. You're a beautiful woman. Any man would be proud to have you as his bride."

"I've spent too much time with you, Jordan. I'm almost on the shelf, and there are younger girls on the marriage mart with far better dowries than mine."

Jordan felt responsible for Melanie's situation, even though he strongly believed she was wrong about her chances for marriage. It was true she did not have a dowry to speak of, but there must be other men who would love her for her beauty and sweetness alone. Not every gentleman needed the money brought to a marriage.

"Melanie, if I could change the circumstances, I would. I will talk to your father. Perhaps there is something I can do that will make your situation easier."

Melanie's face turned red with embarrassment. She knew Jordan meant to offer her father money, and the worst of it was that Mr. Grayson would accept. She felt cheapened, but knew she could not afford to reject his offer.

"I think I should go now," she said in a small voice.

"I'm sorry," repeated Jordan, frustrated that he could do no more.

Melanie did not speak until they reached the ballroom again, where she bade him a quick goodbye.

Jordan searched the room for Nicole. He had left her rather abruptly to dance with a woman who at one time was to become his betrothed. He must find his wife and pretend to be the attentive husband, or the gossips would be speculating on his marriage more than they already were. Lord! What a web of deception he was spinning. He wondered if life would ever return to normal again.

His lips tightened with disapproval as he saw Nicole on the dance floor with Fitzpatrick. He did not like the man's ingratiating ways. There were rumors circulating about Fitzpatrick that made him a less than desirable dancing partner for his wife. Jordan had ignored the man since he was of no importance to him. But if his wife accepted Fitzpatrick as a companion, then he would look into his background. Neither he nor Nicole could afford to bring additional notoriety to their situation.

"You seem to spend a great deal of time with Fitzpatrick," remarked Jordan after they had settled themselves in the carriage for the drive home.

"No more than any other," Nicole replied disinterestedly.

"You have danced with him every evening we've been out."

Nicole did not want to argue with Jordan, but he had no reason to judge her conduct as inappropriate. "And you've disappeared with Miss Grayson each evening we've been out."

"That's entirely different. Fitzpatrick's background is murky at best, while Melanie is a respectable member of society."

"Who was going to be your wife before I returned, and who evidently has not given up yet."

"Melanie is aware there's no chance for us," replied Jordan.

"Then her actions do not suit her knowledge, for she appears to be a woman determined to snare you in the parson's mousetrap despite your already having a wife. I have no doubt she is demanding you divorce me."

"You are misinterpreting her actions."

"Am I? I wonder what I would hear if I intruded into her thoughts?" said Nicole.

"You wouldn't," exclaimed Jordan, forgetting for the moment that he did not believe in her ability.

"I've made it a rule not to delve into other people's minds unless necessary or invited. However, if Melanie continues her animosity, I will have no other choice. No matter what you think, she hasn't given up on you. I think she would do anything to be rid of me, and I won't allow her to harm either me or my child."

"You've changed more than I thought," accused Jordan. "You would never have threatened another person when we met."

"At that time, I was not a mother and I did not feel endangered. I will do what I must to defend myself. If anything should happen to me, Philip would be left alone."

"Nothing will happen to you, but if it should, Philip would have me."

"And you would have Melanie," she replied shortly.

He could not deny it.

"How long do you think she would tolerate my child?" asked Nicole. "As long as it took to send him away," she said, not waiting for an answer.

"It isn't in her nature to be cruel," he objected.

Nicole didn't reply. Jordan would not believe ill of Melanie, but Nicole had felt her anger. Melanie was dangerous, and the next time they met, Nicole would not hesitate to invade her thoughts if necessary.

* * *

Jordan and Philip were in the front hall when Nicole descended the stairs early the next afternoon.

"Mama! We are going to Tats'all to see the horses."

"If you are wondering, he means Tattersall's," said Jordan stiffly. He was still piqued by their argument the day before, but would not allow Philip to see his parents pulling caps with one another.

Nicole kneeled down to hug Philip. "That's wonderful, darling." Looking up at Jordan, she said, "He loves horses so much. Thank you for taking him."

Jordan adjusted his hat and pulled on his gloves. "There's no need to thank me for taking an interest in my own son."

"I know, but it's something I've yearned to see for such a long time."

"Then you should have returned six years ago," Jordan snapped, taking Philip's hand and leading him to the door. He hesitated a moment, battling the shame that filled him after his needless remark to Nicole. It was unworthy of him, he knew, but his stubbornness would not allow him to turn and apologize.

Nicole stood in the hall after the two had left. Pain had lanced through her at Jordan's stinging retort. Touching her cheek, she found it wet with tears. She climbed the stairs again, returning to her room to repair the damage before Alura arrived.

Jordan had been harsh, but she had to consider whether he had told the truth. Perhaps she should have returned when she found she was increasing. She sat before her mirror, reviewing her reasons for leaving. Putting aside the emotions she experienced when she saw Philip and Jordan together, she still felt she had made the right decision. Philip was far better off with the mother she was now, rather than what she would have become had she stayed.

Her spirits revived, Nicole went downstairs to greet Alura.

"What a lovely day for a stroll," said Alura as they followed a path through Hyde Park. "I'm glad you suggested it."

"It is not merely for pleasure," admitted Nicole. "I sent a note round to the Hardestys. We should be meeting them shortly."

"You've found out something, haven't you?" Alura asked, practically skipping along beside her.

Nicole laughed at her antics. "If you don't calm down, you'll be labeled a hoyden, and think what that will do for your consequence."

Alura returned to a sedate walk, but still could not quell the excitement bubbling inside her. "You must tell me or I shall burst with impatience."

"You'll do no such thing. Besides, here are Caroline and Charles, so your curiosity will soon be appeased."

"Mrs. Worth. Alura. How wonderful to see you again," said Caroline Hardesty.

"Please, both of you, call me Nicole. *Mrs. Worth* reminds me too much of my mother-in-law."

"We shall be pleased to," answered Charles for both of them.

"I wanted to meet here where it will seem like an accident," explained Nicole. "If we are seen visiting back and forth, it may get back to Fitzpatrick, and I want to avoid that."

"Do you have news for us?" asked Caroline.

"Some," replied Nicole. "I have convinced Mr. Fitzpatrick to hold a ball in his home. He has promised me an invitation, and I intend to use that opportunity to search for the receipt."

"We are extremely grateful, aren't we, Charles?" said Caroline.

"We certainly are. Is there anything we can do to help?"

"Nothing at this point. I know you want to be involved, but you would only make Fitzpatrick suspicious. In fact, I must ask you to do just the opposite. Avoid him as much as possible. The more relaxed he is, the more likely I'll find what we're looking for. We must also be circumspect. If you need to see me, send a note and we'll arrange a meeting. I'll do the same. If Fitzpatrick sees us together it could ruin my chance at finding the receipt."

"It will be difficult, but we'll follow your instructions," said Charles.

"I'll find a way to keep you abreast of what's happening," she promised.

"Thank you," said Caroline, reaching out to touch Nicole's hand. "This means so much to us."

Charles nodded his agreement, then they turned down a side path and quickly disappeared.

"Shall I take you home?" Nicole asked Alura. "I wish I could stay longer, but I have an appointment with Lord and Lady Goodcastle to inspect the thief's trail again."

"I would like to accompany you above all things," said Alura pleadingly.

"It will be boring," warned Nicole. "I simply mean to repeat what I did the last time we were there."

"Do you think it will do any good?"

"Jordan disapproves of what I do so strongly that he distracted me from my concentration. I missed something the last time, and it's been bothering me since. I can't see what it is, or at least I can't recognize it, so I've decided to return and attempt to solve the puzzle."

"Then take me with you. I will divert Lord Goodcastle if he is there, and you can have the privacy you need to concentrate on the thief."

"As long as you understand it could be tiresome."

"I promise I won't insist upon leaving until you're ready."

Alura might prove a good distraction for Lord Goodcastle, thought Nicole. For all his good-natured personality, he did talk a lot, and she might not be able to find what she had missed with him at her elbow.

"All right, but if Lord Goodcastle talks your ear off, you cannot say I didn't warn you."

Alura laughed and the two set off toward the carriage waiting at the entrance to the park.

"Lord Goodcastle, it is kind of you to allow us back into your house," said Nicole, flashing her most charming smile.

"Not at all. Not at all. I'm happy someone's taking an interest in this whole affair," replied the earl. "Sorry to say, Lady Goodcastle is not here."

"That's quite all right—it isn't necessary I speak with Lady Goodcastle. And I won't take up much of your time, either," promised Nicole. "I'd just like to follow the same route I did the last time. I want to make sure I didn't miss anything."

"Lord Goodcastle, could I trouble you for something to drink?" asked Alura. "We've been walking in Hyde Park and I'm absolutely parched."

"Of course, my dear, of course," he said, signaling the butler and ushering her into the drawing room. "Mrs. Worth?"

"Thank you, my lord, but I'm not thirsty. If you don't mind, I'll go ahead. I know the way—you need not accompany me."

"Well, if you're certain . . ."

"I'll be fine, I assure you," Nicole said, smiling confidently.

After Alura and the earl disappeared into the drawing room, Nicole set off down the hall. She followed the trail once again, through the library, up the stairs, through Lady Goodcastle's rooms, and then downstairs again. If she had missed anything the last time, she had missed it again today, but there was still the drawing room left to visit.

Lord Goodcastle and Alura were at the far end of the room. The earl, intent on Alura's banter, had his back to Nicole and did not see her enter.

This was Nicole's last chance, and she concentrated on what she was seeing. All was the same. The man came into the room, looked around for an exit, and crossed to the long windows set into one wall. He peered out of each, looking for the freest access, Nicole assumed. He chose one, pushed it open, and threw one leg over the windowsill. The last thing Nicole saw was the sole of his boot as he slipped through the window and disappeared into the night.

She shook her head, disappointment filling her. She had been mistaken all along. There was nothing here, nothing new for her to see. But, wait! Something still bothered her. She closed her eyes, willing herself to concentrate on every detail, no matter how small. Then she had it! The boot sole—the last thing she had seen as the thief left. There was a cut on it, an unusual L-shaped gash which would easily identify the thief.

"Alura," she called. "I'm afraid we must go. I just remembered an appointment with my dressmaker. If I don't show up she will never forgive me. You understand, my lord."

"Of course. Dressmakers can be just as crotchety as tailors," he said, adjusting the sleeve of his morning coat.

"Did you find anything?" he asked as he showed them to the door.

"Perhaps," said Nicole. "It's one of those things I need to consider. I know it doesn't help you, but we're doing all that we can."

"I don't mean to complain about your efforts," replied Goodcastle. "It's only that the emeralds have been in the family for generations, and Lady Goodcastle feels responsible for their loss, even though I assure her that she's worth far more than the jewels. I'm just happy that scoundrel didn't harm her."

"As we all are, my lord. Tell her not to give up so easily. There are avenues left to explore before we lose all hope."

"I will pass your words along, Mrs. Worth. I'm sure they will hearten her."

After the polite goodbyes were said and the two women were in the carriage again, Alura turned to Nicole, her eyes shining with curiosity.

"Well? Did you see anything new?"

"I think so, but I'd rather not mention it for I don't know how much use it will be."

"Nicole. How can you tease me so?"

"I'm sorry, Alura, but until something comes of it, I must keep it to myself."

"Oh, all right," said Alura petulantly, reminding Nicole of Philip when he didn't get his way. "But we must stop at Gunter's for an ice to make up for your secret."

"Granted," said Nicole, happy to be let off so easily.

Eight

Nicole drew her shawl around her shoulders and watched the busy streets of London through the window. The carriage felt empty without Jordan's substantial figure by her side. She had not known how much she took his presence for granted until he wasn't there.

Jordan had become angry when she insisted upon attending Fitzpatrick's ball. When she would not cry off, he refused to escort her, slamming the door after him as he left the house.

Nicole wondered if he was with Melanie, complaining of his willful wife. There was no doubt in Nicole's mind that Melanie would commiserate with him. Would they end up in one another's arms? Nicole was glad that she had arrived at Fitzpatrick's; she did not want to think about it.

"Mrs. Worth, I am overjoyed that you could attend. The night would not be complete without you," said Fitzpatrick.

Fitzpatrick had found a distant relative to stand in the receiving line with him and act as hostess. After promising Fitzpatrick a dance, Nicole greeted the elderly woman and passed into the ballroom.

Caroline and Charles Hardesty had been right; the ballroom was lovely. Pilasters decorated with flowers and vines were set along the walls at regular distances. The ceiling was molded, with cupids gamboling amidst additional flowers, around a cloud-swept sky of blue. A small gallery housed the orchestra, which was playing a well-rendered waltz when Nicole stepped through the door.

It was a good hour later before Nicole could separate herself from her current dance partner. She had manipulated this evening in order to give herself an opportunity to help the Hardestys, and she had yet to do one thing to find the receipt.

Nicole slipped into the hall. There were a few couples strolling there, looking for more privacy than the crowded ballroom afforded. She chose what she hoped was the library. Opening the door, she peered in and saw that the room was deserted. A pair of candles burned, dimly lighting the room.

She closed the door, and leaned back against it, breathing deeply, relaxing before she began her work. Suddenly her eyes jerked open and what she saw made her ability seem more like a curse than a blessing. Nevil Hardesty was being murdered, right before her eyes. She could not block the scene before her. Two men burst through the French doors and grabbed Hardesty as he rose from the chair. He struggled but was unable to fight them off. One of the men smashed him over the head with a short club and Hardesty dropped to the floor.

When it was all over, a third man entered the room, stepping around the overturned chair and the smashed ornaments knocked from a small table. He wore a hat and its shadows concealed his face. He searched the top of the desk, then the drawers, tossing aside papers that were of no interest to him. Locating the safe, he took a key from Hardesty's motionless form, opened the door, and began exploring its contents. He evidently did not find what he wanted for he slammed the door and faced the room again, hands fisted on his hips.

The candlelight illuminated his face, and Nicole's breath caught in her throat. The Hardestys were right; it was John Fitzpatrick. And while he might not have struck the blow, he was responsible for their father's death.

Ignoring the body on the floor, Fitzpatrick and the two men quietly inspected the entire room, but found nothing. Dawn was arriving when he called off the search. Fitzpatrick was the last one out of the room. He turned and surveyed the scene a last time, exasperation showing in every line of his body, then disappeared through the door, leaving it slightly ajar.

It took a few moments for Nicole to recover and to gather her thoughts. What she had seen made it even more important to search the house. She began making her way round the room, methodically examining the furniture, paintings, walls, floors, any place that would serve as a hiding place for the receipt.

By the time Nicole finished, she was as frustrated as Fitzpatrick had been. She had been certain that Nevil Hardesty would have hidden the receipt in his library. But it had been a long time, and perhaps Fitzpatrick had found it after he moved into the house and had destroyed it by now.

Nicole could not give up. She had promised Caroline and Charles she would do her best to get their home back. This meant searching the rest of the house, no matter how awkward it might prove to be.

Nicole decided to forego the kitchen area, since she didn't think a man would hide anything there. She inspected the drawing room, then made her way upstairs. She had just finished searching a bedroom when she opened the door and ran directly into Fitzpatrick.

Nicole froze. The last time she had seen him he had casually stepped over the body of Nevil Hardesty on his way out of the library.

"Mrs. Worth," he said, his eyes cold and his voice formal. "Are you lost?"

"I suppose I am," she replied, attempting to sound normal and look suitably embarrassed. "I was looking for the ladies' withdrawing room, but I seem to have taken a wrong turn."

Fitzpatrick's features relaxed. "If you will allow me," he said, offering his arm, "I will show you the way."

She took his arm, subduing the distaste that coursed through her. "I couldn't help but notice that the house is as lovely as I

remembered it. I had not seen any of the bedrooms, but the one
I chanced into was charming," she said.

"You must allow me to show you around," he suggested.

"I would like that very much. Just give me a few moments
to freshen up and I shall rejoin you," she said before he could
reconsider his invitation.

He was waiting at the top of the stairs when she came out of
the ladies' withdrawing room a short time later.

"Shall we begin with the rooms upstairs?" he invited.

The next afternoon, Nicole paced the length of the drawing
room. Caroline and Charles Hardesty would be arriving soon,
and she must decide what to tell them.

If she revealed that their father had been murdered, Charles
might rush out to exact revenge for his father's death. If he did,
he would most likely end up imprisoned, transported, or hanged,
and would never be able to reclaim the estate. Nicole was still
undecided when Caroline and Charles arrived.

"We could barely wait to hear if you had discovered anything," said Caroline as soon as she saw Nicole.

"Why don't we sit down and have some tea?" invited Nicole.

"Caroline doesn't mean to be forward," said Charles.

"You need not apologize for me," interrupted Caroline. "I'm
sorry if I was rude," she said, turning to Nicole. "It's just that
I'm overly anxious."

"I understand," replied Nicole. "But there's something I must
say before I tell you about last night."

The three settled into chairs around the tea tray on a table in
front of them. Caroline and Charles declined tea; Nicole set the
teapot back on the table without pouring a cup for herself.

"I want you to make a promise before I tell you about Fitzpatrick's ball."

"A promise?" questioned Caroline, puzzlement evident in
her voice.

"From both of you, but mostly you, Charles."

"Fitzpatrick killed our father, didn't he?" asked Charles. His hands closed into fists, and his face darkened with rage.

"Charles, you must promise you won't do anything, no matter what I tell you. Remember, there is no proof of what I say except for what I alone can see, and many people give it no credence. We must use what I've seen to bring about justice. Now, will you promise?"

Charles's face reflected his internal struggle. It took several moments, but he finally nodded his head. "I promise. I'll do nothing, but if the time should come when all hope is gone that we shall see justice, then you must release me from my pledge."

"I will gladly do so, my friend. Now," she said, her voice crisp, "let me tell you what I saw." And she did so, as gently as possible.

Caroline was sobbing quietly into her handkerchief and Charles was sitting as still as a statue when she finished her recital of the last evening's events.

"So I didn't find the receipt in the house. Now, I could have very well missed it, but I don't think so. The circumstances surrounding the receipt were so serious that I feel I would have found it if it had been there. That leaves us with two alternatives: either the receipt was destroyed, or it's been hidden in some other place.

"Fitzpatrick did not find the receipt that night . . . the night your father died. He could have found it later, but you had been over the house by then and since you know it far better, I think you would have found it before he did.

"I need your help with the second possibility. Consider your father's routine, where he went, what he did. We will need to search each of the places where he might have hidden the receipt."

"But what if he destroyed it himself?" asked Caroline.

"I don't think he did. He was too happy about paying off his debt. But he must have had some suspicions about what Fitzpatrick might do. He wanted to keep proof that the debt was paid, and had demanded a written receipt. I strongly feel that your father hid it for safekeeping and that it's still in existence."

"So we do nothing?" Charles said woodenly.

"We go home and begin making a list," said Caroline, resolutely wiping her eyes.

"While that blackguard walks around free," he said, eyes flashing hate.

"You've promised, Charles. Fitzpatrick is an evil man. He has men who will kill without thinking twice about it. I've lost Father and our home—I couldn't go on if I lost you, too," Caroline pleaded.

The fire died in his eyes and he passed a weary hand across his face. "I'll keep my promise for the time being. But you cannot hold me off forever."

After the Hardestys were gone, Nicole leaned back into her chair. Using her ability was draining, especially when dealing with such volatile issues.

However, for the time being, she knew she must gather her energy, for she was determined to discover who was stealing the most expensive jewels in London, and locate the Hardestys' receipt.

At the same time, danger was threatening her. It was like a thunderstorm gathering in the distance. She could hear the rumblings of thunder, and while it was still far off, she knew it could move quickly and catch her unprotected in its violence. Nicole shivered. She could feel the cold rain falling on her face, drowning her in its intensity.

"I can't understand why you won't help me," complained Mrs. Worth.

Robert, Duke of Weston, surreptitiously studied his aunt. Her lips were pursed disapprovingly, and he recognized the mournful look on her face from when he was a boy and had gotten into a bit of mischief.

"I would do anything I could for you, Aunt Agatha, but what you ask is too much."

"You will not put yourself out to save your cousin?"

"Jordan didn't look as if he needed saving when I saw him at the Pattersons' ball. He and Nicole seemed to be dealing very well with one another."

"Couldn't you tell it was all a pretense? That woman nearly ruined his life once before, and just when he and Melanie Grayson were all but wed, she comes back. Now poor Miss Grayson has sunk into a decline, while Jordan is futilely wearing his heart on his sleeve."

Robert glanced at Maude, Agatha's maid, who was sitting in the corner, sewing. She had been with his aunt since before he had been born. In fact, she had helped Agatha carry him and his cousin from the burning inn where his parents and Jordan's father had died when they were both infants. Over the years, he had often wondered what she was sewing, but had never worked up the nerve to ask.

Robert did not feel comfortable discussing Jordan's private life in Maude's presence, no matter how long she had been with the family. His aunt evidently did not share in his apprehension since she rattled on about everything in front of the woman without constraint.

"Miss Grayson is upset about losing a very rich man willing to marry her when she brings so little dowry to the union," he said.

"Miss Grayson is a lovely young woman who could have her choice of men," argued Mrs. Worth.

"She is a spoiled, conniving minx who has set out to snare a man to pay her father's gambling debts."

"It may seem that way, but she's really taken with Jordan."

From what he had seen of her, Robert had his doubts whether Miss Grayson could ever care about anyone but herself, but he kept his tongue between his teeth. There was no use arguing with his aunt when she was in her current state of mind.

Robert had never understood Agatha's antipathy toward Nicole. There was no outward cause for it. He was not aware that they had ever argued over anything which would have caused a rift between them. But, from the first, Agatha had been against the marriage. And afterwards, when Jordan had invited her to make her home with him, she had insisted upon staying in the ducal mansion.

Robert did not mind her presence. She had taken the place of his mother when he was growing up, and he could never repay her for her dedication. She doted on his sons, spoiling them excessively. Now, she had a grandson of her own whom she had never seen. Robert hoped Agatha would not let her distaste for Nicole keep her from getting to know Philip.

"It's all meaningless anyway," said Robert. "Jordan and Nicole are legally married, and there's nothing that can be done about it. They'll find a way to get on together. It's done everyday in the *ton*. Melanie will wed someone else, perhaps not as plump in the pocket as Jordan, but someone who will do just as well."

"And Nicole? Will she be allowed to ruin all our lives again?"

"Aunt Agatha," Robert said patiently, "I know you don't like Nicole, but she cannot ruin your life. You can go on with your daily activities just as you did before she returned."

"How can I?" burst out Agatha, dabbing at her eyes with a lace-edged handkerchief. "She put me to shame before, with her strange starts of seeing visions and claims of being able to read fortunes. I will not be able to show my face in public."

Robert laughed, then halted quickly when Agatha glared at him. "What she does is a harmless parlor game, Aunt. Hardly anyone takes it seriously, and those who do will certainly not cause you harm. If you do not wish to socialize with her, then avoid meeting her," he advised. "London can hold the both of you without your often meeting, and when you do, merely nod and pass her by."

"I see you mean to do nothing to help me and your cousin."

"There is nothing to be done, Aunt Agatha," Robert said gently, touching her on the shoulder. "Now, have Maude bring you some tea and try to relax and forget all about this." He gave her a peck on the cheek and left the room with an air of relief.

"We'll see about that," Agatha murmured to herself. "We'll just see about that."

Robert ran into Jordan as he was leaving the house. "Going to visit your mother?" he asked, pulling on his gloves.

"I thought I might try to make amends. She's barely spoken to me since Nicole returned."

"I don't think today would be a good time," said Robert. "I've just left her and she's highly incensed about the whole affair. Suddenly, Miss Grayson has become the perfect wife for you, and Nicole is a troublemaker who won't disappear quietly and let you get on with the wedding."

"She's never liked Nicole," agreed Jordan. "Remember how she tried her best to keep us from marrying? But now her attitude is totally unreasonable. She's aware there's no way for me to dissolve my marriage. I've tried to assure her that Nicole is much more circumspect about her gift." He grimaced as he said the word.

Robert chuckled. "I've never considered Nicole an embarrassment to the family. She's lovely, even more so since she's returned, and she adds spice to any drawing room with her fortune-telling. But don't tell Elizabeth I said so. She's always been envious of Nicole."

"Elizabeth's a charming woman herself," said Jordan, surprised that she envied his wife.

"But she can't see visions," said Robert, chuckling again, and descending the steps to the street. "Make up your own mind about seeing Aunt Agatha, but my advice would be to wait until another day."

Jordan watched Robert climb into his carriage and drive away before deciding to follow his advice. He would visit later when his mother's ire had abated, if it ever did. As for today, he would spend it with Philip.

* * *

Nicole was in her room, dressing for the evening, when the door burst open and Jordan entered. He motioned Betsy out with a sharp gesture of his hand and closed the door behind her.

Nicole had just been ready to slip on the evening gown which lay spread across her bed. She pulled her flimsy wrap more closely around her, determined not to be embarrassed by its thinness. Although it had been long ago, Jordan had seen her in far less. She did not know the cause of his anger, but she would not allow him to intimidate her.

"You could have knocked first," she said, drawing herself up to her full height.

"You are my wife," he sneered. "There is no need."

"There is a need for courtesy in everyone's life."

"And were you courteous when you neglected to tell me about your little adventure for Charles Hardesty?"

"What do you mean?" she asked, playing for time.

"I mean charming Fitzpatrick into throwing a ball so that you could search his house. I should have known you were up to no good when I saw you with him. He wouldn't have been your type seven years ago, but I thought your taste might have changed."

"I remember your telling me that you would not object to any acquaintances I made as long as I was discreet. Have you changed your mind?"

"Don't change the subject," he roared. "It's the reason behind your acquaintance with Fitzpatrick that is under discussion here."

"There will be no discussion until you calm down," said Nicole, turning toward her dressing table.

"Don't turn your back on me," ordered Jordan, grabbing her shoulders and pulling her around. Her skin was soft beneath his hands and he was suddenly intensely aware of her dishabille. They were alone in her room, an intimacy they hadn't shared in a long time.

Jordan loosened his hold, sliding his hands up the silky material until they reached the warmth of her skin. He studied the contrast of his fingers against the ivory tone of her shoulders, wondering what she would do if he slipped the silk down her arms to pool around her feet.

Botheration! What was he thinking? He had come here to set her right. Pulling his hands away as if they were scorched, he stepped back.

"Perhaps I shouldn't have burst in on you, or shouted," he said slowly. Nicole crossed her arms over her chest, her hands covering the imprints he had left on her arms. She remained stubbornly quiet, forcing him to continue. "Or held you so tightly," he conceded. "But I saw Hardesty today at White's. He was drinking himself into a stupor, mumbling about a receipt and Fitzpatrick. When I finally got the whole story out of him, you were right in the middle of it." He glared at her, waiting for a response.

Nicole was not going to allow him to treat her like a child. She had returned so that Philip could have a father; *she* did not need one.

"What's the point of this conversation, Jordan?" she asked coolly. "I must finish dressing."

"The point is that you have no reason to meddle in any matter that involves Fitzpatrick. I don't know everything about the man, but I can recognize that he's not on the up-and-up."

"He certainly isn't," she agreed. "He's to blame for Nevil Hardesty's death and for stealing the estate from Charles and Caroline."

"I suppose you saw this," Jordan scoffed.

"Yes, I did, and it wasn't a pleasant experience at all," she admitted.

"I don't doubt he could do what you say. However, there's no proof of the deed. Except for your vision," he added scornfully.

"I saw what happened, Jordan. Whether you believe it is of no concern to me. I'm convinced that Hardesty hid the receipt for his debts in a safe place before he was murdered, and I intend to find it for Charles and Caroline."

"Surely you don't plan on continuing this foolishness?"

"If you were helping your friends, I wouldn't call it foolish. I expect the same respect I accord you."

"I'm a man. I can protect myself."

"You forget, I have a hidden weapon," she said, breaking her rule and probing Jordan's mind. It was time he was reminded of what she could do. "On the contrary, I do know what I'm doing. I know better than you that Fitzpatrick is dangerous, but I'm going ahead with my search, and no, there's nothing you can say to dissuade me." She smiled at his confusion.

"You're guessing," he accused.

"Think what you wish," she replied, depressed by his thoughts of her. "Now, I really must finish dressing."

"You haven't heard the end of this," he warned, turning toward the door.

"Jordan," she said, as his hand reached for the latch.

He turned. She looked very small and fragile in the soft candlelight.

"If it weren't for Philip, you wish you had never found me."

Jordan was shocked and embarrassed that she knew what he had thought a few moments before. But it was only a lucky guess, he told himself.

"It wasn't a lucky guess," she said, smiling wanly. "I want you to know that if I didn't love Philip so much, I wouldn't have come back to ruin your life. Despite our differences, you'll be a good father, and I wanted him to have that." She turned her back on him and took a seat at her dressing table. "Be good enough to send Betsy in, please."

Jordan did not know what to think. In fact, he was afraid to think, so he left the room as quickly as possible.

Nicole was out of sorts the next day. Jordan had not accompanied her last night, but she had not expected it after their confrontation. Even so, she had missed his solid presence beside her, and had cut her evening short. He was not at home when she returned, and it was early morning before she heard his footsteps and drifted off to sleep herself.

By the time she reached the breakfast table, he was already gone, with no message to say whether he would join her that evening.

After sipping a cup of tea and crumbing a muffin on her plate, she advised Harrison she was at home to no one and took refuge in a small sitting room at the back of the house. Books or embroidery did not hold her attention, and she sat staring out of the window into the small back garden. The day was dull and overcast, and she took comfort that it matched her disposition.

A light knock sounded at the door. "Yes," she said, without turning to see who it was.

"There is a person here to see you, madam," said Harrison hesitantly.

Nicole was irritated that he had ignored her wishes. "I told you I'm not at home."

"She's very insistent. It's . . . ah . . . Mrs. Agatha Worth," he advised her. "And she says she won't go away until she sees you."

"Stop all this hiding away," demanded Mrs. Worth, pushing the door wider and elbowing her way past Harrison.

"I'm sorry, madam," he said to Nicole.

"It's all right, Harrison. I'm sure Mrs. Worth won't be staying long."

"I'll stay as long as it takes," spat out Mrs. Worth, selecting a chair across from Nicole to settle into. "This is my son's home, and the last I heard I was welcome in it."

"That you are, but Jordan is not here now. I cannot understand why you must force yourself on me."

"You're sharper tongued than you were," judged Mrs. Worth. "Comes from being a loose woman all those years, I would suppose."

"It comes from being an independent woman," Nicole shot back. She was glad her poor humor put her in the mood to deal with Mrs. Worth. Otherwise she might have been nicer to her mother-in-law.

"Independent woman," snorted Mrs. Worth. "Some man's lightskirt, no doubt. The father of that brat you claim is my grandson. Well, you don't fool me a minute."

Nicole faced Mrs. Worth, her eyes cold and her voice like steel. "Call me what you like, but never question my son's birth," she warned menacingly. "Remember why you dislike me so—that hasn't changed. I have the same ability as when I left, perhaps even more refined. I won't hesitate to use it to protect my child from harm. You'll do well to remember it."

"Well," huffed Mrs. Worth. "Threatening me in my own son's home."

"What do you want?" asked Nicole, already tired of the woman.

"I want you to leave. I have money. If it isn't enough, I'll get more."

Nicole gave a short bark of laughter. "You could never have enough to entice me to leave. Money isn't the reason I returned. I want my life back—I want Philip to know his father. You can't buy that."

Mrs. Worth stared hard at her. Nicole couldn't resist looking at what she was thinking. It was nothing surprising.

"I'll save you some time," she said. "No, I'm not trying to get you to offer more, and I won't change my mind. And perhaps you're right. Miss Grayson might be easier to handle, but she will never be Jordan's wife."

Nicole watched surprise mixed with fear cross Mrs. Worth's face when she realized that Nicole was addressing her thoughts.

"What is it, Agatha?" asked Nicole, leaning toward the other woman. "What is it you're afraid I'll find out?" she whispered.

"Nothing. Nothing at all," gasped Mrs. Worth.

"I don't believe you. I think you're hiding something." She kept staring at Mrs. Worth until the older woman shifted uncomfortably in her chair. "It's about Jordan, isn't it?" Nicole was jubilant with her success at forcing the reason for Mrs. Worth's animosity into the open.

"No. You're wrong." Mrs. Worth sounded desperate.

"You're keeping a secret from Jordan, and if he found out it would ruin your life. Now, what could be that important?" she mused.

"You're a witch, that's what you are," cried Mrs. Worth. "I've known all along that you shouldn't be with normal people. I tried to warn Jordan, but he wouldn't listen. Now, he'll suffer the consequences."

"You still haven't told me," goaded Nicole, unwilling to let her off so easily. Mrs. Worth's anger had obscured her thoughts before Nicole had been able to ferret out her secret. That was the key to Mrs. Worth's hatred. She feared Nicole because of her ability, not because she was embarrassed by her second sight.

"There's nothing to tell, except that Jordan doesn't want you here. He would be married to someone else if it wasn't for you," Mrs. Worth taunted cruelly, rising to her feet.

Nicole leaned back in her chair, forcing herself to relax. "But he's married to me," she replied languidly.

"Not for long, if I have anything to do with it."

Nicole's breath caught. Mrs. Worth's thoughts were murderous, and she meant to act on them. She stared at the woman who threatened her very life, too wary to let her know she had seen her plans. As long as Mrs. Worth thought they were secret, Nicole had an opportunity to discover the details.

"Harrison," she called, raising her voice.

As she expected, the butler was outside the door and answered quickly. "Yes, madam."

"Show Mrs. Worth out," she said shortly.

Harrison held the door open for Mrs. Worth to pass through.

"You haven't heard the last of me yet," warned Mrs. Worth.

"I would be surprised if I had," replied Nicole wearily.

She surrendered to the throbbing in her head when the door

closed behind Mrs. Worth. The day had begun badly, and Nicole had thought it could not be worse, but she had been proven wrong. A confrontation with her mother-in-law was bad enough, but to find out the depth of her hatred and the lengths to which she would go to be rid of Nicole was crushing.

Nicole leaned her head back and closed her eyes. How she yearned for the peace of her house in the village, where she and Philip had been safe. She wondered whether it was still empty, and fell asleep dreaming of packing her trunks and moving back to the country.

Nine

"The woman is mad!" declared Alura, setting her teacup down with a sharp crack, then checking the delicate china for damage. Finding none, she returned her attention to her hostess.

"Depend upon it, she knows exactly what she's doing," replied Nicole. "She got rid of me once before and she expects to do it again."

"But, why?"

"When Jordan and I first married, I thought she was merely jealous of the woman who was taking her son away. Later I became convinced she was truly embarrassed by my second sight. I was younger then and drew more attention than I should have," Nicole confessed. "But it was little more than a game to me then, and I didn't realize the significance of some of my revelations."

Nicole passed Alura a selection of cakes before continuing. "She poured her venom into Jordan's ear and soon he was convinced. He had seen my predictions come true, and I think it frightened him. Mrs. Worth called me a witch yesterday—perhaps he was beginning to think that, too."

"Nonsense. Anyone who comes to know you couldn't think that was true."

"You're acquainted with my cousin, and are familiar with her ability, so I don't shock you. But if you hadn't known Claire, I doubt whether you would be so accepting."

Alura considered her words. "I don't know," she finally admitted. "It didn't take me long to acknowledge Claire's gift, but then the proof was too substantial to do otherwise. I'd like to think I would have done the same with you, even without knowing Claire beforehand."

"Perhaps," said Nicole, smiling. "But Jordan had no experience in the matter. Men are much more skeptical of what I do. They look on it as an amusing parlor game until they can no longer explain the results. Then they demand it go away, as if it never existed.

"That's what Jordan did. He sided with his mother against me, and ordered me to stop my foolishness. I felt completely abandoned, and was numb for weeks. I don't think I could have been hurt more if I had seen him with another woman."

"I'm so sorry," whispered Alura.

"Don't fret about it," replied Nicole, patting her hand. "It was a long time ago, and I've come to accept that he doesn't believe in me. I came back for Philip's sake, and I expect nothing more from Jordan."

"How sad. You look to be the perfect couple," said Alura.

"Well, if it's left up to Mrs. Worth, I will be gone, and Jordan will marry the lovely Miss Grayson."

"But that can't be. No matter where you go, you'll still be married."

Nicole gave a wry smile. "I'm sure my mother-in-law will get past that one way or another."

"Surely her hate couldn't run so deep merely because of your second sight."

"After yesterday, I'm beginning to doubt it myself. When Mrs. Worth confronted me, she was in high dudgeon. Her loss of control allowed me to see she holds a secret that would turn her life and Jordan's upside down if it became known."

"Oh, Nicole," breathed Alura.

"She's afraid I'll find out that secret and use it against her. In any case, she has inclinations toward me that are extremely unfriendly," said Nicole, unwilling to reveal the murderous intent she had felt emanating from Agatha Worth.

"What do you think she'll do?" asked Alura.

"Anything to be rid of me again, and this time for good."

"Surely she wouldn't hurt you," Alura protested.

"I don't know what the woman will do," admitted Nicole. "I've become an obsession with her, and nothing would surprise me."

"You must tell Jordan immediately."

Nicole laughed. "And what good would that do? He sided with her seven years ago. Do you think it will be any different today? After what I did before, he's probably more convinced than ever that my attic is to let."

A knock sounded at the door, and Jordan stuck his head into the room. "Are men allowed?" he asked, a distinct twinkle in his eye.

"It depends on which men," replied Alura saucily. "Now, if it's the Honorable James Venable, who has a smashing pair of grays and a yellow-wheeled, high-perch phaeton, then he would be more than welcome."

"Has Venable been bothering you?" demanded Drew, pushing his way past Jordan.

Alura gave him her brightest smile. "I would never consider Mr. Venable a bother."

Nicole envied the repartee between the two. She remembered when she and Jordan engaged in the same sort of teasing. It seemed a lifetime ago.

"Nothing to do but show you my pair of blacks are far superior. That is, if you're free," said Drew.

"There's no room for Nicole in your curricle," objected Alura. "And we had planned to spend the day together."

"We thought we'd make a picnic of it," said Jordan, looking at Nicole for her agreement. "Cook's packed a basket, both curricles are at the door, and we only await two lovely ladies to grace their seats."

Nicole knew he spoke for the benefit of Alura and Drew but, nevertheless, she felt a rush of pleasure at his words. She would be a happy woman, if only they were sincere.

"Oh, I would like it above all things," replied Alura with her usual enthusiasm. "That is, if you would," she said to Nicole, remembering their conversation just past.

Propriety demanded Alura have an appropriate chaperone, and Nicole did not have the heart to refuse her. "It's a wonderful day for a picnic," said Nicole, looking out the sun-filled window. "Let me get my bonnet, and we can be on our way."

They picnicked on an estate just outside of London. The owner was a friend of Jordan's, and instructed them on how to reach a stream where the water fell from a high ledge of rocks into a pool below. Woods, dark and mysterious, bordered one side of the water, while the other side opened into a meadow sprinkled with huge oak trees, their widespread limbs scattering shifting patterns on the grass below.

"Would you like to walk?" asked Jordan after they had eaten.

"Exercise is essential after such a delicious meal," groaned Nicole.

"The cook is good, isn't she?" said Jordan, reaching a hand down to help her up.

"Too good," agreed Nicole. "I shall need to let out my gowns before long."

"Balderdash! You've never had a problem with your weight," he commented, pulling her to her feet, his eyes running appraisingly over her figure. Remembering himself, he turned to the other couple.

"Aren't you coming?"

Alura had seen the look that had passed between Nicole and Jordan. "I can't move a step," she said.

"Will do you good," remarked Drew, beginning to rise.

"Oh, no," she said, tugging on his arm. "Why don't we stay here just a little longer. We'll catch up with you later," she said to Jordan. "I fear town life has made me soft."

Nicole had never known Alura to be tired, and quickly caught on to what she was up to. She vowed to set her friend right at the first opportunity.

Nicole and Jordan strolled toward the waterfall and the quaint arched bridge that crossed the stream just below it. They stopped in the middle of the bridge to admire the fall of water that tumbled over rocks, then fell in a sheer wall into the pool.

"You look like a ray of sunshine," said Jordan, touching the sleeve of her jonquil-yellow gown.

The compliment was too intimate for Nicole's comfort. She said nothing, but concentrated on the white foam of water as it flowed over the rocks.

"I heard that my mother visited yesterday," Jordan said, leaning his arms on the bridge rail.

Nicole did not know what he expected from her so she remained silent.

"Don't you have anything to say?" he asked, straightening and turning toward her. His move brought them closer, and he captured the yellow material of her sleeve again, rubbing it between his fingers.

"You're cold," he observed, noticing the chill bumps on her arms. "We should have stayed out of the shade. Your gown may look like a sunbeam, but it's as insubstantial as moonshine. Here, take my coat," he offered.

"No," she said shortly. She shouldn't have come for a walk. Nor should she be this close to him with matters still unresolved.

"I don't need it," he insisted, shrugging out of his coat and putting it around her shoulders.

His warmth immediately surrounded her. She longed to rub her cheek against the material where his scent lingered enticingly. "It really isn't necessary," she murmured ineffectually.

"Now where were we? Oh, yes. I heard my mother visited you yesterday," he repeated, turning her toward him and pulling his coat more securely around her.

So this is why he wanted them to be alone, thought Nicole. He would, no doubt, ring a peal over her head for speaking to his mother as she had. But why take her on a picnic? Why be so courteous and complimentary if his intent was to chastise her? Nicole did not know the answers, but she was determined not to be intimidated.

"She did, but it wasn't by invitation."

An unexpected smile curved his lips. "I never thought it was." He ran his hands up the lapels of the coat and over her shoulders, letting them rest on her upper arms.

"Did she tell you what happened?" asked Nicole.

"She certainly did," he confirmed, rubbing her arms as if to warm them.

"I practically threw her out."

"She probably deserved it," he said, still smiling.

"She called me a lightskirt and a witch."

"I know you're not one, but I'm uncertain about the other," he remarked in an amused tone.

Nicole was too cowardly to ask him which was which.

"She implied Philip was a bastard," whispered Nicole.

He placed a finger under her chin and tilted her head upward until she met his gaze. "I don't believe it for a moment," he replied. He touched his lips to her forehead, then the tip of her nose, and finally her lips, leaving them there long enough to remind her of what they had once shared. "I know you were never unfaithful to me," he murmured huskily.

Tears burned at the back of Nicole's eyes, and she blinked rapidly to keep them from falling. She had convinced herself that Jordan's opinion did not matter. He had just proven her wrong.

Nicole sighed, content to be close to him. "She offered money if I would leave," she revealed.

"And after I told her you were a successful business woman," he chided. His hands caressed her back from shoulders to waist.

Nicole almost purred beneath his touch. Her barriers were falling, and she was glad he wasn't the mind reader in the family. "I threatened her if she tried to harm Philip."

"No more than I would have done," he acknowledged, moving closer and taking her into his arms.

"She wants you to marry Miss Grayson, you know."

"I already have a wife," he replied, bending over her. His lips found hers again, this time lingering until Nicole's knees went weak and she leaned against him for support.

If only this could last, she mused, as the last vestiges of rational thought disappeared.

The ride back to town had been mostly silent. Traveling in an open curricle through the countryside at a spanking pace didn't encourage conversation. Jordan was preoccupied, but pleasant, and Nicole wondered whether he was thinking about their kiss. She certainly couldn't get it out of her mind.

She warned herself not to read too much into one kiss, but found herself dreaming dreams she had long put behind her. When they reached town, he helped her down in front of the house. His manner was polite, everything a woman could hope for—if she were not his wife, and had not recently shared a passionate kiss with him. Nicole's brief flight of hope was dashed. She reminded herself that the only thing they had in common now was Philip. Jordan was being kind to the mother of his child, his kiss simply a token of respect.

It was evening, and Nicole had been sitting in front of her mirror far too long. Her hair had been done for some time. The dark strands were pulled softly away from her face, emphasizing her high cheekbones and displaying to advantage her dark eyes set beneath delicately arched brows. Glossy curls, threaded through with ribbon the shade of her gown, were gathered at the crown of her head, while softly curled wisps softened the neckline.

Betsy had spread the azure ball gown across the bed so it wouldn't wrinkle. Matching slippers were ready to be eased on over embroidered silk stockings, and gloves were waiting to conceal her arms to the elbow. Betsy waited patiently for Nicole to signal she was ready to finish dressing.

After spending the better part of the day with Jordan, Nicole dreaded going out alone that evening. Jordan had been escorting her quite often of late, but he had said nothing to her about this evening when they had parted. She was seriously considering telling Betsy to put away the gown, and choosing a good book for company.

Sunk in thought, Nicole didn't hear the knock at the door, nor did she see Betsy answer it.

"It's Mr. Worth, madam."

"What?" said Nicole frowning.

"It's Mr. Worth," Betsy repeated. "He's down below waiting for you. He wants to know if you'll be much longer."

Nicole's heart raced. She turned to face Betsy. "He's going with me?" Energy coursed through her body, when moments before she had been too lethargic to move.

"Send word I'll be down shortly."

Before Betsy could relay the message to the footman, Nicole bounded from the dressing table to the bed, snatched up the gown, and began struggling into it.

"Oh, madam, don't," wailed Betsy. "You'll wrinkle it so, and I spent ever so long pressing it." She rushed to Nicole's side and pulled the gown down around her hips, smoothing the skirt and clucking over imagined creases.

"I mustn't keep Mr. Worth waiting. You know how he hates to keep the cattle standing," Nicole chattered nervously.

"I know, madam, but he wasn't overly anxious," soothed Betsy, helping Nicole into her dancing slippers and handing her the long gloves.

"Do I look all right?" asked Nicole. "I shouldn't have worn this gown, should I? It's all wrong. Neither the fit nor the color suits," she fretted. "Is it too late to change?"

"You look a picture," Betsy assured her. "And the gown is beautiful. Do you want your diamonds?"

"No, that would take too much time, and I can't keep Mr. Worth waiting any longer." She snatched her shawl from Betsy's hands and hurried out the door, pausing only when she reached the top of the stairs. She descended slowly and regally; it wouldn't do to let Jordan think she was rushing to meet him.

* * *

Jordan watched as Nicole came down the stairs toward him. She seemed lovelier than ever tonight, but perhaps he was seeing her differently after the kiss they had shared earlier in the day.

Jordan's feelings toward Nicole had been bouncing back and forth ever since she had returned. He had lost Melanie and hated her for that; but he had gained a son, and he felt indebted to Nicole for such a perfect little boy.

When Nicole first returned, he had convinced himself that they could be cordial to one another for Philip's sake. Since then, Jordan had been in Nicole's company more often, and his resentment over the loss of Melanie was fading more rapidly than he wished to admit. But it was their kiss today that had erased the memory of every other woman but Nicole from his head.

He was probably the greatest fool alive, but after they had returned to town, Jordan had spent a great deal of time selecting a gift for Nicole. It was no more than he would have done at Philip's birth if he had been there, he assured himself.

"You're looking lovely, as usual, this evening," he said, taking her hand and raising it to his lips.

"Thank you," she said, grateful that her voice emerged firmly from her quivering body.

"But there is something missing."

"What is it?" she asked, craning her head, trying to see every part of herself. Surely, Betsy had not let her leave without being fully dressed.

"I don't know exactly," murmured Jordan, studying her intently. "It's your diamonds," he finally said. "You're not wearing them this evening."

"I've worn them too often," said Nicole, glad it wasn't something more. "Besides, I know you don't like them."

"If you've given them up for me, then it's only right that I replace them." He pulled a box from his evening coat and handed it to her.

"What . . . what is it?

"Open it and find out."

Nicole slowly lifted the velvet lid and gasped in delight. Sapphire and diamond gems sparkled up at her. The necklace was made up of large sapphires, set off by diamonds, with a teardrop sapphire falling from the center front. The earrings consisted of single teardrop sapphires dangling from larger sapphires, also surrounded by diamonds.

"They're magnificent," she said in a hushed tone.

"Let me help you on with them," he said, taking the necklace from the box and moving behind her.

His fingers were warm on the nape of her neck as he fastened the clasp and adjusted the necklace. His hands settled on her bare shoulders and he leaned down to whisper in her ear. "I'm afraid you must do the earrings." His nearness caused a flutter of excitement inside her, making her feel more vulnerable than she had in many a day.

Reluctantly, Nicole stepped away from the warmth of his body to a mirror on the hall wall. Laying the box on the small table below it, she put on the earrings and stood admiring the jewels until Jordan's reflection appeared in the mirror behind her.

"Beautiful," he said.

"Yes, they are," she agreed, touching the necklace.

"I didn't mean the sapphires," he said, smiling.

Nicole blushed as the meaning of his words washed over her. "I think it's time we leave. We're going to be extremely late as it is."

He took her hand and placed it on his arm. "The coach is already at the door. Are you ready to go, Mrs. Worth?"

The use of her married name falling from his lips was more precious than the jewels he had given her. She felt as light as a butterfly as she floated through the door and down the steps.

"They aren't here," gloated Melanie. "Perhaps he changed his mind after I talked to him. He could never withstand my tears," she bragged.

"Or they could be enjoying a quiet evening at home together," said Agatha Worth, unable to resist baiting the woman who thought far too much of herself.

"Surely not," replied Melanie, unable to believe any man would choose another woman over her.

"Or they could be at any one of the many other events going on this evening."

"But this is the most important and *that woman* would be here if she were going to be anywhere," argued Melanie.

"You're absolutely correct," agreed Mrs. Worth, nodding toward the other side of the room where Nicole and Jordan had just entered.

"That witch," said Melanie, borrowing Mrs. Worth's epithet. Her hands clutched the sides of her skirt in fury.

"I agree. But from the way Jordan is looking at her, he doesn't agree with our view. And I would wager our task has just become more difficult. Notice the sapphires she's wearing. They're something a besotted husband would give his wife."

A hiss escaped from Melanie's lips. "How could he? He doesn't love her—he loves me."

"If that's true, you need to remind him, but it won't be enough. She's determined to stay, and that calls for more drastic measures."

"What are you going to do?" asked Melanie.

"Don't bother your head with my plans. You concentrate on Jordan, and I'll get rid of Nicole."

"You've said that before, and nothing happened," accused Melanie.

"I didn't know she was going to be so difficult to deal with. When I finish this time, we won't have to worry about her ever again."

The look on Agatha Worth's face caused Melanie to take an involuntary step backward. She vowed never to make the woman her enemy.

"I'll attempt to catch Jordan alone," she said, anxious to get away.

"Yes, you do that. He'll need someone to lean on once he loses his wife again. You should be available when that happens," instructed Mrs. Worth.

Agatha was too busy planning Nicole's fate to notice Melanie skittering away into the crowd. She was unable to carry out her plans alone, which meant she would need to hire someone, and that was a risky business.

John Fitzpatrick was standing at the edge of the dance floor and she beckoned him over. Fitzpatrick was anxious to be accepted by the *ton,* and she could make that come about—for a price.

"Mrs. Worth, what a pleasure," Fitzpatrick said when he reached her side.

"I'm surprised to see you here, Mr. Fitzpatrick."

"Since my ball, I've found my social life has improved a bit," he replied truthfully.

"It could be much better," said Agatha, satisfied when he immediately looked interested.

"I would like nothing better than to travel in higher circles," he admitted with unusual candor.

"I could possibly be of some help. You're aware that I live with my nephew, the Duke of Weston."

Fitzpatrick nodded, waiting for her to continue.

"If you were seen in his company, there would be no question that you would be accepted in all circles."

"If that could be arranged, I would be most appreciative," responded Fitzpatrick, waiting to hear the price for such consideration.

"I'm sure you would be, Mr. Fitzpatrick, but I couldn't accept anything from you. Except . . . perhaps . . . no, it's too much to ask."

"Please. You must tell me, Mrs. Worth," urged Fitzpatrick, playing the game.

"I do need some help with a problem I've recently encountered."

They had finally arrived at the reason Mrs. Worth had called him over, and Fitzpatrick felt in control again. He had always attributed his success to his ability to make deals that were beneficial to himself, and tonight would be no exception.

"I will do whatever I can," he replied.

"This, of course, must be completely confidential."

"Naturally," Fitzpatrick agreed, his curiosity growing.

"If not, I can ruin you as well as make you," warned Agatha.

Fitzpatrick did not take well to threats, but he only nodded again. He was determined to find out what the woman was planning. Even if he chose not to be involved in her scheme, it was possible the information could be used at another time. Mrs. Worth might be known as a dragon in society's small circle, but she did not have a chance up against him.

"It is essential I get rid of someone—permanently," revealed Mrs. Worth. "I can't be involved in it myself, so I need to hire someone who will do it for me. I don't know anyone like that . . ."

". . . But you think *I* do."

"Well, you do have a certain reputation. Not that it's mentioned in polite company," she added.

"And what do you suggest should happen to this person?"

"I don't care. Have her transported, sell her into slavery. It doesn't matter, as long as she never returns to England."

He should have known it would be a woman, thought Fitzpatrick. "And if neither of those choices is available?" he asked, wanting her to say the words.

"I told you, there should be no chance that she would ever return. You understand what I mean."

"I'm afraid I don't!"

"Kill her," she hissed, her face twisting in hate. As hard as Fitzpatrick was, he was glad her venom was not directed at him.

"I might know someone who could help you," he admitted, now that she was as much in his trap as he was hers.

"Good. I will be at the Marchcamps' musical, two nights hence. There's a garden, with a door in the wall that opens onto the mews. I will go out for some air at ten o'clock. Make sure he's there. I will give him instructions at that time."

"I could act as intermediary, if you wish," Fitzpatrick offered. "A lady might get in a pelter dealing with such a matter."

Agatha's eyes were filled with scorn. "I am not so delicate that I cannot deal with it on my own. I want the thing done right."

Fitzpatrick did not insist. He could find out the details from the man he sent, and Mrs. Worth would never be the wiser. As soon as the deed was done, he could use the knowledge of it to bend her to his will. With the Duke of Weston's endorsement, he could gain access to any house in England.

"Then I will arrange it," he said with a small bow.

Nicole caught a glimpse of Mrs. Worth and Fitzpatrick with their heads together and wondered what two such disparate people had to talk about.

"Would you like to dance?" asked Jordan. "It's a waltz, I believe."

Nicole was overjoyed at the chance to be held in his arms again, and as they stepped onto the floor, she completely forgot about the odd pair she had just seen.

Jordan searched the dancers, hoping for a glimpse of Nicole, but the blue of her dress had been swallowed up in the crowd. He remembered how beautiful she was with the sapphires sparkling around her neck and at her ears. Since he had admitted he and Melanie had no future, his heart and mind had opened to a reconciliation with Nicole. Today had proven he was as attracted to her as ever. He still felt a residue of bitterness because she had deserted him and kept his son a secret from him, but he was certain he could overcome any problem to bring his family together.

He and Nicole had once loved one another with an intensity he had never experienced before or since. Surely they could revive some part of that feeling. They had taken a step closer today, he thought. The kiss they had shared had ignited a physical need in Jordan, and he wondered whether Nicole felt the same way. He longed to be back in the shadowy confines of the coach with her sitting next to him. There was an endless range of possibilities that could be explored before they reached home.

His musing was interrupted by a tug on his sleeve.

"Jordan. Jordan. You're so oblivious, you must be thinking of me," said Melanie, smiling just enough to show her dimples.

Jordan wondered how best to answer. To agree would only encourage her attentions, but to contradict her claim might very well bring on a bout of tears. If they had been anyplace other than a crowded ballroom, he could answer truthfully and admit he had been thinking of Nicole. If he were able to do so, she might finally understand that there could be nothing between them.

"It's unfair for me to expect an answer in such a public place," she said before he could decide upon a reply. "But come dance with me. Surely there can be no objection to that since *she* is dancing with someone else."

Jordan searched again in vain for a flash of blue. Feeling like a trapped animal, he followed Melanie onto the dance floor.

Nicole had just danced with Lord Thornton, a short, rotund man who never seemed to tire and had an abundance of tales to amuse her. She was vastly enjoying the evening.

She touched the sapphire teardrop, lying warm against her skin, remembering the moment when Jordan fastened it around her neck. Up until today, she had not allowed herself to seriously hope that their marriage might become what it once was. She had kept her heart safely guarded so that she would not go through the pain she had experienced before.

But Jordan had been a different person today. No, not different, but more like the Jordan she first knew. He had held her and kissed her with the old ardor, and had spent a small fortune on a gift that seemed to indicate his feelings were changing.

She made her way around the edge of the room, greeting friends and indulging in idle chatter while searching for Jordan.

She finally saw him dancing and moved to the edge of the dance floor to catch his attention. She longed to feel his arms around her again, and hoped they could share the next dance. He turned and Nicole saw that he was dancing with Melanie, who was staring up at him, adoration clearly written on her face.

Nicole's blood ran hot, then cold. Her mind was numb, and she looked around her to see if anyone had noticed her confusion. John Fitzpatrick was nearby, and as much as she abhorred him, she flashed a smile which immediately brought him to her side.

"Mrs. Worth," he said, as the music ended. "Am I fortunate enough to find you without a partner for the next dance?"

"You are, Mr. Fitzpatrick."

"Would you do me the honor?"

"Certainly, sir," Nicole said, placing her hand on his arm.

Jordan had finally freed himself from Melanie's clutches and was eagerly looking around for his wife. He spotted her in the crowd and began making his way toward her just as the orchestra began playing. By the time he reached the place he had last seen her, she was walking away with Fitzpatrick.

Nicole was clinging to Fitzpatrick's arm and laughing at him. A wave of jealousy and anger surged through Jordan. He had thought today had meant something to them both, but evidently he had been wrong. Nicole was not anticipating another dance as he had been. Instead, she was with a man she knew Jordan disapproved of. How many times must he be taken for a fool before he learned Nicole cared nothing for him? Not one more, he vowed.

Agatha Worth's eyes narrowed as she watched Fitzpatrick and Nicole take their places for the next dance. She wondered how he would feel if he knew he was dancing with a woman who would soon be dead.

Ten

Nicole was astonished when she had learned Jordan had left her with only a casual message sent by Drew. He was bored, he had told his friend, and was going on to his club. Please tell Nicole that he had left the carriage for her.

Drew seemed embarrassed, but Nicole accepted the message as if it was something that happened every evening. She kept her feelings contained until she reached the privacy of her room and began to take off the sapphires. Then the tears came.

It was midmorning before she made her way downstairs, her eyes still sore from crying and her heart heavy from Jordan's insensitive actions. If he had regretted the day he had spent with her and the gift he had given her, he could have told her in private. It would have been far kinder than an off-hand message sent by a third party.

Nicole avoided the breakfast room; the thought of food made her swallow convulsively. She ordered tea brought to the small sitting room, settled into her favorite wingback chair, then leaned back and closed her eyes.

"Did last evening tire you, madam?"

Nicole leaped from the chair, her heart pounding from the suddenness of Jordan's voice.

"You startled me," she said, holding a hand to her breast.

"My apologies," he said coldly.

Nicole gathered her ragged nerves and breathed deeply. "To answer your question, I left soon after I received your message."

He raised on eyebrow quizzically. "I'm surprised. When I last saw you, you and Fitzpatrick were quite involved."

"We were dancing," she said, unable to keep her voice from rising.

"It looked like more to me," he accused.

"Then your eyesight is poor. I have danced with Mr. Fitzpatrick many evenings when we attended the same function, and you've never complained."

"That's because . . ." He could not tell her that those times were before his feelings had begun changing. He would not allow her to gloat over his weakness.

"Because what?" she asked. "Because you've always had your sweet Melanie by your side? Then last night shouldn't have been any different, because the last time *I* saw *you,* she was in your arms, hanging on to your every word."

"I had no choice but to dance with her," he shot back.

"Hah! I suppose she forced you onto the dance floor."

"As a matter of fact, she did. There are times when a gentleman cannot say no to a lady."

"You've said it enough times to me—you should be in perfect practice."

"Dammit! Why am I making excuses, when you're the one who left me standing while dancing with half the men in London."

"That's ridiculous. I danced with you first and you gave me no indication you wished to dance with me again."

"You should have known I did."

"How? You've never danced more than one dance with me. Just one each evening to prove our marriage is all that it should be. How was I to know last night would be different?"

"Last night *was* different," he growled, reaching out to grasp her by the arms and pull her to him. "And you know it as well as I do." His lips came down on hers in a fierce kiss that Nicole returned with just as much intensity. The anger quickly turned to passion, and Nicole slipped her arms around his neck, burying her fingers in his hair.

"I shouldn't have left you as I did last night," he said a few moments later.

"It was a misunderstanding," said Nicole, resting her head against his chest.

"I was too hasty in my judgement," he admitted, breathing in the perfume of her hair. "But I don't trust Fitzpatrick."

Nicole was surprised at his admissions, and hope reasserted itself in her breast. "He's always acted the gentleman with me," she said, striving to reassure him of her safety.

"And that is all it is, merely an act," he growled.

"I believe he's only toadying up to me. I understand his fondest desire is to be accepted into society."

"True, but the way he's going about it is suspect. Many of the people who invite him to their homes would never do so in the natural course of events. He's holding something over their heads, but I don't know what, and the people involved aren't talking."

"Perhaps I could find out," she suggested.

"Don't even think of meddling with the man—he's dangerous."

"I could take precautions."

"I've seen men obsessed with a desire before," said Jordan. "He'll do anything to obtain his goal. It's best to stay away from him."

"I can't give him the cut direct or people would expect an explanation," she reasoned, hoping to find a basis to keep up her acquaintance with Fitzpatrick until the Hardestys' problem was solved.

"You can avoid him," suggested Jordan. "You're good at that. After all, you eluded me for seven years."

Nicole was relieved to see him smiling. "Six years and ten months," she corrected him with a corresponding smile.

Nicole was encouraged by Jordan's concern. Perhaps she could find other ways to investigate Fitzpatrick without direct contact. It would be well worth it if it would help revive her marriage.

"I will try my best to evade him," she said. "But if I can't, I hope we won't be at daggers drawn again."

"I will attempt to be patient."

"Thank you," she said, reaching up to caress his cheek.

"Now, where were we?" he murmured.

His lips were only inches away from hers when a knock sounded at the door. "Dammit!" he complained in a low voice. He released her and stepped away. "Come in."

Harrison opened the door. "Miss Hardesty is waiting in the drawing room for you, madam."

"Tell her I shall only be a few minutes," said Nicole. The butler nodded and closed the door.

"I assume you have plans for today," said Jordan.

"Just a shopping expedition, but I'm afraid there's no way to get out of it," she said apologetically.

"Which reminds me, I haven't received any bills from your *modiste.*" His appreciative glance took in her striped morning dress. "Although she should be paying you for displaying her creations so charmingly."

"Fustian!" replied Nicole, though pleased at his compliment. "I am well able to pay my own bills. You need not worry about that matter any longer."

Jordan was reminded of Mr. Grenville's visit. Perhaps he hadn't been merely flattering Nicole. She must be doing very well if she could afford the extensive wardrobe she had ordered. He felt vaguely uncomfortable that Nicole could get on so well without him.

"It doesn't trouble me at all. I've always enjoyed buying fripperies for you."

But those were days when Nicole knew that he loved her. She was determined to pay her own personal expenses as long as their present situation continued. "I had forgotten Caroline," said Nicole, changing the subject in order to avoid another disagreement.

"Miss Hardesty's a nice young woman. Much more acceptable as a companion than Fitzpatrick."

"I'm not certain she would consider that a compliment, so I won't pass it along. But I will attempt to cut my social tie to Mr. Fitzpatrick. However, it may take several evenings to do so."

Jordan frowned, but nodded. "I hope you can do it quickly."

"And you?" she asked, unwilling to let him off so easily. "What of Miss Grayson?"

"She's aware there's no future for us, but I'll tell her again. Although it may take several evenings to do so," he said, using her own words to tease her.

Nicole returned his smile, pleased that he could jest about ridding himself of Melanie. "I mustn't keep Caroline waiting."

She hesitated, wondering whether to ask him about his plans for the evening. She had not done so before, thinking he would consider it an invasion of his privacy. He usually sent her word whether he would be attending whatever event she had chosen. No, she would not chance breaking the fragile bond that was growing between them. She turned to make her way from the room.

"Nicole?"

The warm sound of her name on his lips sent a shiver through her. She turned to face him.

"I suppose you've made plans for the evening?"

"Yes."

"Is there room in the carriage for me?"

"Of course. You would be welcome."

"Then I shall see you this evening."

He was so handsome standing there, dressed in his riding clothes and highly polished Hessian boots. Nicole had always found it difficult to believe she was married to such a man. Even during the worst of their times together, she had continued to admire him, and her feelings had not changed over the years.

"This evening," she repeated before leaving to join Caroline.

* * *

A short time later, Nicole and Caroline were matching ribbons and exchanging information.

"We've tried to think of every place Papa may have hidden the receipt," said Caroline, handing Nicole a folded sheet of paper. "He went to his clubs, visited his friends, rode, and, of course gambled, but it doesn't make sense that he would hide anything in any of these places."

"I agree, but I'll look at all of them I can. The most logical place would have been your home, but I've already been over most of it. Would your father have left anything with a friend of his, or perhaps his man of business?"

"I don't think he would have had time, and I'm sure his friends would have come forward by now," mused Caroline. "Could you have missed it when you searched the house?"

"It's possible. There was quite a crush. In addition, Fitzpatrick was at my elbow most of the time, so my concentration wasn't all that it should have been. Perhaps I'll try again."

"How can you get into the house without arousing Fitzpatrick's suspicions?"

"I'll think of something." If another visit to Fitzpatrick's house became necessary, Nicole wondered how she would explain it to Jordan.

While Nicole and Caroline were shopping, Jordan approached the Graysons' residence. It was a call he didn't look forward to and one he hoped would be over quickly. He and Chester Grayson had never developed an easy rapport during the time he had been planning to marry Melanie. Grayson had welcomed him into his home for one reason only: money.

Chester Grayson was a man who would bet on anything, and usually lost. His pockets were constantly to let, and in Jordan he saw an endless supply of money. Once married to Melanie, Grayson speculated that Jordan wouldn't let his father-in-law end up in debtors' prison.

Now that the marriage was off, Jordan didn't expect a warm

reception. He would state his business quickly. Once Grayson knew money was coming his way, he'd be more agreeable. Jordan climbed the steps, ignoring the curses of two drivers arguing in the street behind him. He knocked on the door, wishing to be anywhere but where he was.

Alura's carriage was stuck behind two coaches whose wheels had become locked. She was late for a fitting of several new gowns, and tapped her fingers impatiently on the plush squabs. Glancing out of the window to judge how far they had to go, she saw Jordan alight from his carriage. She was ready to call out his name until she recognized the house he was approaching. Alura wondered if Nicole knew her husband continued to call on his recently affianced.

Grayson's debts were larger than Jordan had expected, and he returned home more than satisfied that he had paid any obligation he had incurred due to his inability to marry Melanie.

Jordan considered whether he had left anything undone. He had told Melanie there could be nothing more between them, and had made monetary amends to her father. He could think of nothing else. The relief left him feeling as light as a feather.

He felt the need to celebrate, and could think of no better way than taking his wife and son for a drive in the park.

Harrison advised Jordan that Mrs. Worth had just returned and was in the nursery. Jordan found her there, sitting on the floor with Philip, her skirts spread around her in jumbled disarray, displaying a trim ankle and a generous length of a silk-covered leg.

Philip ran to him and he scooped the boy up in his arms. "It's a beautiful day."

"Yes, it is," Nicole said, looking out the window to admire the sunshine.

"Much too nice to be stuck inside. Don't you agree, Philip?"

The little boy didn't know exactly what his father meant, but he felt it was something good, so he nodded his head.

"Would you like to go for a drive?" Jordan asked.

"Yes. Yes," Philip cried enthusiastically.

"He is horse mad," said Nicole, laughing. "He will enjoy this afternoon so much. Let me get his jacket."

"I meant for you to come, too," Jordan said. The look in his gray eyes reminded her of the kiss they had shared that morning.

"I . . . are you certain?" she asked.

He nodded.

"Then I will meet you downstairs in five minutes," she said, rushing from the room to collect her spencer, bonnet, and gloves.

We are together as a family, thought Nicole a short time later when they turned into Hyde Park. Tears threatened to fall, but she blinked them away, replacing them with a brilliant smile. Perhaps her future was not so bleak after all.

But the owner of a pair of blue eyes had followed their progression down the street and into the park and did not share Nicole's assessment. Melanie was not at all happy with what she had seen: Jordan, that woman who claimed to be his wife, and that brat of a son, driving through town as if they belonged together.

Jordan may have told her there was no hope for them, but he did not mean it. Melanie was determined to have him, no matter what the cost. She remembered Mrs. Worth's vow to do away with Nicole for good, and wished her well.

Nicole was already regretting she had chosen to attend the Marchcamps' musical that evening. She had thought it would be a change of pace from the balls they had been attending, but all of the people she wished to avoid had also shown up. She wondered if it was simply bad luck or whether *they* could read *her* mind and were accepting the same invitations in hopes of keeping her at home.

At present, Agatha Worth was quieter than usual. She sat near the French doors, which were opened slightly to admit fresh air. Her attention was not on the music as she stared out into the small garden, seemingly preoccupied with her own thoughts. Nicole shrugged, happy for the respite from her mother-in-law's usual vitriolic criticism.

John Fitzpatrick stood at the back of the room, behind the last row of delicate gilded chairs. He, too, was quiet this evening. He had not approached Nicole before the music began, and now seemed to be focusing his attention more on Mrs. Worth than anyone else.

Nicole remembered seeing them together several nights earlier and wondered what they had in common. She decided to find out if the opportunity presented itself.

Nicole and Jordan were sitting with Alura and Drew in the last row. The closeness of the room had made them all thirsty, and at the first intermission, the two men went to procure some refreshments.

"Oh, no," said Alura, looking over Nicole's shoulder.

"What is it?" asked Nicole. Turning slightly, she saw Melanie and Jordan standing closely together. Melanie's hand was on his sleeve, and she was gazing up at him with a look that was hard to mistake. What she was saying Nicole did not want to know; what was apparent to anyone seeing them was that Melanie was still pursuing Nicole's husband.

"I'm so sorry," said Alura. "I can't believe that woman is so forward. It's bad enough that she encourages him to call on her when everyone is around and about and can see him, but to make such a spectacle at a public gathering is beyond all that is proper."

"He calls on her?" said Nicole, confused at what she was hearing.

"I saw him myself, just a day or so ago when I was on my way to the dressmaker's. He was knocking at her door as bold as brass." Alura saw the stricken look on her friend's face. "Oh, my. I'm sorry. I thought you knew," she said in a hushed voice.

"It's all right," said Nicole, consoling the young woman.

Questions buzzed through her head. She wondered why Jordan had kissed her, had given her jewels, had indicated he wanted a future with her, if he had not given up Melanie. He had said Melanie knew it was over between them, but it looked as if that was far from the truth. If anything, Melanie looked more obsessed with Jordan than ever.

Nicole was proud that her hand was steady when she accepted the cup of punch from Jordan. She would not let him see that she was upset; she had brought it on herself. She had let down her defenses in the warmth of Jordan's attentions. She had told herself time and time again not to hope, yet she had. Now she was paying the price.

She would not think about it until she was in the privacy of her room. There were other things with which to occupy her mind. The Hardestys still did not have their receipt, and although the jewel thief had not stolen anything in the past few weeks, he was probably plotting his next robbery at this very moment.

It seemed an eternity until the music came to an end. Pleading a headache, she urged Jordan to stay and have supper with Alura and Drew, but he was adamant about escorting her home. She spoke barely a word in the carriage, and once she reached the house she went upstairs with only a short word of goodnight.

When Nicole turned the corner at the top of the stairs, Jordan stood watching from the bottom, a puzzled look on his face.

Nicole had not felt one qualm of guilt as she planned her entry into Fitzpatrick's stable to search for the receipt. Jordan had broken his promise not to see Melanie again, so she considered herself released from her promise to stay away from Fitzpatrick.

Nicole had crossed off as impractical many of the places on the list that Caroline had given her. She had checked out all the rest and found no receipt. Only Fitzpatrick's stables were left.

The previous afternoon, she had joined the parade in Hyde Park until she chanced upon Fitzpatrick. They had paused and chatted briefly. Nicole had complimented him on the excellence of his horse, and had gone on about how she admired such a fine animal. Flattered, Fitzpatrick had bragged of his other cattle and invited her to see them. Nicole had immediately accepted, and they had made an appointment for the next morning.

Nicole had dressed carefully in a new chocolate brown gown, the skirt decorated with a double band of biscuit-colored ribbons. She wore a matching spencer and bonnet with feather trimming. The rich, dark brown made her eyes seem even more mysterious, and she was extremely pleased with the effect.

As she accompanied Fitzpatrick to the stables, she was well aware that he was admiring her. Now if he would only remain distracted while she went about her business.

To Nicole's disappointment, she wasn't able to detect any sign of the receipt as she wandered through the stables. She had given up and was ready to leave when Fitzpatrick drew her attention to a horse he had acquired at Tattersall's the week before. He insisted on putting the animal through its paces so she might judge its excellence for herself.

The horse was a tall gray that looked better equipped for the hunt than for a ride in the park. The animal was quickly saddled and Fitzpatrick made ready to mount. Nicole moved away from the horse and, as Fitzpatrick swung his booted foot over the animal's back, what she saw drove all thought of the receipt from her mind. The bottom of Fitzpatrick's boot bore a familiar L-shaped cut, exactly like that on the jewel thief's sole.

Nicole smiled and nodded as Fitzpatrick paraded the gray back and forth in front of her, all the while wondering if she had been mistaken. After all, she had only had a brief flash; she could have been wrong.

When Fitzpatrick brought the horse to rest in front of her, Nicole moved to its side, patting its neck admiringly. Unable to think of anything else at such a short notice, she allowed her reticule to slip from her fingers. Admonishing Fitzpatrick to hold the animal still, she bent to retrieve it, stealing a look at the bottom of his boot. She had been right; an L-shaped cut marred the sole of his Hessian. It was proof, but she wanted more.

Nicole and Fitzpatrick strolled back to his house, talking of horses and the latest *on-dits* of the *ton*. She hoped her appearance was disarming and that he would drop his defenses.

"I hear several people have lost a great many jewels to a thief lately," she casually mentioned, concentrating on Fitzpatrick's thoughts.

"So I understand," he replied.

Nicole felt satisfaction and amusement when he answered, but she saw nothing.

"I was speaking to Lord and Lady Goodcastle last week and they were terribly upset. It seems the thief took emeralds that had been in their family for generations."

"They were upset, were they?" he asked. Pure exultation flowed from him.

Then, suddenly, came a scene so vivid that Nicole felt she was actually there. Fitzpatrick sat at his library desk, emeralds spilling between his fingers onto the mahogany surface. He laughed out loud as he fondled the jewels. "This will pay you for giving my mother the cut direct, my top-lofty Lord Goodcastle," he said while admiring the emeralds. "You and all the others who ignored her have paid with what is dear to you."

Nicole must have made all the right answers, because she was back in her own carriage without Fitzpatrick showing any sign of suspicion. The carriage rolled through the streets of London while Nicole wondered what to do with her newfound knowledge.

Eleven

Nicole was highly troubled as she dressed for the evening. She had still not decided what to do about Fitzpatrick. Since Jordan had broken his word about Miss Grayson, she did not feel any compulsion to confide in him, which left her with Drew. But she did not want to endanger Drew's life should he become angry and decide to confront Fitzpatrick by himself. She would think on the problem; Fitzpatrick was not going anywhere.

In the meantime, the problem of Jordan and Melanie was staring her in the face. In a short time, Jordan would be downstairs waiting to join her for the evening. She decided that she couldn't pretend any longer. If Jordan wanted to be with Melanie, then she would not make a fool of herself by appearing with him and feigning that all was well.

"You look lovely this evening," said Jordan as Nicole came down the stairs dressed in an ivory gown, heavily embroidered around the hem.

"Thank you," Nicole replied, toying nervously with her ivory and silk fan.

"The carriage is ready if you are," said Jordan.

"I would like to terminate our agreement," Nicole said abruptly, unable to approach the subject with any sort of subtlety with all the emotion swirling within her.

Jordan's eyes narrowed as he stared down at her. Motioning

Harrison away, he waited until the butler had disappeared down the hallway before he spoke.

"And what agreement is that, madam?"

"Our agreement to be seen together. I think it's gone on long enough. I've been accepted back into society, and there doesn't seem to be any gossip circulating about us."

"So now we're successful, and you see no need to continue?"

"Yes."

"Odd. I thought there was more between us than just fulfilling the terms of an agreement," he commented, watching her closely.

"I can't imagine what made you think that," she said.

"Perhaps it was the kisses we shared," he mused.

"They were only meant to make ours look like a normal marriage," Nicole replied, flushing slightly.

"Even though they were in private?" he murmured.

"I would think you'd be happy to be free again," she said, ignoring his question. "You no longer need attend balls or musicals, but can frequent your clubs and enjoy the companionship of your friends." And Melanie, Nicole wanted to add, but held her tongue. She had her pride. She would not mention the woman's name, nor allow him to see how hurt she was.

Their agreement was made to make Philip's future better. The fact that she had allowed her feelings to become engaged was her own dilemma. She could not blame youth for the problems in her marriage this time; she was old enough to know better than to fall in love with her husband again.

"And if I've found I enjoy dancing with my wife more than drinking with my friends?"

"Then you will need to find another partner," she answered brusquely. "I'm certain there are scores of ladies willing to dance with you." There was a bitter taste in her mouth from the thought of Melanie's blond head resting against his black evening jacket.

Jordan studied Nicole closely, but her face was expressionless. He could think of nothing that had occurred that would have caused this change. His hopes for their marriage were dashed for the moment. He had thought the time was right and had planned on convincing her to share his bed tonight, but now she seemed even more aloof than when she first returned. He would let her go for the time being, but he was determined to find out the reason for her change of feelings. He had not been mistaken when he felt her response to his kisses. What had gone wrong?

"Harrison," he called, then remained silent as the butler hurried down the hall from the back of the house.

"Please show Mrs. Worth to the carriage," he said.

Harrison's face was an expressionless mask as he opened the door for Nicole and stood waiting for her to precede him.

Nicole looked up at Jordan, holding his gaze, seeming to want to say something. Changing her mind, she quickly hurried to the door and disappeared from his view.

Jordan heaved a great sigh, attempting to release the stiffness in his shoulders. Did other men have as much trouble with women as he did? he wondered. Then he retired to his library for a large glass of brandy before setting out on his solitary path for the evening.

"I'm sorry, but I couldn't find anything," said Nicole to Caroline and Charles Hardesty. She had been at the ball an hour or more, but her thoughts were still on Jordan. She had felt his shock when she had told him she did not want his company this evening, but he had quickly covered his feelings and she could see no more. She wondered whether his astonishment came from being free to see Melanie again. Perhaps the woman had agreed to become his *chère amie* just to obtain the money her father needed. At this point, nothing would surprise Nicole.

"Fitzpatrick must have destroyed it, then," said Caroline.

"Which means we'll never right the wrong, unless I take it in my own hands," added Charles, his face dark with anger.

"No, Charles, please," begged Caroline. "It isn't worth risking your life."

"There *is* something I found out," Nicole said, hoping to distract Charles from seeking revenge, at least for a short time. "I can't talk about it yet, but it could rid England of Fitzpatrick for all time."

"When will you know?" asked Caroline, her hands clasped in front of her.

"Within a fortnight, I should expect," Nicole answered.

"We've waited this long, Charles. Surely another two weeks is not too much to ask," said Caroline, looking at her brother with anguished eyes.

"A fortnight, then," agreed Charles. "But I will wait no longer," he said harshly, turning abruptly and leaving the room.

"I'm sorry, Caroline," apologized Nicole. "I did the best I could."

"Don't blame yourself. The receipt could have been destroyed long ago. Or Fitzpatrick could have hidden it someplace where we could never find it. Thank you for giving me two more weeks to talk some sense into Charles."

"I wasn't just spouting nonsense," revealed Nicole. "I did find out something else about Fitzpatrick while I was looking for the receipt. If handled right, it could bring more down on his head than your receipt could, but I need some time to plan."

"Oh, Nicole, I pray you'll be successful."

"As do I. Now, let's see if we can find two entertaining gentlemen willing to dance with us."

Nicole danced every dance, but could not help missing the steadiness of Jordan guiding her through the steps. There were no gray eyes to meet as she gazed over the shoulder of a particularly inept partner, no smile to share when he was trapped by a nosy dowager, and no embrace to warm her on the dark ride home.

"You should thank the thief who stole your betrothal ring, Drew. He saved you from a worrisome fate. Women were not made to be understood."

"Women or Nicole?" asked Drew, amused at his friend's pessimistic state of mind.

"Everything was going along just fine. At least, I thought so. Then suddenly she tells me we should go our separate ways."

"What did you do to change her mind?"

"Nothing," said Jordan, offended at the suggestion.

"Had to be something. Nicole's not a woman to take strange starts," insisted Drew.

"I tell you there was nothing. We'd been attending all manner of events, and having an enjoyable time." Jordan thought about the rides home and was reminded of just how pleasing the evenings had been. "Not every aspect of our lives was back to normal, but we were progressing rapidly."

"What about Miss Grayson?"

"Nicole knows about her—everyone knows about her. It's public knowledge that we were going to marry. But Melanie hasn't been willing to give up. She's been approaching me every time we attend the same function, demanding I do something about Nicole so we can continue with our plans. I finally convinced her it was over between us. I'm certain her persistence has been mainly due to her father. The man doesn't have a feather to fly with, but gambles like Prinny himself."

"And they're both broke and owe everyone in London," added Drew.

"I took care of that," said Jordan, then laughed at Drew's expression. "With Grayson, not Prinny. It seemed the right thing to do," he explained. "Melanie has refused offers of marriage while waiting for me, which would have gotten her out from under her father's thumb. I agreed to pay her father's gambling debts so he wouldn't be so harsh with her."

"What was her reaction?"

"What could it be? Nicole and I are still married and there's no way to change that. Settling her father's debts could only make life easier for her and buy her a little time so she wouldn't be forced to accept the first man who offered for her.

"I was glad I had done it, because Nicole's been spending

more time with John Fitzpatrick than I like. When I broached the subject, she accused me of being in Melanie's company just as often. We made a promise to one another that we would avoid their company from now on."

"Did you keep it?"

"Of course. Well, I did go to the Grayson home to make arrangements with her father, but I didn't even see Melanie. And then, the other evening at the Marchcamps' musical she stopped to thank me. Said her father's been much more pleasant since my visit. Should be, too, as much as it cost me," grumbled Jordan.

"Nicole see you and Miss Grayson?"

"I . . . I don't know," said Jordan, attempting to remember if Nicole could have observed Melanie with him. "I suppose she could have. Do you think that's what's wrong with her?"

"Don't know. But if someone made me a promise, then broke it, I wouldn't like it one whit."

"But I didn't break my vow. Melanie was only thanking me," protested Jordan.

"Willing to bet an onlooker couldn't tell the difference."

Jordan remembered Melanie grasping his hand and staring up at him with glistening blue eyes. Perhaps it would look suspicious if a person didn't know what was being said. If that was it, he could straighten out the misunderstanding with a short explanation. If he could get home in time perhaps his plans for the evening were not ruined after all.

He swallowed the remainder of his brandy. "Thanks, Drew. You've given me hope. I'm going home to see if I can repair the damage."

"Good luck," Drew called after him.

"By the way," said Jordan, turning back for a moment. "I hope you get your ring back. Perhaps marriage isn't all bad after all."

"But sometimes confusing," murmured Drew as he filled his glass again.

* * *

Jordan arrived home before Nicole and paced the drawing room, watching for her return. He left the door leading into the hall open so he wouldn't miss her arrival. While waiting, he reviewed his explanation of his meeting with Melanie at the musical, and his visit to her home. He would state the facts; surely, Nicole couldn't help but see the truth.

He heard the clatter of hooves in front of the house and was at the door when it opened to admit Nicole.

"Come into the drawing room—I want to talk to you," he said pleasantly.

"It's late, Jordan. Can't it wait until tomorrow?"

Jordan thought of the night he had planned. "No, it can't. It's important to me that I say this now. Surely you can spare me a few minutes," he cajoled.

"Oh, all right," she grumbled, "but I hope it won't take long. I have a headache."

"This might cure it," he teased, holding the door for her, then closing it behind them.

Nicole did not sit down, but turned when she reached the far side of the room and watched warily as he approached. "It isn't Philip, is it?" she asked suddenly as the possibility of an accident to her son occurred to her.

"No, no. Nothing like that," he said, taking her hand and patting it reassuringly.

Nicole pulled her hand from his grasp. "Then what is it?" she demanded.

"It concerns the promise we made the other evening about Fitzpatrick . . . and Melanie."

Her hands tightened on her reticule. "I don't think we need to discuss it any further," she said, her eyes cold and her voice brittle. "Since we aren't playing the parts of devoted husband and wife, I see no need to worry about a promise."

"Does that mean you're seeing Fitzpatrick again?" Jordan asked, anger causing his voice to rise.

"You don't need to shout," replied Nicole. She took a deep breath before continuing. "Jordan, I'm here at your request, but if it's about me and John Fitzpatrick, then I have nothing to say." She had taken several steps toward the door before he grabbed her arm.

"Don't go," he said.

Nicole looked down at his hand, then jerked free.

"It isn't Fitzpatrick I want to discuss. It's Melanie."

"I already know more than I care to about Miss Grayson," snapped Nicole. "My sleep is more important than anything you could tell me about her."

"Did you see us together at the Marchcamps' musical?" he asked.

Nicole looked at him, attempting to judge where the conversation was leading. "Yes," she finally admitted.

"And you thought the worst, no doubt," he said.

Nicole pulled her shawl around her shoulders. "I didn't think about it at all."

"You thought I had broken my promise, but I didn't. She had approached me . . ." he began to eagerly explain.

"I don't want to hear it," said Nicole, holding up her hand to stop him. "What you and Miss Grayson do, or say, is no business of mine."

"It is if it upset you, if it caused you to reject my company this evening. I had such wonderful plans for tonight," he said, starting toward her, his eyes aglow.

"Plans!" she said, outraged, stepping aside to avoid his embrace. "If you think I'll have anything to do with you you're an addlebrained blockhead!"

Jordan stared at the lovely woman who had turned into a virulent termagant before his eyes. He was bewildered by her reaction; he only wanted to make love to her. She was his wife. They had been getting along very well until this small misunderstanding. If only she would listen to his explanation, she would realize she had misinterpreted his exchange with Melanie.

"Do you think I care whether you and your golden-haired angel gaze longingly into one another's eyes in public? You're only making a fool of yourself and gaining sympathy for me. No, it isn't what you do in public, it's the sneaking around that angers me. Did you think I wouldn't find out about your visiting her at home? Did you suppose no one would see you?

"I thought at least we could deal honestly with one another," she went on without seeming to stop for breath. "You told me when I returned you wouldn't object to any acquaintances I made as long as I was discreet. You said you'd do the same. Well, nothing you've done involving Miss Grayson has been discreet. And you come from her to me with plans for tonight? You can forget your plans with me, Jordan. You can forget them forever. But I'm sure that Miss Grayson will be amenable to anything you might suggest," she said scornfully. "I would only advise you to be more private about it in the future."

She was gone before the echo of her words died.

"I'm glad you could take tea with us," said Caroline. "We wanted to thank you for all your help."

"I'm sorry it came to nothing," replied Nicole, sipping the fragrant brew.

"You confirmed what we thought," said Charles. "Fitzpatrick is guilty of . . . of murder, and of stealing our home and probably much more, if truth be known. There are rumors going around that he owns the new gambling hell. If that's right, he's robbed more men than I could count."

"Why isn't something done about it?" asked Caroline.

"Deuced hard to prove," said Charles.

Nicole stored the information for further use. She began to raise her cup again, but something nudged at her mind. She searched the room for the cause.

"Is something wrong?" asked Caroline, noticing her distraction.

"Not really," she said, and was rewarded by being prodded a little harder. "Do you mind if I walk around?" she asked.

The Hardestys were surprised by her question. There was not much to see in their small drawing room.

"Of course not," answered Caroline, suppressing her curiosity.

The room was unnaturally silent at she paced the outer edges, but Nicole did not notice. She wandered aimlessly, touching things here and there, a book, a lamp, a decorative box. She picked up a small Buddha statue from the mantel.

"Ugly little fellow, isn't it?" remarked Charles.

"I don't know why, but it was a favorite of Father's," added Caroline. "It was the only thing Fitzpatrick allowed us to take from the house. He said he had no use for it, and didn't want to appear completely heartless. I remember, he laughed when he said it." She lowered her eyes, struggling for composure.

Charles reached across and clasped her hands, which were folded tightly in her lap. "Trust me, Caro, things will come right," he vowed.

"He may have done you the greatest service imaginable," murmured Nicole, cradling the small statue in her hands.

"What do you mean?" asked Charles, a puzzled expression on his face.

"Do you mind if I remove the bottom piece?" Nicole asked, already picking at the fabric covering the bottom of the statue.

"N—no," stammered Caroline, uncertain of what was happening.

"Here, let me help," said Charles, his interest rising.

Nicole held the statue as Charles used his knife to loosen the bottom covering. He pulled it away, revealing the opening to the cavity of the Buddha. It was small, but Nicole worked her fingers into the hollow, feeling around until she grasped what she already knew was there. She pulled the paper from the statue and handed it to Charles.

"I believe this is what you've been searching for," she said, a glorious smile on her face.

Charles unfolded the paper with shaking hands and spent a

few brief moments reading it through. Caroline waited, hands pressed over her lips, as if to hold back cries of disappointment.

Charles finished and raised suspiciously bright eyes to Caroline. He blinked rapidly, then nodded. "It's the receipt," he croaked out, his voice cracking with emotion. "We have our home back."

"Oh, Charles," cried Caroline, tears streaming down her face. She leaped to her feet and threw herself into his arms. He lifted her from the floor, spinning in circles of joy.

"Oh, Nicole, we're ignoring you," said Caroline when her feet were once again on the floor. "And you're the reason we can go home again. We'll never be able to thank you enough."

"She's right, you know," said Charles. "And at a time like this, propriety be damned." He grabbed Nicole in a huge hug, lifting her off the floor and turning in circles as he had with Caroline.

They were all giggling like children by the time he set her feet on solid ground.

"I'm so happy for both of you," said Nicole once they were quiet again. "What I'm going to ask you will be difficult, but when I tell you the full story you'll see how important it is."

"Let's sit down," suggested Charles.

"As it stands now, you will be able to reclaim your estate," said Nicole after they were seated. "But there is no way that Fitzpatrick will pay for the murder of your father."

"How can that be?" asked Caroline in an alarmed voice.

"I know that Fitzpatrick hired someone to murder your father, but there is no proof of it. No one saw your father murdered but me, and I will tell you now that my story will not be accepted as the truth."

"Then my solution is the best way," said Charles, his face grim.

"You remember, I mentioned a few days ago that I knew something about Fitzpatrick that could rid England of him forever?" The Hardestys nodded. "I want to tell you what that is, but I must have your promise that you won't reveal it to another person, no matter what you ultimately decide to do."

Caroline and Charles glanced at one another. "We want Fitzpatrick punished for what he's done."

Nicole nodded. "There is one way to do it. Fitzpatrick is obsessed about being one of the upper ten thousand," she explained. "He spends every hour of every day working toward that end. If you want to punish Fitzpatrick, exiling him from England and forcing him to give up that society would be worse than death. I think we can use what I know to do exactly that."

"We'll do whatever we can to help," vowed Charles.

"Wait until you hear what I have to say before you promise anything," said Nicole.

"I don't know why you want to see me now," said Melanie resentfully. "It's too late to do anything about Jordan. He's told me there's no way to get rid of that woman."

"He may not be able to, but I can," said Agatha Worth, unable to conceal a certain amount of smugness.

"What can you do that Jordan can't?"

Agatha was irritated that Melanie still looked skeptical. "I've made certain arrangements that will remove Nicole from our lives forever," she bragged.

Agatha's confidence gave Melanie a little hope. "What can I do to help?"

"Nothing, right now. I've put the plan in motion—now we wait for the results. Make yourself ready to rush to Jordan's side to console him. You'll be able to win him back very quickly."

Melanie's eyes widened as the enormity of Mrs. Worth's words washed over her. "What have you done? I only wanted her to go away—I never mentioned killing her."

"And neither have I. But if an unfortunate accident should occur, there's nothing to say you can't take advantage of it."

"What if she can see what you're planning?"

Mrs. Worth gave a hollow laugh. "Don't tell me you're beginning to believe all that faradiddle about being able to read minds and predict futures?"

"Many people do."

"Then they are fools. The woman can no more read minds than I can," she scoffed.

"Then why do you fear her so?" asked Melanie with a sudden flash of insight.

"I'm not afraid," replied Agatha scornfully. "The woman has made us a laughingstock with her fortune-telling. She's kept Jordan from living a normal life for the past seven years—then she suddenly reappears expecting to be accepted with open arms. Well, I for one won't do it."

"From what I hear, you didn't do it before," retorted Melanie. "And I've never once heard you worry about Jordan. You even refused to live in his house."

"There's nothing mysterious about that. I was settled in at Robert's. It's been my home since he and Jordan were babes, and Robert has children I can fuss over."

"That's still not reason enough to arrange to . . . to do away with her. She knows something about you, doesn't she?"

Melanie's question came too close to the truth for Agatha. "Don't be ridiculous. We have never gotten along, and Nicole's made Jordan's life miserable. I think it's time she disappeared from our lives for good."

"And what if she finds out? What if she uses her powers and reads your mind?"

"I've told you, she has no such powers. Now, listen closely. When you hear of something happening, go to Jordan. Don't let anyone stop you. You must be there to help him through the difficult times. As soon as propriety will allow, you and Jordan will be married and all of our lives will be smooth again."

Melanie was still doubtful about Agatha's plan; however, she desperately wanted to marry Jordan. He was by far the richest untitled gentleman in London. The other men who had shown an interest in her could not approach his wealth or looks. Even though Jordan had settled her father's gambling debts, it would only be a matter of time before Chester Grayson would find himself without a feather to fly with again. As soon as that occurred, he would resume insisting that Melanie accept the next offer that came her way. She would do anything to avoid that fate.

Twelve

"I hope this won't take too long—I have an engagement," said Jordan as he strolled into the drawing room. Nicole had asked him earlier in the day if he would join her for a short time. He had been curious, but evinced no interest in the meeting other than agreeing to be there.

He had been polite, but aloof, since their argument after the ball when he had tried his best to mend the rift between them.

"I suppose the length of time will depend upon your reaction to my news," Nicole replied.

"Shall we get on with it then?" he asked, adjusting the sleeve of his evening jacket.

"I've invited Drew and Alura and the Hardestys," she revealed. "They should be arriving any time now."

The look of boredom disappeared from Jordan's face. "What is this about?"

"The jewel thefts," said Nicole, confirming his suspicions, "but I'd rather explain it only once."

Drew and Alura arrived in a swirl of perfume and evening clothes. "We're on our way to Vauxhall Gardens," exclaimed Alura, excitement brightening her hazel eyes.

"If you don't wear yourself out before we get there," said Drew, smiling at her indulgently.

Caroline and Charles Hardesty followed hard on their heels, and a few minutes later they were seated. Jordan had chosen to stand with his elbow resting on the fireplace mantel, overlooking the small group.

"Since we all have plans, let's get to it," suggested Jordan in a bored voice.

Nicole doubted whether any of them would continue on their way after she revealed what she had learned, and felt a little guilty about ruining their evening.

"What I have to say is about the jewel thefts and the loss of Caroline and Charles's home," Nicole began. "Jordan, I invited you because you once had an interest in finding the thief. Lately, you have urged me to stop looking for him, and you also have disapproved of my search for the Hardestys' receipt. So if you would rather not be a part of this, I'll understand."

Jordan felt a very curmudgeon as all eyes turned to him. "It isn't that I didn't want you to help—I feared for your safety," he explained. "And yes, I would like to be a part of whatever you've uncovered." It hurt like the very devil to think that she might have been successful where he had failed.

"Very well," she said, nodding agreement. She began by relating the details of her second visit to the Goodcastles' home and the cut she had seen on the thief's boot. She told of encouraging Fitzpatrick to hold a ball, then searching his house without success. She moved on to the list provided by Caroline and Charles, and her visit to Fitzpatrick's stable.

Jordan's lips tightened and his scowl deepened. He had not known the half of it when it came to Nicole putting herself in danger.

"When I saw the same cut on the sole of Fitzpatrick's boot," said Nicole, unaware of her husband's feelings, "I was shocked. I hadn't expected to discover that not only had he cheated Caroline and Charles out of their inheritance, but that he had stolen some of the finest jewels in London."

"It's unthinkable!" burst out Alura.

"Damnable blackguard," growled Drew.

"We couldn't believe it either when Nicole first told us," said

Charles. "But she convinced us to hold off claiming our home until he could be charged with stealing the jewels."

"How do we find out where they are?" asked Drew.

"I'm certain they're in the house. If we can surprise him with the receipt and immediately claim the house, then I can locate the jewels before he has time to move them," said Nicole.

"You can't mean to let this entire operation rest on your fortune-telling?" said Jordan, amazed at her audacity.

"Why not? My fortune-telling found the thief and the receipt," countered Nicole.

"You tell us of some cut on Fitzpatrick's boot and expect us to go rushing off?" said Jordan.

"There is one more thing I haven't mentioned. When we were in the Goodcastle home, I detected a unique scent. None of you gentlemen were wearing it, and neither was Lord Goodcastle. Last night, Fitzpatrick asked me to dance, and he was wearing the exact scent."

Jordan made a sound of disgust. "And probably half the other men at the ball."

"No. The scent was unlike any I've ever encountered. When I complimented Fitzpatrick on it, he told me he had brought it from France."

"It isn't that I'm defending Fitzpatrick. God knows, I'd like nothing better than to see him locked away forever. But we can't do it on visions and perfume," mocked Jordan.

"Then what about the receipt? It will give us an opportunity to go into the house and search for the jewels. That's the reason I asked Caroline and Charles to wait before confronting Fitzpatrick," explained Nicole. "As far as your being involved, if you'll remember, I told you before I began that you need not be a part of this, Jordan."

"No matter what my feelings, I intend to be involved in whatever is decided."

"Very well," said Nicole. "Does anyone have any ideas on how to make a stronger case against Mr. Fitzpatrick?"

"We could find out if he knew the people who have been

robbed, whether he's been in their home and familiar enough with them to know where the jewels are kept," suggested Charles.

"If he doesn't know them, he might be acquainted with someone who does," added Caroline. "They could have told him where the jewels were kept without thinking. It's amazing what people reveal in general conversation."

"You two are solidly accepted by society. No one would think twice if you asked a few questions about Fitzpatrick," said Nicole.

"I know many who are more than willing to gossip about any subject," said Caroline. "But we would need to separate the truth from hearsay."

"We should be able to do that," replied Nicole. "What else?"

"The gambling hell," said Jordan, looking at Drew. "We never looked into it. Rumor has it," he said to the others, "that Fitzpatrick is behind the new gambling hell in town. Men have lost fortunes at the tables. It would be extremely tempting for a man to exchange information for his vowels."

"Just so," agreed Drew.

"I'm feeling an urge to gamble," said Jordan. "Would you like to come along?"

"Be delighted," replied Drew.

"But what can I do?" asked Alura, determined not to be left out.

"Come with me," invited Nicole. "I'm going to revisit Lady Goodcastle and the others who have suffered losses. We'll attempt to find out whether Fitzpatrick has been in their home recently, and we'll ask for a guest list where possible to see if anyone matches with what the others find."

"Be careful," warned Jordan. "If it is Fitzpatrick, and he finds out that we're on to him, he'll do anything to save himself."

There was a moment of silence as Jordan's warning reminded everyone that this wasn't a parlor game they were playing.

"I suppose that's it then," remarked Nicole, breaking the silence. "I assumed none of you would have eaten yet, so I asked cook to prepare a cold collation. We can work out the details of our plan while we eat."

When the collation was laid out on a table at one end of the room, Jordan motioned Nicole aside. Her four guests were busy filling their plates and talking among themselves, so she moved to the far end of the room with Jordan.

"Let's step outside," he said, indicating the French doors.

"I can't think of any reason we need to be so private," she objected.

Jordan had decided to try to reason with Nicole again. Despite all her nonsense, his feelings for her had not died. "There are some things I want to say to you that I'd rather the world not know. Our private life has been too public by far."

"Couldn't it wait until later? We have guests."

"They are well occupied," he argued. "I'm only asking for a few minutes of your time, Nicole. Is that too much for a wife to give her husband?"

"That isn't fair," she said.

"I never promised to be fair." He grinned charmingly. "Please," he said, holding the door open. "Just a few minutes?"

"Oh, all right," she agreed with little grace, stepping out into the small garden. "But I don't like it."

"You still think I lied to you about Melanie, don't you? That's why you don't want to be alone with me."

"This has nothing to do with you or Melanie. I just don't like being here," she said, looking around. "There's something wrong."

"I suppose your second sight is telling you that."

"Let's go back inside," she said, her voice urgent. "This is wrong, all wrong," she repeated, taking his arm and tugging him toward the door.

"My valet would swoon if he saw you wrinkling my coat," he teased, allowing her to pull him along.

"No!" Nicole screamed all of a sudden, pushing him aside as a shot rang out.

They landed in a heap near the doors. Jordan thought it pleasant to be lying all tangled up with Nicole until a searing band of pain set his side on fire. Dammit! Nicole had been right; there had been danger and he had led them right into it.

The door burst open and light spilled out into the night.

"Nicole? Jordan? Are you all right?" said Drew, bending over them.

"Nicole hasn't moved," said Jordan, fear chilling him to the bone, making him forget the pain that still throbbed in his side.

"Let's take her inside," said Charles, lifting her easily and carrying her into the drawing room.

Drew took Jordan's arm and pulled him to his feet. Jordan staggered a bit, and Drew steadied him as they followed Charles through the door.

"Hurt worse than you think," judged Drew, seeing the red stain spreading on Jordan's white shirt.

"I'm only a little shaken," he replied, watching as Charles carefully laid Nicole on the settee.

"More than that," argued Drew, pulling open Jordan's jacket to inspect the damage. "Looks like you've been shot," he said calmly, guiding him to a chair.

A cluster of servants filled the door. "Better send for the doctor," said Drew. Harrison hurried away to follow his order.

It was several hours later, and Nicole had the very devil of a headache from striking her head when she fell. A bullet had creased Jordan's side, which the doctor said would be painful but not life-threatening.

The Hardestys were gone, taking a protesting Alura with them, while Drew stayed behind to help where he could.

Jordan was stretched out on his bed, remaining as still as possible so as not to reopen the wound. Nicole sat by his side, with Drew standing nearby.

"I can't believe Fitzpatrick got on to us so quickly," said Jordan.

"I don't believe it was Fitzpatrick," said Nicole, wondering how much to tell him.

"Then who could have done this? And for what reason?" asked Jordan. "I'm unaware of any enemies who would resort to such a cowardly method to settle a score."

Nicole realized she had to be honest with him. "The bullet was meant for me."

"You are, no doubt, joking," said Jordan.

"I'm afraid not," she replied. "I saw it."

Jordan stared at her for a long moment. "Someone attempted to kill one of us tonight, Nicole. Surely you realize the outcome of this situation is far too serious to rest on your visions."

"That is exactly why you must hear me out," said Nicole.

"Should listen to her," interjected Drew.

"Of course you would agree with her," replied Jordan. "You have encouraged her from the beginning." He shifted his gaze to Nicole. "What makes you think that the bullet was meant for you?"

"You will remember I didn't want to go out into the garden," she said. "I couldn't determine what was wrong until the moment the man raised his pistol to fire. Then it was almost too late." She shuddered, thinking how close to death Jordan had come.

"At the moment he fired, I saw the scene through his eyes. His sight was on me. If I hadn't pushed you, perhaps you wouldn't have been shot."

"But *you* might have been," he replied, reaching for her hand. Jordan could see she unequivocally believed what she said. And, at this point, he had nothing better to suggest. There would be no harm in indulging her for the moment, he decided.

"We'll talk about this later when we both feel more up to it. Right now, you should be lying down," said Jordan, seeing the paleness of her face.

"I'm fine. It was just a bump on the head, and you've told me often enough it's too hard to hurt."

"This is no joking matter, Nicole. Make her lie down, Drew."

"How do you expect me to succeed where you have failed?" Drew asked.

"I shall go as soon as you drink this," said Nicole.

"What is it?" Jordan asked, sniffing at the glass suspiciously.

"Something that will help with the pain."

"You promise you will lie down if I drink this?" he asked.

"Nothing like trust in a marriage," remarked Drew, which earned him a frown from Jordan.

"I promise," said Nicole.

Jordan drained the glass. "What a vile concoction," he remarked. "I've kept my part of the bargain, now it's your turn."

"I'll only stay until you fall asleep," she said, reaching out for his hand.

He wrapped his hand around hers. "Perhaps that would be acceptable after all. How is Philip?"

"Fast asleep," Nicole reassured him. "All the upheaval didn't even wake him."

A short time later, Jordan drifted off to sleep, a smile on his face.

"You were both lucky tonight," commented Drew.

"It was more than luck. I knew something was going to happen, but I saw it a little too late."

"Are you certain the man who took a shot at you was a stranger?" asked Drew.

Nicole nodded. "Yes. He had been hired to kill me."

"Do you know who's responsible?"

"There's little doubt in my mind, but I must be certain before I make an accusation," she said.

"Understand," said Drew. "Call on me if you need assistance."

"Thank you, but I don't think I'll be doing much for a while. Jordan comes first. I'm to blame for this, and I must make sure he's all right."

"You're not to blame for anything," objected Drew. "You tried to convince Jordan not to go into the garden—he told me so himself. He would suffer this and much more to keep you safe."

"How can you say that when you know our story?" she asked.

"That's why I can say it. Last time I saw Jordan, he had just visited Grayson to settle the man's gambling debts. Wanted to make some gesture since he couldn't marry Miss Grayson. He was on his way to tell you that all the loose ends were tied up and that Miss Grayson was out of his life for good."

Nicole remembered their argument, and how she would not listen when Jordan wanted to explain. If the bullet had been a few inches to the right, she would have never heard his voice again. When he woke, she vowed to listen to anything he had to say.

"He's asleep," observed Drew. "Should keep your promise. You need to rest as much as he does."

"I don't want to leave him," she said, suddenly afraid that something would happen to him during the night.

"Willis will be here," said Drew, indicating Jordan's valet standing on the other side of the bed. "And I'll stay until morning. Not much left of the night anyway."

"I'll go lie down for a while then. Promise you'll call me if he wakes."

"I will. Now go ahead," he said, taking her place beside the bed.

Nicole woke early the next morning after a few short hours of restless sleep. Jordan was still asleep, with Drew and Willis serving as sentinels on either side of the bed.

The doctor arrived, and Nicole waited in the hall while he examined Jordan. Her husband had a slight fever, said the doctor, which was not unusual with his injury. He was to keep to his bed and rest for the next few days, if she could keep him there.

Today would be no problem, thought Nicole. He was still

groggy from the laudanum, and his wound was painful when he moved.

She spent time with Philip, explaining to him that his papa was sick and wouldn't be able to see him for a few days. He was downcast, but she promised him a picnic as soon as his father improved, which helped him recover his spirits.

Drew returned at midday, seeming to suffer no ill effects from his sleepless night. Alura, Caroline, and Charles arrived shortly thereafter. Nicole advised them of what the doctor had determined about Jordan's condition, and assured them she was well.

"Charles and I were wondering what we should do about the plans we made last night," said Caroline.

"Nothing's changed," replied Nicole. "If we're all agreed, I propose we go ahead." Looking around the small circle, she saw everyone nod.

"Jordan will kick up a dust if he thinks we're going on without him," commented Drew.

"Then we won't tell him," said Nicole. Receiving a skeptical look from Drew, she added, "If he doesn't ask."

"You're the only one Jordan's injury affects," she said to Drew.

"I can gamble without him," remarked Drew.

"Do you think it was Fitzpatrick who tried to kill Jordan last night?" asked Charles.

"I know it wasn't," said Nicole. "Fitzpatrick doesn't know we're on to him yet, and we must keep it that way." She hesitated, wondering how much to reveal, then decided they deserved to be assured they were in no danger. "The bullet was meant for me, for a purely personal reason. So you have no reason to fear the same thing will happen to you."

"Who could want you dead?" gasped Alura, unable to hide her astonishment.

"Shouldn't be so nosy," said Drew.

Alura turned on him, her face pale. "This isn't about the current *on-dit*. Nicole is my friend, and someone tried to kill her."

Nicole was touched by Alura's response. "Don't worry," she said. "I know who was behind it, and I plan to deal with it very shortly."

"Would like to help," declared Drew, repeating his offer of the night before.

Nicole had not had friends who cared about her for such a long time, and she fought back a sudden rush of tears. "I don't think it will be necessary, but I thank you."

"Jordan would never forgive me or himself if anything happened to you," said Drew.

"I'll be very careful," she assured him.

A short time later Caroline, Charles, and Drew departed, more determined than ever to carry on with their part of the investigation. Alura stayed behind to accompany Nicole to Lady Goodcastle's.

"Let me pour you another cup of tea—then I'll check on Jordan and gather my bonnet and gloves," said Nicole.

"You go ahead—I'll pour my own tea," replied Alura. "I'm certain you're anxious to see how Jordan is doing."

Nicole hurried up the stairs, grateful for Alura's understanding. While the doctor had assured her Jordan was in no danger, she needed to look in on him to convince herself all was well.

"He's still asleep," said Willis when she eased the door open and peered around the edge. "He was getting restless and I gave him a little more laudanum so he wouldn't break open the wound."

"How long do you think he'll sleep?"

"Probably for the rest of the day," judged Willis.

"I need to go out this afternoon," said Nicole. "Don't leave him alone."

Willis looked slightly affronted. "I would never do that, madam."

"I'll sit with him this evening and you can get some rest."

"That won't be necessary . . ." Willis began.

"I insist," broke in Nicole. "It will be one of the few times

I'll have the upper hand." Leaning over the bed, she placed a kiss on Jordan's forehead, then reluctantly left the room as quietly as she had entered.

The afternoon had been a tiring one for Nicole, especially when she had wanted nothing more than to sit by Jordan's side. She and Alura had called on Lady Goodcastle and three of the other families who had suffered losses at the hands of the burglar.

Lady Goodcastle had confirmed that Mr. Fitzpatrick had been present at their home. Her nose wrinkled when she said his name and Nicole had felt safe in continuing her questions.

The countess told them that her husband had insisted she send Fitzpatrick an invitation. When she objected, he said he had promised Viscount Thornton he would invite Fitzpatrick. After all their years together, Lady Goodcastle knew her husband never went back on his word, so she sent Fitzpatrick an invitation and put him out of her mind.

Fitzpatrick had been in one of the other homes where robberies had taken place. Nicole had asked for a copy of the guest list for any recent entertainment, and also a list of people hired to help with the event.

Before the afternoon was over, Nicole and Alura had collected a considerable number of sheets filled with names. They returned to Nicole's home and retired to the drawing room.

"I didn't realize this would be so tiring," said Alura, sipping from her cup of tea.

"I'll never accuse the Bow Street Runners of being paid too much for their services," remarked Nicole, leaning her head against the chair back and closing her eyes.

"Should we go over these today?" asked Alura, indicating the stack of lists on the table between them.

"I don't think I could give it the attention it deserves at present. At all events, I want to sit with Jordan for a time, and comparing names will be a long and, undoubtedly, tedious task."

Alura nodded in agreement, relieved that she could go home and rest before dressing for the evening. "I could sit with you," she volunteered, suddenly feeling guilty about going out while Jordan lay abed with Nicole nursing him.

"Thank you, but Willis would never forgive me if I pushed him aside entirely. I think he resents my sending him away for any length of time," she said, smiling. "Why don't we plan on working on the lists within the next few days? By then, Jordan will be much better and might be able to help us. It will give him something to occupy his mind until he can be up and around."

"Is there nothing I can do?" insisted Alura.

"Nothing at the moment," said Nicole. "The best thing you can do is go out this evening, have a good time, and forget about this. You're here to enjoy the Season, not to be embroiled in these problems."

"You forget that it was Drew and I who involved you in the robberies and the Hardestys' dilemma," she said, suddenly downcast.

"But it wasn't either of those that caused Jordan to be shot."

"Are you certain?"

"Absolutely," replied Nicole. "Now go ahead. You have only one first Season, and you shouldn't miss it. After that, they all look the same."

"I'm still not convinced as to that," said Alura, grinning. "I'll stop by tomorrow and catch you up on all the *on-dits,*" she promised.

Jordan was awake when Nicole entered his room.

"He won't drink this," complained Willis, indicating the cup of beef broth.

"I want some real food," growled Jordan from his bed.

"This is what the doctor ordered," replied the valet, standing his ground.

Nicole restrained a grin of relief. If Jordan was complaining about food, he was out of danger.

"Perhaps we could stretch the doctor's orders to include some lightly buttered eggs and toast," she said in a conciliatory voice.

Neither man was completely happy, but Willis left to get a more substantial meal for his master.

"How is Philip this morning?" asked Jordan. He missed spending time with his son and didn't want Philip to think he no longer cared about him.

"Pouting that you're too sick to be with him today. But I promised him a picnic when you're better and he's already planning the menu. I'm afraid it's going to be a very sweet lunch," she said, reciting the long list of various cakes that Philip insisted they take.

"Since you're the one who promised, you must join us," said Jordan, enjoying the lighthearted banter. "I don't think I can deal with the results that such a repast would have on me or Philip."

"We'll see," she replied, pausing a moment before continuing. "Jordan, I'd like to have a footman stay with Philip and Betsy."

"You mean to guard them?"

"Yes."

"Why?" he demanded, pulling himself up, then grimacing and falling back against the pillows.

She leaned over him, concerned that he might have reinjured the wound. "Be careful," she warned sternly.

"What is it? Has Philip been threatened?"

"No, but I don't want to take the chance. I still contend that the bullet was meant for me. There is someone who wants me out of the way very badly. I've heard it said that Philip is the reason you allow me to stay. The logical conclusion would be that if Philip was gone, then I would soon follow."

"And what do you think?" he asked.

"It doesn't matter. What does matter is Philip's safety."

"Do whatever it takes to protect him. Use as many men as you require. We'll hire more if need be."

"Thank you."

"There's no need to thank me for safeguarding my own son. And Nicole . . ." He waited until she looked at him. "To answer your question—although Philip is very dear to me, he is not the only reason I want you to remain."

A flush appeared on Nicole's face, but she did not reply.

Jordan decided not to force the subject. "You seem to have suffered no lasting effects from last night's events," he said, attempting to shift his position.

Nicole adjusted his pillows until he was comfortable again. "You sound disappointed," she teased. "I do have a headache, if it makes you feel better."

"Nothing of the sort," he said, looking chagrined. "When I saw you lying there so quietly, it was worse than when I found you gone before."

For the first time, Nicole realized what she had put Jordan through when she walked out of his life seven years ago, and she was ashamed.

"Jordan, I'm sorry . . ."

"Shush. I'm not ready for a deathbed confession yet, be it yours or mine. We'll have plenty of time for apologies when I'm back on my feet." And he did not plan on being in this large bed by himself for long. But now he was too weak and sore to carry through with his plans, so it was best to avoid the subject.

"Whatever you want." Nicole rose as Willis came in, carrying a tray.

"Don't go," he said, reaching out for her. "That is, if you have nothing better to do."

The last time they had talked at any length they were at daggers drawn. She thought he was still dancing attendance on Melanie, and would not listen to his explanation. He had been shot attempting once again to mend the breach, and although she seemed to view him in a more benevolent light, he did not know how far her goodwill extended.

Willis arranged the tray, which contained what Jordan considered a meager fare of buttered eggs, toast, and tea, then looked at Nicole.

"I'll stay for a while," she said, nodding at Willis and indicating that he could leave, "but you need your rest."

"That's all I've done today, and I've had my fill of it. If it weren't that I might open this blasted wound again, I would have been up this morning."

"You mustn't do anything foolish," she pleaded, leaning toward him.

Her concern was real, and Jordan's hope that there might yet be a chance for him grew. "I won't if you'll stay and tell me what has happened today. Willis has kept me totally isolated, without a bit of news from outside this room. He says it's for my own good, but I have my doubts. I think he enjoys having me at a disadvantage."

"It's very possible," agreed Nicole, laughing at his impatience. "There's not too much to tell. After the doctor left last night, we decided to put it about that you had come down with a case of influenza. I didn't want the whole town buzzing about who had shot you and why."

Jordan sampled the eggs and found them better than the broth. "That was a good decision," he said after taking a few bites.

Nicole was more pleased than she should have been with his compliment. "After that, we decided to go ahead with our plans even though you couldn't be actively involved."

"You didn't do anything foolish?" he asked, almost upsetting the tray. "You shouldn't go out at all if this man is trying to kill you."

"I don't feel any danger from that direction any longer."

They were getting on too well for Jordan to argue about her second sight. It would not hurt to humor her a little longer. "But how can you know for sure?" he asked. "You were almost too late in recognizing it last night."

"No, I felt the danger—I just couldn't determine where it was coming from. But today it's completely gone."

"You could be right," he said thoughtfully. "If a man of that ilk fails, he usually has no stomach to try again. But you must remain vigilant," he warned.

"I will," she promised.

"Now, tell me what you did today."

"No more than we had planned. Alura and I visited Lady Goodcastle and three of the other homes that had been burglarized." She went on to explain what had come of her visits.

"I was hoping you would be willing to help us with the lists since there are so many of them. I know it isn't the active role you intended to play, but it will only be a few days until you're up and around again."

"I suppose it's better than doing nothing," he grumbled.

"It will be a great help," she said, removing the tray and placing it on a table nearby.

"Is there any use asking for a brandy?" he said hopefully.

She folded her arms across her chest and hardened her heart. "None at all."

"You and Willis are tyrants," he accused.

"It's for your own good."

"The last time I heard that was just before a thrashing at school."

"Be assured you have nothing to fear on that score."

"Oh, I don't know," he said, a devilish glint in his eye. "When I think of you administering it, a thrashing takes on a whole new light."

Nicole was thankful for the dimness of the room. She had been married to Jordan and had borne his child, yet he still had the ability to bring a blush to her face.

"I'm afraid you're not fit for sport of any kind," she said sharply, hoping such a set-down would show him his words had no effect.

But he only laughed, then grimaced as his wound objected to such activity.

She rushed to his side, bending over him to see whether the wound was bleeding again. "Have you hurt yourself?"

"No." He reached up to touch a curl that had tumbled over her shoulder. Rubbing it against his cheek, he closed his eyes and inhaled deeply.

"You still wear the same scent." He opened his eyes and caught her staring at him. "I've dreamt about it," he murmured. "Dreams so real I'd wake, thinking you were beside me again."

Nicole was mesmerized; his gray gaze so close, catching her, unwilling to let her go.

"Stay with me tonight, Nicole. Lie beside me again."

"I can't," she whispered. "I would hurt you."

"It hurts me more that we're apart." She didn't answer. "I only mean for you to stay with me," he explained in a lighter tone. "I'm afraid anything more would probably hurt like the devil," he teased, breaking the tension between them.

Nicole straightened, relieved to be free of his spell. "I will sprinkle some of my perfume on your pillow. Perhaps that will suffice."

"I'm afraid it wouldn't be the same. No, I'll wait until I'm better and see if we can come to a mutual accord."

Nicole's skin felt warm, and she backed away from the bed. "I'll call Willis. It's been a tiring day."

Jordan immediately felt guilty. Nicole had been knocked unconscious last night. He was sure she had gotten very little sleep, and had more than a full day today. "I'm sorry," he said, embarrassed at his lack of sensitivity. "I'm being selfish. You, no doubt, feel worse than I do."

"Balderdash!" she replied, a twinkle in her eye. "You're doing it up a bit too brown, Jordan."

"I mean it," he said, indignant that she questioned his sincerity.

Nicole studied him a moment. "Then I thank you. You are the last person I can remember worrying about me, and that was seven years ago. I'm sure you can understand my skepticism," she explained gently.

"You will never be without anyone again, if that is your desire," he said. "That's what I wanted to talk with you about last night."

"Shush," she said, laying a finger against his lips. "Don't say any more now. Wait until all of our problems are behind us."

"If it's Melanie, everything is over between us. When I went to her home I was only . . ."

"It isn't only Melanie," Nicole said, interrupting his explanation. "There are other problems we must overcome. Now, I'm going to call Willis and let him settle you for the night. I'll see you tomorrow."

She unexpectedly leaned over him and placed a kiss on his lips. Jordan wanted to put his arms around her and hold her until they had resolved all of the problems she thought kept them apart. What was she talking about, anyway? He could think of nothing between them but Melanie, and he had done all he could to separate himself from the Grayson family. It was true that his mother still did not approve of Nicole, but that had been the case since they had first met and it had not kept them from marrying.

Jordan fell asleep searching for obstacles that might keep them apart once he was well again.

Thirteen

Nicole looked in on Jordan the next morning. Willis had given him a mild dose of laudanum the night before and he was resting comfortably.

Advising Willis that she would be back to relieve him in an hour or so, Nicole ordered the carriage brought around.

It was still early and the London streets were as yet uncrowded when Nicole set off on her mission. She was soon stepping down in front of the Duke of Weston's home.

Her knock was answered by the butler, who advised her Mrs. Worth was not receiving.

"I'm her daughter-in-law," she reminded him, concealing her temper beneath a calm facade. "She will see me."

"Nicole, how good of you to visit," said Elizabeth, coming down the stairs.

"Elizabeth," said Nicole with relief. "I've come to see Mrs. Worth. Do you know where she is?"

"Why, she's usually in her sitting room at this hour," answered Elizabeth without turning a hair at the early hour or the abruptness of her visitor.

"This way?" asked Nicole starting down the hall.

"At the back, on the left," called Elizabeth after her departing back.

* * *

The room was pink and green and hot. Even with the pleasant weather outside, a small flame blazed in the fireplace. Mrs. Worth's face registered surprise when Nicole entered without knocking.

Nicole had wished to catch Agatha off guard. She hoped the story about Jordan's having influenza had been credible. She hadn't wanted the older woman to have learned the truth and have had time to compose herself.

"What are you doing here?" demanded Agatha.

A few short steps brought Nicole to rest in front of Mrs. Worth. "I've come to bring you news."

"There's nothing you could tell me that I would be interested in. You're interrupting my morning tea, and will probably cause me indigestion."

"Oh, no doubt," Nicole agreed cheerfully. "Particularly after you hear what I have to say."

"I've told you, I don't want to hear anything from you."

Nicole selected a chair across from Mrs. Worth. It was covered in a violent shade of pink, which seemed appropriate to Nicole's state of mind. She leaned back, appearing to be completely at ease, knowing it would further incense her mother-in-law.

"Jordan has been shot," she said abruptly.

Mrs. Worth's cup and saucer clattered to the floor, coming to no harm on the thick carpet but spilling the remains of her tea.

"You should call someone to clean that up or it will certainly leave a stain," recommended Nicole in her best housekeeper's voice.

Mrs. Worth's face was as white as her lacy cap. "Is he alive?" she asked.

"Jordan?" asked Nicole, as if she didn't know who they were discussing. She didn't feel at all guilty about wanting the woman to suffer. "He'll live, but an inch or so the other way and he wouldn't have."

Mrs. Worth closed her eyes and drew a few deep breaths. Opening them, she fixed her gaze on Nicole, glaring at her across the small space that separated them. "You've brought your news, now go," she ordered.

"You probably won't believe me. At least you never did before," said Nicole, as if they were enjoying a harmless chat. "But I had the strangest feeling—you remember my feelings, don't you?—that the bullet wasn't meant for Jordan." She paused, looking at Mrs. Worth for a response, but the other woman only stared fixedly as if mesmerized by a swaying cobra.

"In fact, I'm convinced it was meant for me. You wouldn't know anything about that, would you?"

Mrs. Worth reached for a bell and rang it vigorously. Maude rushed into the room to her side. "Put out that fire and open the window. This room is too hot to breathe in."

The two women were silent while Maude followed her orders. After she had left the room, Mrs. Worth turned her attention back to Nicole. She had regained her composure, and responded to Nicole's last question calmly.

"I know nothing about anyone wanting to shoot you or Jordan."

Nicole had opened her mind to Mrs. Worth's from the moment she had entered the room. She had found the usual feelings of anger and hate that she had always encountered from the woman, but there was something worse. Mrs. Worth wanted her dead and the knowledge chilled Nicole to the bone.

"You hired someone, didn't you?" she asked, concentrating intently. She saw a dark garden with mews behind it, then a door opening and two shadowy figures whispering together. The figures parted and one returned to a house. Nicole recognized a statue that she had admired while at the Marchcamps' musical. Then the figure stepped into the light from the door; it was Mrs. Worth, a malicious smile on her face.

"Don't be foolish—this is just one of your strange starts," accused Mrs. Worth.

"It was at the Marchcamps'," said Nicole, ignoring her remark. "You met him in the mews behind the house and arranged for him to kill me. Then you slipped back into the house without anyone knowing the difference."

"You should be in Bedlam," gasped Mrs. Worth.

Nicole remembered the murderous intent she had felt the last time they had met. "No, I'm not insane. This is not the first time I've seen the fate you want me to suffer. Why do you want to be rid of me so badly? You seldom see Jordan—I don't think you even like him very much. So why would you want to keep us apart? Why is it necessary to do away with me? When I first married Jordan, you said I embarrassed you with my second sight, but that's no reason for murder. You could have laughed that off and no one would think any more of it."

"You're talking nonsense," charged Mrs. Worth.

"I don't think so," responded Nicole. "The last time we discussed this, I accused you of keeping a secret from Jordan. I still believe that's the truth. What is it? What is so important that it's worth taking a life?"

Mrs. Worth's thoughts burned behind Nicole's eyes. She saw a blazing building, with figures running from it. Two babies wrapped in white blankets, smudged with soot, and a young Agatha bending over them.

"The fire," whispered Nicole. "Something about the fire that killed Jordan's father and Robert's parents."

"You're a witch," charged Agatha, looking at her wildly. "I don't want you here. Get out!"

"I'll leave," agreed Nicole, rising from her chair. "I have what I came for. You are the cause of Jordan's being shot. Your hatred of me almost killed your own son," she hissed, her love of Jordan releasing a hatred as strong as Mrs. Worth's. She breathed deeply and walked the short way to the door. "You want to be rid of me for good," she said, turning to face her mother-in-law. "But I'm on to you now and it won't be so easy." Nicole began to open the door, then turned back for a parting shot. "You think this room is hot, madam? Just wait until you reach hell!"

* * *

"I should go downstairs—the news of your illness is getting about. Harrison said people have been calling and flowers have been arriving all morning. It amazes me how fast news travels in London."

"Will you come back later?" Jordan asked.

"As soon as you've eaten and Willis has wielded his razor," she said with a radiant smile.

He nodded and watched her leave, thinking of their exchange the night before. Except for the gibberish about the problems besetting them, she had seemed in a receptive mood toward their reconciliation. And today there was a look about her that hadn't been there before. He couldn't explain what it was, but it made him think that it was possible to put their lives right after all.

In his mind, the one thing that stood in their way was Nicole's second sight. She was convinced that it was real, as were many of their other acquaintances, including his best friend. And she was quite adamant that she would never renounce her gift.

The issue had been the breaking point in their marriage before, and Jordan would not allow it to keep them apart any longer. If he could not believe in it, then he must learn to live with it.

He would make a conscientious effort to hide his skepticism whenever Nicole alluded to her second sight. He felt he had made a good start by not totally rejecting her idea that the bullet was meant for her. And when she had announced that the danger was over, he believed he had done a creditable job of accepting that also. However, he was still determined to put the Bow Street Runners on to the shooting to see what they could come up with. In the meantime, he would insist she be particularly cautious.

After she left Jordan's room, Nicole welcomed several of his friends who called to inquire about his condition. Some of Nicole's acquaintances also stopped by to offer suggestions on how to hasten his recuperation. The drawing room and hall were rapidly filling up with flowers, and the kitchen was overflowing with favorite healing concoctions sent by well-intentioned friends.

The drawing room finally emptied, and Nicole told Harrison to turn away any further callers while she went upstairs to sit with Jordan. She had reached the top of the stairs when there was a commotion at the front door.

"Mrs. Worth is not receiving at present, ma'am," Harrison intoned in his best butler's voice.

"It isn't *that woman* that I want to see," said Melanie Grayson, catching Harrison by surprise and pushing past him. "I understand Mr. Worth is ill. I demand to see him immediately."

"Mr. Worth is confined to his room for the time being," replied Harrison. "If you will leave your card . . ."

"I'm not leaving until I see him for myself," she declared, her voice rising. She started toward the stairs.

Harrison was momentarily baffled. He had never faced a lady who was forcing her way into a place she wasn't wanted. He dared not lay a hand on her, and did not know how to stop her ascent to his master's room.

Nicole watched from the top of the stairs and silently berated the hand fate had dealt her. She and Jordan were teetering on the edge of reuniting, and now the enemy was climbing her stairs. She did not need to read Melanie's mind to know that she had called not only because Jordan was ill, but to make another attempt to win him back. Even though Jordan had made it clear there was no chance for them, Melanie had not yet given up. She would grasp at any excuse to rush to Jordan's side, reminding him of what he had lost.

Nicole felt the urge to throw boiling oil over the banister, like warriors of old protecting their castles. Instead, she motioned to Harrison to leave the woman alone.

"Miss Grayson, I understand you would like to see my husband."

Melanie's blue eyes didn't look at all angelic as she glared at Nicole, who didn't bother to waste her time searching for her thoughts; they were all too apparent.

"I came to call on Jordan, and I won't leave until I see for myself that he is all right."

"I wouldn't expect you to," replied Nicole agreeably. "Only let me inquire as to whether he's dressed to receive visitors." Nicole kept her smile from changing into a smirk as she slipped into Jordan's room.

Jordan was propped up in bed against a mound of pillows. Willis had shaved him and changed his shirt, and except for a drawn look to his face, he seemed much better.

"I was wondering where you had taken yourself off to," he said, halfway complaining.

"We've had a flood of people coming by to inquire after your health. The drawing room has turned into a garden of flowers, and the kitchen . . . well, I can only say that you have enough beef broth to last a fortnight."

Nicole laughed at the face he made.

"Promise that I won't see another bowl of that swill," he said.

"I think you're well enough to avoid that fate, but we've received two barley waters and a quince jelly if you're interested."

His face became even more contorted. "Both sound worse than the beef broth. Sit down and tell me who called," he invited.

"Oh," said Nicole, raising her hand to her mouth as if she had forgotten. "You distracted me. There's a visitor waiting to see you."

"Couldn't you put him off until tomorrow?"

"Um. I'm afraid not. She says she won't leave until she sees you."

"She?"

Nicole nodded.

He leaned back against the pillows and closed his eyes. "Tell me it isn't my mother," he pleaded in a long-suffering voice.

"Perhaps you should see for yourself," said Nicole. She opened the door, and an angry Melanie flounced in.

"Oh, Jordan," she wailed when she saw him. "My poor dear,

what has happened to you?" she said, rushing across the room
to his bed and throwing herself halfway across it.

Jordan grunted as the wound in his side protested Melanie's
treatment. "Please, Melanie. You could reopen the . . . I mean,
I'm not feeling quite the thing."

"Oh, I'm sorry," she said, pulling back to stand beside the
bed, tears trickling down her face. "I've been so worried, Jordan.
As soon as I heard, I rushed right over. I had to see with my
own eyes that you were alive."

"Well, you can now rest assured," he replied, rearranging his
pillows with Willis's help.

Melanie wiped away her tears with a dainty, lace-edged handkerchief. "You must let me stay and nurse you," she begged.
"I make the most fortifying beef broth. Father swears by it."

Nicole lapsed into a fit of coughing, which earned her a frown
from Jordan.

"I'm sure he does," Jordan replied. "But the doctor says I
can eat regular food this evening. Besides, you could come
down with my illness if you stay."

Melanie looked uneasy with the idea, but she would not re-
linquish the battlefield. "I am willing to sacrifice my health for
your comfort."

"Really, Melanie, there is no need at all for you to do so,"
objected Jordan.

"Let me stay and read to you," she suggested. "Remember
how you enjoyed it so when I read from my book of poems? I
could send for it and we could spend the rest of the day reminiscing."

Nicole slipped out of the room. Even though Jordan had assured her he had completely broken with Melanie, references
to what they had shared still hurt. There was no way to pretend
that Melanie had not existed, but Nicole had no desire to hear
the details.

Jordan was well enough to decide whether he wanted Melanie
to stay or go. She would retire and count the containers of beef

broth until Miss Grayson left the house. She hoped she would not be forced to spend the remainder of the day in the kitchen.

To her surprise, Nicole hadn't nearly finished counting the beef broth when Harrison had advised her that Miss Grayson had departed.

Nicole did not return to Jordan's room that evening, nor did she visit him in the morning. She had no idea what effect Melanie's visit had made on Jordan, but she decided to delay finding out as long as possible.

However, it was now early afternoon and she had promised Jordan they would begin going over the lists she and Alura had collected from the hostesses who had been robbed.

Nicole collected the lists and reluctantly approached Jordan's door. Since her return, she had constantly shifted back and forth between acceptance that her marriage was over in all but the legal sense, and hope that not all feeling had died between them. Her resilience was worn to a nub, and if Jordan greeted her with gray eyes as cold as icy shards, she did not know what her reaction would be. She tapped lightly on the door before she entered.

Jordan was clearly a disgruntled man. He lay propped against his pillows, scowling at nothing in particular and everything in general. His tray of buttered eggs and toast sat untouched by his side, while Willis had taken refuge in the dressing room.

"I think I might prefer beef broth to a steady diet of this," he said without preamble when Nicole entered. "And where have you been all morning?" he demanded before she had a chance to say a word.

"And a good afternoon to you, too," she said, smiling wickedly.

"Keeping a man locked in his room without a decent meal is not a laughing matter." He spoke gruffly, but the scowl had disappeared from his face. "Willis has hidden himself away and will not even discuss bringing me something more hearty."

With Nicole present, Willis grew bold enough to return to the bedroom. "I'm only doing what the doctor and madam have ordered," he replied in an aggrieved voice.

"Our patient sounds as if he could use something a little more substantial, or else he might decide to take a bite out of us," she teased. "Cook should have some roasted chicken prepared by now, and fresh-baked bread. Bring up a bit of that, along with some potatoes and asparagus, if you would, Willis."

"Yes, madam," he said, relieved to no longer be the focus of his master's ill will.

"And Willis," she called as he reached the door. "Also bring a glass of that white wine I had with luncheon as well."

"You have saved my life," Jordan announced dramatically as she took a seat beside his bed.

"You aren't by chance auditioning to replace Mr. Kean?" she asked, speaking of the popular actor who filled the Theatre Royal Drury Lane every night he appeared.

"I would need to look over Mr. Kean's daily menus to determine that."

Nicole found she enjoyed teasing Jordan. "I doubt whether he has a better cook than you do."

"It does me no good if I am fed nothing but barley water and quince jelly," he retorted, drawing a laugh from Nicole.

"I have kept the barley water and quince jelly below stairs. But perhaps if you continue complaining, you won't get off so easily."

"You have me, madam. I will do battle no longer," he quipped.

Their glances caught and held. His eyes were not cold as she had expected, but showed an intensity of warmth that made her think Melanie's visit had not endangered the progress they had made in healing the breach between them.

"Worse than the lack of sustenance is the visitor you allowed to get by you yesterday," he complained. "I am not strong enough for women to be throwing themselves on me. Except for one," he added, causing the heat to flood her face.

"And how am I to determine which one that might be?"

"Come now, Nicole. Even in my salad days, I was never known to keep several women dangling at once. I've tried to explain that everything is over with Melanie, that I even settled Grayson's gambling vowels to atone for any embarrassment the family might have suffered. But you won't listen."

"I have heard you, Jordan, but we face more serious problems than Miss Grayson's pursuit of you."

Jordan was exasperated and didn't bother to hide it. "You continually repeat that, but you refuse to reveal what they are."

"I can't—I don't yet know everything myself. If you'll just give me a little more time," she pleaded, "things will come about. I'm sure of it."

"And in the meantime, I'm to sit here like a bacon-brained bumpkin until you decide to share your doubts with me?"

Willis entered, bringing a tray and a trail of tantalizing aromas with him.

"But you will be a well-fed bacon-brained bumpkin," she remarked, laughing as the scowl returned to his face. Nicole was enjoying their banter, and prayed that it would last. "Now, no more complaining or I'll drink the wine myself."

"You know the way to bend me to your will," he replied as Willis arranged the tray. "What is that you have?" he asked after he had sampled everything on his plate.

"These are the lists Alura and I collected. She's coming over later, but I thought we could begin going through them. Then when the others finish their tasks, we can compare all our results."

Jordan buttered the bread, still warm from the oven. He took a bite and closed his eyes. "Umm."

"Well, what do you think?"

"I think that cook is worth far more than I'm paying her."

"No, I mean about my suggestion."

"I think it's wonderful. I think cook is wonderful, and Willis is wonderful, but most of all I think you're wonderful," he said, his eyes sparkling with laughter.

Nicole did not know how to interpret his statement, so she said nothing.

"As soon as I finish this delicious meal, we'll get on with the lists," promised Jordan, taking a sip of wine.

Nicole was still wondering about his comment some hours later while she was taking tea in the drawing room and waiting for Alura. They had gotten a good start on reviewing the list, noting the people who had been at all the homes within the allotted time, and the ones that Fitzpatrick had attended. They had compared the people from outside the residence who had been used for various services, and whether extra help had been hired for the night of the event.

When she saw Jordan was tiring, Nicole had insisted that she and Alura could finish the lists. He had protested, but not strenuously. He had seemed sincerely sorry to see her go, and had made her promise she would return that evening.

"Miss Grayson is here to see you, madam," said Harrison, interrupting her musing.

"Again?" Nicole asked wearily.

"Yes, madam. Shall I say you are not at home?" he asked hopefully.

Nicole considered avoiding Melanie, but if the woman was determined to confront her, she would rather it be in private.

"No, Harrison. Show her in." She was certain the butler was disappointed at not being able to refuse Miss Grayson entry.

"I'm surprised you agreed to see me," said Melanie, a stubborn set to her chin as she sailed through the door Harrison held open.

"Miss Grayson, how delightful of you to call again so soon," greeted Nicole.

"Don't pretend to be happy to see me," responded Melanie. "It would be no more true than I am to see you."

"Then if this makes neither of us happy, why are you here?"

"To do what everyone else will not. To tell you that Jordan

does not want to be with you. We were on the verge of being wed when you arrived, and that is still what he wants. I know that Agatha Worth has offered you money . . ."

And a bullet in the head, thought Nicole.

". . . to leave, but you didn't accept. I'm here to find out what it will take to get rid of you."

The little angel gets right to the point, observed Nicole. "Please. Sit down," she invited, indicating a chair across from the tea tray, proud of her control in the face of such an unusual confrontation. She was unaccustomed to bartering for her husband. Perhaps it was possible that women would one day rule the world if they could decide proprietorship of husbands this civilly.

"I think there's a misunderstanding, Miss Grayson," she said once Melanie had been seated. "My husband told me he had broken off with you, and had made a settlement with your father for any inconvenience he had caused."

Melanie's face turned red. "You forced him to say and do what he did."

"How could I do that? As you probably well know, Jordan is a strong man. I've never seen anyone compel him to do anything against his will."

"You have a child you claim is his son to hold over his head."

"Philip *is* his son," answered Nicole in an icy voice. "You need only look at the boy to see that. And you'll do well to leave him out of this, Miss Grayson. I'll not have my child slandered by you or anyone else."

Melanie had never confronted a mother protecting her young, but she was wise enough to back away. "Jordan would have gotten rid of you when you first returned, but he could not drag his family's name through a divorce. If you have as much pride as you claim, you would not keep an unwilling man tied to you."

"And what would you have me do? I will not leave my son behind, and Jordan refuses to let him go with me. If you can convince him otherwise, I'll leave—for all the good it will do you. For you know as well as I that as long as I'm alive, you cannot marry, and I must be gone another seven years to be considered dead. So what is the solution to our problem, Miss Grayson?"

"You have done this for money, haven't you?" charged Melanie. "You know Jordan's a wealthy man. You probably had no one to support you and decided to take advantage of Jordan."

Nicole laughed. "I don't need Jordan's money, Miss Grayson. Perhaps Agatha didn't pass along the information that I have money of my own. Oh, not as much as Jordan has, to be sure, but enough to allow me to live comfortably, as I was doing when Jordan found me."

"How can you do this?" cried Melanie, jumping from her chair to stand in front of Nicole, her hands clenched.

"What is going on in here?" demanded Agatha Worth as she barged through the door, followed closely by her maid and Harrison.

"I'm sorry, madam," said Harrison.

Nicole was sympathetic for the butler who, for the past several days, had tried to order a household beset by gunshots, a wounded master, and a deluge of beef broth, flowers, and hysterical women. "That's perfectly all right, Harrison. Please see that we're not disturbed."

"As if anyone would," she heard him murmur as he closed the door.

"Melanie, what are you doing here?" the older woman demanded.

"Attempting to talk some sense into her," she replied, indicating Nicole.

"In order to do that, you'd need to have some yourself, and that I doubt," snapped Nicole. "And why are *you* here?" she asked Mrs. Worth.

"I came to see my son. You will allow that, I suppose?" she said sarcastically.

Nicole had reached the limits of her patience. She could not block out the overpowering emotions of hatred, envy, and spite that battered her, and she bowed beneath their weight.

"Mrs. Worth, you and Miss Grayson may do whatever you wish," she replied wearily. "I am going to my room to rest. You may stay as long as you desire. Visit Jordan, debate my future, even order dinner, I no longer care. I will merely remind you once and for all: I am married to Jordan. He will not divorce me," she said to Miss Grayson. "And I will not allow you to kill me," she said to Mrs. Worth.

With a screech of rage, Melanie threw herself at Nicole, striking out with gloved fists. Unwilling to be involved in a common brawl, Nicole backed away until Agatha's maid rushed forward to throw her arms around Melanie, effectively crushing her attack.

"She is distraught," said Mrs. Worth.

"Evidently," agreed Nicole.

Agatha gazed with unsympathetic eyes at Melanie sobbing in her maid's arms. "If we may have some privacy, we will attend her," she offered.

Harrison had appeared immediately at the sound of Melanie's screams. He stood in the doorway, his mouth agape at the scene before him.

"Harrison, show the ladies to a spare room and supply them with water, tea, or anything else they desire." He nodded, and Nicole wondered how long it would be before she would be searching for a new butler.

Fourteen

It was evening and the house was quiet. Nicole hoped it would last until morning, but looking back over the past several days, she had her doubts.

She had not asked Harrison whether Mrs. Worth or Melanie had visited Jordan that afternoon, and he did not offer the information. The butler had merely informed her when both ladies had left the house.

If they had talked to Jordan and influenced him against her, she did not want to hear about it until the morning. By then, Nicole hoped her spirit would be renewed and she could face whatever came her way.

She and Alura had finished with the lists late that afternoon, and then Nicole had dined alone before retiring to her room.

Nicole groaned in pleasure as she sank into the softness of her bed. Drifting into sleep, she once again dreamed she was back in her country house, living a simple village life.

But she awakened with someone tugging at her arm, calling her name.

"Ma'am! Ma'am! Oh, wake up! The whole house is burning down around us," cried Betsy.

"I must get Philip," said Nicole, trying to make sense of what was happening.

"He's all right. Mr. Jordan gave him to Harrison to take downstairs.

Nicole grabbed a wrap and rushed into the hall. Smoke

poured out of the room across the corridor from hers, and she coughed as its harshness bit her throat and burned her nose.

She and Betsy hurried down the stairs where the staff was gathered in the hall.

Harrison handed a sleepy Philip to Nicole. "I'm going up to help the master," he said. Then he turned to the footmen who came hurrying to the front of the house with their clothes thrown hastily on. "Bring buckets of water," he yelled over his shoulder as he hurried up the stairs. Nicole had never seen him move so fast.

"Shouldn't we go outside?" asked Betsy nervously.

Nicole attempted to concentrate on what was going on upstairs, but was unsuccessful. "Not yet. There was a great deal of smoke, but I didn't see any flames when we passed the room. Perhaps they put it out before it got started," she said soothingly. "I'm worried about Jordan, though. He could hurt himself again."

"Willis will watch out for him," Betsy assured her.

"When he sets his mind, no one can tell him anything," fretted Nicole.

Harrison came to the top of the stairs. "Mr. Jordan wanted you to know that the fire is out. We're opening the windows to clear the smoke now."

"I'm going up," said Nicole, handing Philip to Betsy. "Wait in the drawing room with Philip until I come for you."

Even with the windows open, the upstairs retained a haze of smoke and the smell of burning fabric. "Jordan," called Nicole. "Where are you?"

"In here," came the muffled answer from the bedroom. "Where's Philip?"

"Downstairs with Betsy. Are you all right?" she asked, stepping through the door.

Jordan's face and clothing were smeared with soot and ashes from the fire. "I fared better than the room," he said, looking around at the charred bedclothes, now a sodden pile on the floor. Smoke had discolored the walls and left a dirty film over everything else.

"It can be cleaned," said Nicole. "Who discovered it?"

"I did."

"What were you doing up in your condition?" she asked.

Jordan was not about to tell her he had been on his way to her room when he had smelled smoke. He had suffered through an uncomfortable visit from his mother, while Melanie, she claimed, lay prostrate with grief in the room across the hall. The thought of spending time with Nicole had sustained him, then Willis brought him word that Nicole would see him in the morning.

Jordan had brooded for several hours until deciding to take matters in his own hands. He was determined to see Nicole, if only for a short time. He had eased himself up and was sitting on the side of the bed when he caught the first whiff of smoke.

"I couldn't sleep," he said, evading the truth of the matter. "I smelled smoke and woke Willis to investigate. We saw it was coming from this room. A servant must have left a candle burning. The spread and then the bedclothes were smoldering when we arrived. We were lucky—a few more minutes and we might not have been able to stop it."

Nicole knew a servant's negligence wasn't to blame for the fire. Melanie had retired to this room in order to collect herself. It was no accident that the candle was left burning. The accident was that they had lived.

Nicole was suddenly distracted. "Your side," she cried out, looking at his shirt where a red stain was rapidly spreading. "You've broken open your wound. Come back to your room."

Jordan's burst of strength was quickly ebbing and he willingly followed her. She and Willis cleaned and rebandaged his wound, washed the soot from him, then insisted he lie down again. Jordan asked her to sit with him for a while. It was selfish of him, since the last days had been busy for Nicole, and she needed rest as much as he did. But he wanted her near him, confirming that she and Philip were safe. He squeezed her hand

and closed his eyes, content for the first time since he had last seen her.

Several days later, the house and its occupants were practically back to normal. The bedroom had been cleaned, and the damage from the fire repaired. The windows had been left open and the odor of smoke had almost completely disappeared.

"You were extremely lucky not to have been burnt alive," said Caroline Hardesty, shuddering at the thought.

"We were indeed," agreed Nicole, looking around her circle of friends. Drew, Alura, Caroline, and Charles had met to share the information they had collected over the past several days.

Jordan had been well enough to join them downstairs. "I won't need you for a while," he said to Willis, who was hovering beside his chair.

"Now, what have I missed?" he asked.

"Few nights of unprofitable gambling," answered Drew. "Dashed difficult to win at the new gambling hell."

"Did you find out anything other than that you're a poor gamester?" Jordan asked with a grin.

"Confirmed that Fitzpatrick owns the place. It's been suspected for some time, but seems he's been offering to sell it for a considerable sum. Heard he has enough money now and doesn't want to jeopardize his standing with the *ton.*"

"If he's rich, then why chance ruin by stealing?" questioned Alura, a puzzled frown on her face.

"It's more than money," said Nicole. "When I saw him with the emeralds, I understood that he was delighted because he was paying back Goodcastle and others of his kind for some slight that they had dealt his mother."

"Know something about that, too," said Drew. "On occasion, elderly relatives are a blessing. My aunt remembers Fitzpatrick's mother. Seems she became involved with someone unacceptable to her family. Said Fitzpatrick was born on the wrong side of the blanket, but the man responsible was finally convinced it was in his best interest to marry her. They went to France and weren't heard from until Fitzpatrick came of age. When he was young, my aunt says he made no attempt to hide his contempt of the people who turned their back on his mother."

"So he's taking revenge for her," concluded Alura.

"Seems that way," replied Drew.

"You've learned a lot in the short time you've had," said Charles.

"Heard a few more things. Strong rumors that when some men fell into deep debt at the gambling hell, Fitzpatrick would make a special arrangement with them. He would return their vowels for introductions to high-ranking people, or invitations to events where he would never be accepted otherwise."

"That's what we suspected," said Nicole. "But there's more, isn't there?"

"There is a whisper, and not much more, that other bargains were made. Man who told me doesn't know much. Only that a friend of his was in his cups one evening, told a rambling story about betraying someone to redeem his vowels. Something about revealing the location of a fortune."

"Did he say who it was?" asked Jordan.

"Viscount Thornton," replied Drew.

Jordan and Nicole exchanged glances. "He was responsible for Fitzpatrick being invited to the Goodcastles' ball," said Nicole. "He was also on the guest list for two of the other homes where burglaries occurred."

"So it was Viscount Thornton who told Fitzpatrick about the jewels," mused Alura.

"Perhaps not every time," responded Jordan. "There were most likely others, but unless they decide to confess—which I very much doubt—we'll probably never know."

"In going over the lists, we also found that most of the people who entertained usually brought in additional staff to help," contributed Nicole. "If Fitzpatrick knew in advance who was hiring extra servants, it would be easy to pay one of them to make sure a door or window was left open, or perhaps to steal a spare key, as was the case at the Goodcastles' home."

"But how would he know where the jewels were kept?" asked Alura.

"Different ways," said Drew. "Could be good guesses. People aren't too inventive when hiding valuables. Most safes are in similar locations. He could have paid someone for the information, or threatened one of the men who owed him money."

"Again, unless he confesses, we'll probably never know," said Jordan, shifting to a more comfortable position in his chair.

Nicole looked at him, a worried expression on her face.

Jordan met her gaze and was pleased she was concerned. It proved she still held some feelings for him despite everything she had gone through. He smiled reassuringly and she turned back to the others.

"Then what have we accomplished?" asked Charles. "We are certain that Fitzpatrick is behind the burglaries, but we can't prove it."

"We can if we can catch him with the jewels in his possession," said Nicole.

"You didn't find them when you were in his house before," Charles stated.

"I wasn't looking for them at the time," she replied. "And Fitzpatrick didn't give me any indication they were there. He guards his thoughts very carefully. It was only when he allowed himself to think about his hatred that I was able to see the jewels. At the time, he was sitting at his desk in the library. However, that doesn't mean they're still in the house. He's a shrewd man and could have hidden them elsewhere."

Charles rose and paced the length of the room and back. "We can charge him with stealing our inheritance."

"That might not be enough to have him transported," said Nicole. "But if we caught him with the jewels, he would have no chance to stay and redeem himself. If I could get back inside the house once more I could—"

"No!" said Jordan, jerking upright, and earning himself a

sharp pain in his side. "I won't hear of it. You've put yourself in too much danger as it is."

Nicole's anger flared. He was ordering her life again and she would have none of it. "I will do—" she began.

"You will do what the mother of our child should do," he broke in. "If something happened to you, what would become of Philip?" He held her gaze and concentrated on Melanie, for the first time hoping that Nicole's gift was real and that she would read his thoughts. Perhaps it wasn't fair, but he would use any means to keep her safe.

A blond-haired, blue-eyed image filled Nicole's mind. Surely he would not, she thought. But try as she might, she could see nothing else. She would not let Melanie Grayson raise her son, and if she believed Jordan's thoughts, that was exactly what would happen if misfortune befell her.

"Perhaps you're right," she agreed.

Jordan hid his self-satisfaction. There was a way for him to use Nicole's gift as well, he thought, relieved she had not insisted on going through with her plan.

"If I could talk to Fitzpatrick at some of the entertainments we attend, perhaps I could jolt him into revealing where the jewels are hidden. Surely you wouldn't object to that," she said, looking at Jordan.

He did not like it at all. He wanted Nicole to have nothing to do with the scoundrel, but he also wanted to be rid of the man as much as anyone else in the room. And Nicole would at least be within sight where he could keep an eye on her.

"As long as you don't go off somewhere with him," stipulated Jordan.

"And what if you don't find out where they are?" asked Charles.

"Then I suppose it is up to you as to how to seek justice. But I don't think Fitzpatrick is worth being hanged for murder."

"He must be caught first," Jordan said, a grim look on his face.

"Do not be overly hasty," cautioned Nicole. "Give me time to try again."

Jordan remained in his chair while Nicole showed their guests out. When she returned he was dark and brooding.

"You look as if you're having a fit of the dismals," she teased.

"I don't like your being involved with Fitzpatrick in any way," he complained. "He's a dangerous man who will stop at nothing to gain what he desires."

"I will be very careful," she promised. "And you will be there to watch me, I'm sure."

"There is no doubt about that," he vowed. "When do you plan to start?" he asked, after a small silence.

"As soon as you're able to be up and about again."

"Then let's get it over with. I shall escort you tomorrow evening."

"Done," agreed Nicole, a shiver of excitement rushing through her. The hunt was on—and this time, Jordan would be by her side.

"I'm so glad you could come today," said Elizabeth as she handed Nicole a cup of tea.

"The house seems to have settled down somewhat," replied Nicole. "Jordan's wound is much better, the smoke smell is almost completely gone, and I've thrown out the beef broth."

Elizabeth laughed. "I'm glad I didn't send any. I'll remember your experience if I'm ever tempted."

"Will Agatha join us?"

"I am not such a pea-goose as to bring you two together again," said Elizabeth. "She's on a short trip to a friend who lives not far from town. I thought it an excellent opportunity for the two of us to visit without interruption."

Nicole breathed a sigh of relief. She had not looked forward to another confrontation with Agatha so soon.

"Let's stretch our legs," said Elizabeth, after they had been sitting for some time. "We have a new family portrait and I'm anxious to have someone admire it."

"It's lovely," commented Nicole when they stood in the gallery before the large painting.

"You should have one done," said Elizabeth.

"I don't know whether Jordan is ready for a family portrait just yet, but I would like one of Philip."

"Did you ever see the one of Robert and Jordan?"

"Yes, but it was years ago, before Jordan and I married."

"It's here, at the end," said Elizabeth, leading the way to the painting.

"They looked remarkably alike as boys, didn't they?"

"They are of a size, and similar hair coloring," agreed Elizabeth. "And next to them is a painting of their fathers when they were about the same age."

Nicole studied the picture of Robert's father, Francis, and Jordan's father, Richard. Except for the clothing, they could have been the same two boys.

"There is an extraordinary resemblance to their fathers."

"It seems to have always been that way," said Elizabeth, strolling down the gallery past a long line of Worths.

"Ma'am," said a maid, giving a brief bob in front of Elizabeth. "Maggie says Master Will is crying for you."

"Do you mind if I leave you for a few minutes, Nicole? Will has an earache, and is a bit cranky."

"You go ahead. I'll find my way back to the teapot," said Nicole, giving her an understanding smile.

Nicole passed the library on her way back to the drawing room, and, being a voracious reader, decided to investigate the contents. The collection of books was varied, from leather-bound, gilt-edged volumes to ancient tomes cracked with age.

As she perused the shelves, her eye was caught by a small book bound in red leather. When she opened it, she saw it was handwritten. The flowery script inside the front cover identified it as the diary of Susan Elliot Worth, the late Duchess of Weston.

She should have felt guilty reading such personal thoughts, she supposed, but somehow reading of Susan's experiences as a newly-married young woman forged a bond of understanding between Nicole and the deceased duchess.

She was reading about the birth of Robert when she came across something puzzling. She closed the diary, marking the place with her finger as she stared out the window.

"There you are," said Elizabeth. "I thought you might have given up on me and gone home."

"On the contrary, I've been greatly entertained. I wonder, may I borrow this book for a few days?"

"Take whatever you want," invited Elizabeth. "They're seldom used at all. Robert isn't much of a scholar, and neither am I."

"Thank you. I shall return it in good repair," Nicole promised.

"I've ordered fresh tea," said Elizabeth, linking her arm through Nicole's. "And after dealing with Will, I can certainly use it."

The women spent another hour of pleasant conversation, sharing accounts of the years that had separated them. But Nicole's eyes kept straying to the red leather book, her thoughts questioning its contents.

Nicole longed to begin reading the diary as soon as she arrived home, but tonight she would commence her quest to pry the location of the jewels from Fitzpatrick. She had stayed too long with Elizabeth, and she had a dozen things to do before dressing for the evening. She laid the book aside and went to spend some time with Philip.

The ball at Lord and Lady Richardson's was at its height when Nicole and Jordan arrived. A continuous line of carriages delivered ladies and gentlemen dressed to the nines to the front of the stately brick mansion.

Nicole and Jordan made their way through the receiving line and into the ballroom.

"It will be difficult to find anyone in this crush," murmured Nicole.

"All you need do is stand still—Fitzpatrick will come to you," advised Jordan, sounding not at all pleased with the idea.

Nicole suppressed a giggle. "Not if you're standing by my side, glaring."

"Then I shall remove myself and procure a cup of punch for you," he said with a feeble attempt at raillery.

"I saw the Hardestys talking with Drew and Alura when we came in. Perhaps you should reassure them that all is well."

"I don't know that I can honestly do that, but I will try."

Nicole felt uncomfortably exposed after Jordan left her side. She was becoming too accustomed to having him with her, but there were still too many unanswered questions between them for her to assume that he would always be there. She would continue to presume she was on her own until it was indisputably proven otherwise.

"You brighten the room considerably," said Fitzpatrick, appearing out of the crowd to bow over her hand.

"Why, thank you, sir," she replied, steeling herself not to jerk away from his touch.

"Would you do me the honor of this dance?" he asked.

"It's such a crush, and the room is insufferably stuffy," she complained. "Perhaps we could simply talk for a while. I do find your conversation most interesting."

Fitzpatrick preened visibly. His weaknesses were his desire to be accepted and his overblown conceit. He suspected Nicole of nothing more than having spent enough time with him to have fallen victim to his heretofore unappreciated appeal.

"I would deem it an honor," he said, guiding her away from the dance floor.

Nicole concentrated intently on Fitzpatrick. "Aren't Lady Richardson's diamonds magnificent? I'm surprised she wore them with the thief still about."

"I think the Richardsons' feel they are above such vulgarities," commented Fitzpatrick.

But they will find out differently, he thought, and Nicole heard him perfectly.

"It's certainly a mystery how the thief knows exactly where to find the jewels."

A number of images flashed before her eyes. She recognized Viscount Thornton, Mr. Peterson, and Lord Berryton's son; all had a reputation for heavy gambling. There were other people, dressed in servants' garb, whom she did not recognize. One was opening a window, the other a French door, the last was removing a key from what looked like the Goodcastles' home.

"He must be extremely intelligent," remarked Fitzpatrick.

"A common thief?" scoffed Nicole.

"Perhaps he's not so common. After all, he's gotten away with some very valuable pieces of jewelry, right beneath the noses of the owners."

"It's said he even entered Lady Goodcastle's dressing room," whispered Nicole.

"Shocking! He didn't harm the lady did he?"

"Oh, no. She didn't even awaken."

"Then she's fortunate."

Nicole saw the darkness in his mind, felt the danger, and knew that only Lady Goodcastle's uninterrupted slumber had saved her. It was then that she realized the risk of being with Fitzpatrick and was thankful that Jordan had insisted she see the man only in public. She glanced around the room, but was unable to sort out Jordan's comforting figure from the throng.

Nicole decided to do her best to jolt Fitzpatrick into giving her more. She might never again have the opportunity to speak with him about the robberies without raising his suspicion.

"It is very confidential," she said, lowering her voice until he had to lean toward her to hear, "but I understand that the identity of the man is known."

Nicole swayed beneath the intensity of Fitzpatrick's reaction. She felt confusion, disbelief, and rage swirl in his mind.

"Impossible. He's been too shrewd to be caught."

She saw some of the same images she had seen before. A man entering a house, garbed all in black, taking jewels and disappearing without a trace. His face was still covered, but Nicole now knew the man was Fitzpatrick.

"I heard it from a reliable source," she insisted, praying his thoughts would betray him and reveal the whereabouts of the jewels.

Fitzpatrick was standing stiffly, his face pale and damp. If he were ever going to disclose the location of the jewels, it would be now.

"And just this afternoon," she confided in an undertone, "I was privy to the information that it's known where the stolen jewels are hidden."

Nicole could hardly contain her elation. She had a clear flash of the jewels in their resting place.

"And where did you hear that foolishness?"

"I am under oath not to breathe a word," tittered Nicole, "so I can't divulge the person's name. But he was very confident in his knowledge, and I have no reason to doubt his word."

"I hope you will excuse a hasty departure, Mrs. Worth, but I am engaged to dance with Miss Worthingham."

"And a very lucky lady she is," said Nicole, as anxious to be rid of him as he was of her.

Fitzpatrick bowed and quickly disappeared into the crowd. He was barely out of sight before Jordan appeared, a cup of very warm punch in his hand.

"I know where they are," Nicole announced triumphantly, her eyes sparkling in victory.

Jordan wasn't sure when he had begun placing credence in Nicole's gift. Perhaps he had always had a feeling that she did more than make lucky guesses. Perhaps seeing that people he respected believed in her had swayed him even more. But, whatever the cause, he did not question her absolute certainty of the location of the jewels.

"Say no more," he ordered, looking around for a place to

dispose of the punch. Finding none, he poured it into the nearest flower arrangement, grasped her arm, and guided her toward the door, nodding and smiling as they went.

"Oh, dear," she exclaimed, attempting to suppress her laughter. "You may have found a unique way to keep flowers fresh."

"This is no laughing matter," he muttered, continuing to force a smile.

"Of course it isn't," she agreed. "But you have not just spent time inside the head of a thief and murderer. The relief of escaping its confines can be exhilarating."

Jordan stopped, staring down at her. For the first time, he realized that this was not a game to Nicole; it never had been. It could not be amusing to be dragged into other people's minds, sharing their darkest thoughts and emotions. If she did have the ability she claimed, he did not envy her at all.

"No, I haven't," he said. "And I'm sorry you had to experience it." His hold loosened and he guided her firmly, but far more gently, to their carriage.

Nicole made no reply. She did not want to break the delicate balance between them. It appeared that Jordan had finally accepted her as she was.

Once they were inside the carriage, Nicole began to repeat her discussion with Fitzpatrick, but Jordan silenced her, motioning toward the driver.

They spoke of inconsequential matters until they reached home. When they arrived, he led her into the drawing room, closed the doors, and drew her down on the settee with him.

He took her hands between his. "Now, tell me what you have discovered."

"The jewels are in the house."

"Are you certain?"

"I saw it very clearly. There is an armoire in his bedroom. It's a massive piece. Inside, there's a panel in the back that can be removed. That's where the jewels are hidden."

"Then we can set our plan in action. Tomorrow Charles,

Drew, and I will confront him with the paid receipt. We'll reclaim the house immediately and recover the jewels."

"You can't do that."

"Why not? That's what we've planned on from the start."

"Tomorrow will be too late," she said urgently. "Fitzpatrick is going to move the jewels as soon as possible."

"Dammit!" exclaimed Jordan, rising to pace the floor. "There's nothing to do but confront him."

"No," said Nicole. "The man's a cold-blooded killer. He would have murdered Lady Goodcastle had she awakened while he was in her room. He would do the same to you."

"He must catch me unawares first, and I will be ready for him," argued Jordan.

"Please," she begged, going to his side and looking up at him. "I will ask you the same question you asked me—what will happen to Philip if you are killed?"

Before he could answer, there was a commotion in the hallway. The door to the drawing room opened to reveal Caroline, Charles, Alura, and Drew.

"We saw you leave and couldn't wait to hear the news," exclaimed Alura.

"I'm glad you didn't," said Jordan. "Your impatience may have saved the jewels."

"What do you mean?" said Charles, stepping into the room behind the women.

"Nicole says that the jewels are inside the house, but that Fitzpatrick is going to move them as quickly as possible. We can't wait until tomorrow—we must move tonight."

"My carriage is outside. Suggest we use it," said Drew.

"Let me get my pistols," said Jordan, and hurried out of the room, followed by Charles and Drew. A few minutes later the front door closed behind them.

Nicole, Alura, and Caroline looked at one another. "I do not intend to sit here placidly and wait," said Nicole.

"Nor do I," said Caroline.

"And I won't either," chimed in Alura.

"Harrison, have the carriage brought around again, and tell them to hurry," ordered Nicole. A short time later, the carriage was rolling over the dew-dampened streets toward the Hardestys' former home.

Fifteen

Everything looks so ordinary, thought Nicole as they came to a stop in front of the house. There was nothing about the brick facade or the lights in the windows to indicate the portentous confrontation being played out inside.

The door was standing slightly ajar, and the women entered to find the front hall deserted. If there had been servants about, they were presently nowhere to be seen.

The drawing room was lighted, but empty. Nicole led the way toward the library, with Alura and Caroline following close behind. They halted in the doorway, taking in the scene before them.

Fitzpatrick sat behind the desk; Jordan, Drew, and Charles had stationed themselves around it. A stranger stood further away, but was keeping a sharp eye on Fitzpatrick.

Fitzpatrick looked up from the paper he was studying and saw them gathered in the doorway. "Well, ladies, what a pleasure it is to see you. I assume you're here for the entertainment."

"I don't consider any of what has happened enjoyable, Mr. Fitzpatrick," replied Nicole, stepping farther into the room.

Jordan frowned at Nicole. "You should have stayed at home," he said. From the expressions on Charles and Drew's faces, he also spoke for them.

"Don't blame Nicole," said Caroline. "This is my home, too, and I have every right to be here." She raised her chin defiantly, daring any of them to challenge her.

"Your mother would kill me if she knew you were here," said Drew to Alura.

"She will not know unless you tell her," Alura reasoned. "I've been involved in this and I deserve to see the outcome."

"And you, Mrs. Worth?" chided Fitzpatrick. "Are you here to support your husband?"

"My husband is perfectly competent to carry on without any help."

"How charming," sneered Fitzpatrick. "It must be rewarding to have a wife who holds you in such esteem, Worth."

"It's time we got on with this," said Charles. "You have the receipt in your hands. You can no longer deny my father repaid you."

"Of course I can't," agreed Fitzpatrick. "I would never have denied it if you had shown this to me at the very first."

"You killed my father trying to find it," charged Charles.

Drew laid a restraining hand on his arm to keep him from attacking Fitzpatrick.

"I did not lay a hand on your father."

"Some of your men did, though."

"You cannot prove anything or you would have done so by now. The only thing you have is a receipt allowing you to reclaim this house, and I am not contesting it. This was all a mistake," Fitzpatrick said, flicking the paper with the tip of his finger. "As you probably know, I own a gambling hell where vast sums are won and lost every evening. Your father's repayment was simply overlooked. A regrettable mistake, but a mistake nevertheless." His expression was smug as he met Charles's glare.

"I will, of course, vacate the house first thing in the morning to allow you access."

"You will leave immediately," growled Charles.

"How discourteous of you, Mr. Hardesty. Hardly the action of a gentleman. Surely you will allow me time to gather my belongings and arrange to have them moved."

"Would some of those belongings be the jewelry you've stolen over the past months?" asked Jordan.

Fitzpatrick was stunned by Jordan's question, but he quickly recovered. "I have no idea what you mean."

"Then if I should go upstairs to your room and open the secret panel inside your armoire, you would know nothing about the jewels I would find there?"

Fitzpatrick was no longer the confident man who, a few moments before, had declared they could prove nothing. His face was pale and his mouth agape. "Who put you on to me?"

No one spoke, and he searched their faces for the answer. His gaze returned to Nicole. "So, it's true what they say. I didn't believe the *on-dits*—I thought it was just gossip. I was wrong, though. All the time you spent flattering me, you were trying to get inside my mind. You lied to me this evening, didn't you? You knew I'd attempt to save the jewels and you saw where they were hidden. It's the only way anyone could have known where they were."

"It doesn't matter how we know," said Jordan. "You may be able to avoid a murder charge, but you cannot deny stealing the jewels. Can you imagine what the owners will demand as punishment? You will never see the light of day again. Either that or you will be transported to Australia in the hold of a ship where you will be fortunate indeed to live long enough to see the shore again."

"You can't do this to me," blustered Fitzpatrick. "I have money, plenty of it. I'll make it worth your while to let me go."

"Now that you mention it, I think Mr. and Miss Hardesty should be reimbursed for the hardships they have suffered. Not that money can replace their father, but their home and belongings were taken from them by deception."

Hope lit Fitzpatrick's face. "They can have it all," he promised.

"We wouldn't want to take everything from you, for you'll be needing a little for yourself. You see, although we have an eyewitness account, it's true we could never prove that you ordered the murder of Mr. Hardesty. But we have caught you red-handed with the jewels, and there is no way you can deny that. The owners of the jewelry will be happy just to have it back. Justice for the Hardestys, however, is another matter."

"I told you they can have the money," said Fitzpatrick.

"And see you walking the streets of London a free man?" said Charles. "I think not."

"What more do you want?" asked Fitzpatrick.

"This is what we have decided," said Jordan. "We will take the jewels tonight and return them to their owners. Our story will be that we found the cache but that the thief escaped. I doubt that anyone will question their good luck.

"We know that you put a great deal of store in being accepted as a gentleman, Mr. Fitzpatrick. So what we propose to do is bypass the usual course of punishment for a crime such as yours and offer you a gentleman's agreement.

"Let me introduce Mr. Warren," said Jordan. The man who had been standing outside the circle took a step forward and made a small, sharp bow.

"Mr. Warren is a Bow Street Runner. I have known him for five years or more and he is one of the best. He has failed only once, but that was by no means his fault."

Nicole gathered that this was one of the men who had helped Jordan search for her, and looked at him curiously. He caught her eye and gave her an imperceptible nod. She acknowledged him, then turned her attention back to Jordan.

"Mr. Warren will keep you company for the evening. Then in the morning, Mr. Hardesty will return and the three of you will go to ascertain the amount of money you currently possess. At that point, Fitzpatrick, you will turn over the amount Mr. Hardesty demands. He will leave you enough to get out of the country."

"What . . . what do you mean? I am going nowhere," objected Fitzpatrick.

Charles stepped forward and, leaning over, placed his hands on the desktop, allowing the full force of his hatred to spill across the mahogany expanse to the man sitting on the other side.

"My inclination was and still is to kill you," said Charles. The coldness in his voice froze everyone in place. "However, I do not want to cause my sister any more distress. I have been convinced by my friends that the loss of your fortune and banishment from England would be a far worse punishment than death for you. So if you value your life, you will do as we say. Not many in your position would get such a chance." He held Fitzpatrick's attention a moment longer, then straightened and stepped away from the desk.

"You can see that emotions run high against you, Fitzpatrick," said Jordan. "You would do well to accept our bargain. Turn your money over in the morning, then leave England. If you return, you will be punished for stealing from some of the more prominent members of society. And they will insist you serve a harsh term indeed."

"And if you think we'll have no proof," added Drew, "you will spend part of this evening writing a confession until Mr. Warren is satisfied it will be accepted in court."

"You cannot do this to me," gasped Fitzpatrick.

A smile finally creased Charles's face. "I believe we just did."

"There is one other thing I'd like to know," said Nicole.

"I shouldn't think I'd need to tell *you* anything," Fitzpatrick answered, his voice flat.

"Just a confirmation," she replied. When he did not answer, she continued. "An attempt was made on my life. Will you tell me what you know about it?"

A bit of life returned to Fitzpatrick's eyes. He remembered Mrs. Worth's arrogance and the promises she had made, but would no longer be forced to keep. "It would be my pleasure, but in return for an answer to a question."

"If I can," agreed Nicole.

"Where did you find the receipt? I know it was you, because it didn't turn up until after you arrived."

Nicole glanced at Charles and Caroline. They both nodded. "It was in a small Buddha statue."

"That ugly little thing I allowed you to take from the house?" he asked of Caroline.

"The *only* thing you allowed me to take from the house," she confirmed.

Fitzpatrick threw his head back and roared with laughter. "Ah, Fate has a sense of humor," he said, wiping his eyes.

"And now will you answer my question?" asked Nicole.

"I will give the answer only to you and no one else," replied Fitzpatrick.

"I will not leave you alone with him," protested Jordan.

"It isn't necessary for you to leave the room. You see, I understand your wife very well," Fitzpatrick remarked, his words meant to provoke.

Fitzpatrick stared at Nicole, and the room fell quiet.

Nicole saw Fitzpatrick and Mrs. Worth together, she heard the bargain they made, and watched as her mother-in-law met with the man who would attempt to kill her. She had been right all along. Now she knew who had put her in touch with the assassin and why.

"Thank you, Mr. Fitzpatrick," she said sedately.

Fitzpatrick studied her. "You're not surprised," he stated. Then he hesitated a moment. "You already knew, didn't you?"

"I'm afraid I did," she agreed with a sad smile. "I merely wanted to make certain I wasn't mistaken."

"Enough of this," said Jordan, uneasy with the rapport between Nicole and Fitzpatrick. "Mr. Warren, you will see to Fitzpatrick's statement and secure him for the remainder of the evening."

"Certainly will, sir," said the Bow Street Runner, speaking for the first time.

"Mr. Hardesty will be by in the morning. You will accompany them to withdraw the funds. Then you will escort Mr. Fitzpatrick to the coast and see him off to a destination as far from

England as possible. You will also pay the captain to see that he remains aboard."

"I know several captains personally, sir. I'll make sure he has no chance to slip away."

"You would be foolish even to try," Charles said to Fitzpatrick. "For my promise not to kill you holds only until you leave England. If I ever see you again, one of us shall die. If it should be me, then you will still spend the rest of your life locked up—my friends here will make sure of that." Drew and Jordan nodded their agreement.

It was nearly noon before Nicole descended the stairs the next morning. She had paid a brief visit to Philip and promised to take him to the park as soon as luncheon was over.

"Mr. Worth wanted to know as soon as you came down, madam," said Harrison.

"Oh? Do you know where he is?"

"In the library, I believe, madam."

The door was standing open when she arrived at the library, and she was able to observe Jordan for a short time before he became aware of her.

He was such a handsome man, of the perfect height and form for her tastes. She remembered everything about him and their short time together as man and wife. She had heard other women complain about their husbands' demands, but she had never considered Jordan's lovemaking a burdensome duty. Her face grew hot, remembering their evenings together.

"There you are," said Jordan, looking up and discovering her watching him. He rose and came around the desk to greet her. Taking her by the shoulders, he brushed her cheek with a light kiss. Releasing her, he took her by the hand and led her to a settee, settling himself close beside her until the warmth of his thigh permeated the fabric of her gown.

"Have you had breakfast? Or would it be luncheon?" he asked, looking at his watch.

Nicole laughed. "It's a bit late in the day for breakfast."

"Then I shall join you for luncheon," he said. "That is, if you do not object."

"You need not ask to dine at your own table," she replied.

Jordan stared at his highly polished Hessians. "After last night I am embarrassed to face you at all, whether it be across a luncheon table or as we are now."

Anger struck at Nicole's heart. "I will not apologize for my actions last night," she said heatedly.

"No! No! I meant nothing of the sort," he said, taking her hands and keeping her by his side when she would have risen. "I am talking about *my* inadequacies. That a murderer and thief should know my wife better than I do is a failing of which I am not proud."

"What are you talking about?" Nicole asked, bewildered at his admission.

"Fitzpatrick did not distrust your ability. He believed in you without question, while I have doubted you all these years. I have always known that your visions were too accurate to be merely good guesses, but I would never admit it. I cannot escape the fact that you knew where the jewels were, but it is still extremely difficult for me to believe."

Nicole entwined her fingers with his. "You are an Englishman," she said with a smile. "You like your beef and potatoes— they are standard fare. But when you are dished up something a little more exotic, you will have nothing to do with it. At least, for a time, until you become accustomed to a different taste."

He flashed a mischievous smile, then quickly took her in his arms. "I know I developed a taste for you long ago, and I have been starving these past seven years."

Nicole's breath caught as he rained kisses on her face, around the shell of her ear, and down the side of her throat. His lips finally met hers and she slipped her arms around his neck, pulling him against her as she sank back into the curve of the settee. His hands roved her body, exploring the tempting contours hidden beneath her thin morning gown. His breathing was labored when he released her lips.

"I am going to smash you," he murmured in her ear, his breath causing another shiver to course through her.

"I couldn't choose a better way to leave this world," she replied with a girlish giggle.

Jordan pulled back so he could stare directly into her eyes. His gaze held the same warmth as it had when they had first met. "I would like nothing better than to have my wife back," he said, his voice husky with emotion.

"And I would like nothing better than to have my husband," she whispered, feeling as if they were exchanging vows anew.

He kissed her again, a gentle kiss that pulled her soul from her body to merge with his. She was not reading his mind, but no words were needed from either of them. They had come full circle.

Reluctantly, Jordan pulled himself away. "This is an extremely public place for such carryings on, Mrs. Worth. You look like a woman of wanton spirits in delicious disarray," he teased, looking down at her.

Nicole rose and began straightening her gown, slapping his hands away and laughing when he tried to help. "And who has done this to me?" she demanded.

He took her into his arms again. "I suppose I must admit to being just as wanton as you. However, as unromantic as it seems, you have not eaten today, and I will not take advantage of a famished lady."

"Oh," she exclaimed, returning to the everyday world. "I promised Philip an outing in the park as soon as I had lunch. I even promised I would hurry, and that was some time ago."

"It's been time well spent."

"I agree," she said softly. Her gaze dropped to the firm line of his mouth, remembering the feel of his lips on her skin.

"If you continue looking at me like that, I'll lock the door and we won't leave this room until dinner."

She reached up and ran her fingertip down the length of his cheek. "Do you still plan to join me for luncheon?"

"You could not keep me away."

It was early evening and Nicole was in the sitting room, her embroidery in her lap. However, she was dreaming far more than she was stitching.

She and Jordan had enjoyed a quick luncheon before collecting Philip and driving to Hyde Park. They had returned to change and dress for dinner at home before joining a party, which included Drew and Alura, for an evening at Vauxhall Gardens.

Jordan had insisted Nicole move to sit beside him during dinner, contending that conversation was impossible with one of them at either end of the long table.

Their increased proximity made for a much more intimate dinner, and they lingered longer than usual. They were enjoying a glass of claret when Drew was announced.

"Sorry to interrupt."

"We were just finishing, and can be ready to leave in a few minutes," said Nicole. "But where is Alura? Surely she would not miss a visit to Vauxhall. She's been eager to see the gardens since she first arrived."

"She has gone ahead with the rest of the party. Didn't want her to miss out on it again."

"Is something amiss?" asked Jordan.

"Nothing that can't be handled. Afraid it might take both of us, though. It's Charles."

"What is it? Has he been hurt?" asked Nicole.

"Nothing like that. He's having second thoughts about allowing Fitzpatrick to go free. Says he should have done away with him while he had the chance. Threatening to go after him and finish the job."

Jordan rose from his chair. "Where is he now?"

"At White's, well on his way to being foxed."

"Then perhaps he'll come to no harm until we get there."

"It's a loose tongue I worry about more than physical injury," said Drew.

Jordan reached for Nicole's hand. "I'm afraid I won't be able to accompany you to Vauxhall, my dear."

"I shall be well satisfied resting this evening. The last few days have been wearing."

"I don't know when I will be able to return. Shall I knock if it isn't too late?"

His eyes held her in thrall, asking a question that reminded Nicole how it had felt to be in his arms that afternoon.

"Yes," she whispered.

He raised her hand to his lips and pressed a kiss against her fragrant skin. "I look forward to my return with great anticipation." He gave her hand a slight squeeze, then left the room with Drew.

After that, Nicole had wandered dreamily into her sitting room, thinking that her life was finally coming right at last. She could not concentrate on her embroidery and laid it aside, looking around the room to find something else to keep her mind occupied until Jordan returned.

The red leather diary popped into her head. It seemed ages ago that she had borrowed the book from Elizabeth. The events that had occurred since then had driven it out of her mind. Her curiosity was renewed, and she decided it was just the thing to keep her from watching the clock slowly tick off the minutes until Jordan returned.

Reaching her room, she lit the candles and settled into a chair to read Susan's diary. Later, she paused long enough for Betsy to help her get ready for bed, then once more became engrossed in the book. She read and reread a portion of the diary, then marked it with a ribbon.

What she had read did not make sense. Or perhaps it did, she thought, after some consideration. Perhaps it explained everything that had happened to her since she had first married Jordan. Perhaps it was the reason she'd been forced out of her marriage into a seven-year exile.

If what she thought was true, Nicole knew why Mrs. Worth hated her. She knew why the woman had attempted to bribe her, and why, as a last resort, she had hired a murderer to do away with her unwelcome daughter-in-law. In short, Nicole knew Mrs. Worth's secret, and she meant to reveal it in order to save her family.

Nicole looked down at her nearly transparent gown. She had meant for Jordan to see her in it tonight, but now she could not carry through with her intentions. What she knew could change everything between them. If she gave herself to him and then lost him again, she did not know whether she could continue, and she must remain strong for Philip.

The clock chimed, reminding Nicole of the lateness of the hour. She hurriedly snuffed out the candles and crept into bed. She lay stiffly, her mind spinning with what she must do on the morrow, until she finally drifted into sleep. She had not needed to hurry to bed, for dawn was almost breaking when Jordan moved stealthily past her room, threw off his clothes, and fell heavily across his bed.

Jordan was still asleep when Nicole left for the ducal mansion the next morning. She did not know exactly what she was going to do when she got there, but she had to see Mrs. Worth, and it must appear to be an accidental meeting.

She was in luck, for when she reached the Duke of Weston's house, Elizabeth had already left for an appointment with her dressmaker.

When she was advised of this by the butler, Nicole asked for Mrs. Worth, hoping the older woman would be at home, resting from her journey.

Mrs. Worth received her in the drawing room. Nicole smiled, wondering if it was because she had likened the green-and-rose sitting room to hell.

"What is it you want?" asked Mrs. Worth ungraciously.

"I came to call on Elizabeth, but she is not at home. Since I was here, I thought I would take the opportunity to thank you for assisting Miss Grayson the other day. I don't know what I would have done if you hadn't arrived at that moment."

"She's an overwrought, spoiled chit who's been denied a new toy," admitted Mrs. Worth, being unusually honest for the moment.

"I don't know whether Jordan would appreciate being called a toy," said Nicole, smiling at the thought.

"Not that Melanie wouldn't make him a fine wife," Mrs. Worth added quickly. "She knows her place, and wouldn't go about embarrassing him with any strange starts."

"But children usually tire of a toy and want another," pointed out Nicole.

"She knows how to be discreet."

"She hasn't demonstrated much of it to me."

"This is an altogether different situation," pointed out Mrs. Worth. "Now, why are you really here?"

Nicole prayed that her scheme would be successful and she would leave with the information she needed. "I know that we'll never be friends, but I would like to come to some sort of accord so that we can at least be cordial to one another in public."

Mrs. Worth studied Nicole with suspicion.

"I visited with Elizabeth while you were gone," admitted Nicole. "Our conversation reminded me of what you've done for Robert and Jordan. You've sacrificed your life for them. You were young enough to remarry when you lost your husband in the fire, but you devoted your life to raising Robert, and Jordan, all by yourself. No matter what has happened between us, I do admire you for that."

Mrs. Worth visibly relaxed. Evidently, Nicole did not suspect she had a hand in the bungled attempt on her life. It would do no harm to go along with her.

"It wasn't easy," Mrs. Worth acknowledged. "They were quite a handful, particularly when they became older."

"I can imagine," agreed Nicole, thinking of Philip. "The fire and being caught in a burning building must have been a terrible experience." Nicole concentrated intently on the other woman when she began to speak.

"I've never forgotten it," said Mrs. Worth. "One moment I was trying to quiet Jordan—he was teething, you know—and the next moment I was feeling my way down a hallway thick with smoke."

"You couldn't get to your husband, or the duke and duchess?"

"No," said Mrs. Worth, shaking her head. "There was a wall of fire between us. My only thought was to save the children."

Nicole could see the flames and smell the smoke. She could feel the fear of being burned alive, and it took a great deal of effort to speak normally.

"How did the fire start?" asked Nicole.

"We were never sure. I think it was the kitchen stove, but others said it started from a candle. There was even a rumor that someone in his cups had fallen asleep while smoking. The building burned to the ground, so there was nothing left to tell us anything." Her words drifted off and she was silent for some time, lost in her thoughts.

Nicole sat rigid in the chair. She was reliving that night, and what had followed, with Mrs. Worth. She was seeing what had happened over thirty years ago, seeing the truth behind the lies that Mrs. Worth had woven over the years, and was paralyzed with the knowledge.

Nicole pulled herself from the nightmare and glanced at the small watch pinned to her spencer. "I've stayed far too long. You must still be fatigued after your trip."

Mrs. Worth was suspicious of her solicitude. "You never told me why you really came here today."

Nicole rose, gathering her reticule and gloves. "Yes, I did.

You just don't believe me. I'm glad we had this chat—I think I understand you better for it."

Mrs. Worth stared at the door long after Nicole had disappeared though it, wondering what she meant, and why a sense of foreboding had settled in her breast.

Sixteen

Nicole was in her room, dressing for the evening. When she had returned home from visiting Mrs. Worth earlier in the day, Jordan was gone, leaving a message that he would be back in time to accompany her to the Carringtons' soiree.

Other than spending time with Philip, she had kept to herself for most of the day. What she had learned from Mrs. Worth lay heavy on her heart. When revealed, the knowledge she had acquired would drastically change her life and the lives of those around her. She attempted to picture the consequences, but her talent failed her. She did not need to look into the future to know that the outcome could ruin more than one life and would change the future of generations to come.

If it hadn't been for Philip, and her desire for her son to know his father, she would never have discovered Mrs. Worth's secret.

She and Jordan had lost seven years together, and Jordan had missed the first six years of his son's life, because of Mrs. Worth's devious schemes. A shiver ran through her when she thought how close they had come to losing one another forever because of one selfish woman. She vowed to complete their reconciliation when all this was over, if that was what Jordan desired.

She knew, almost to a certainty, that what she had seen was true; but with the fate of so many lives resting on it, she needed to verify one last detail in order to confirm her suspicions. She would do that when she returned home this evening. Then the die would be cast.

Betsy finished arranging red rosebuds in Nicole's hair. At her maid's urging, she stood while Betsy slipped the ball gown over her head. It was crimson in color, with a low decolletage and tiny sleeves, made especially to be worn with her mother's rubies.

She sat before her mirror again while Betsy fastened the necklace. Then she attached the earrings, slipped on her gloves, and clasped the bracelet around her wrist. She looked every inch the wife of a prosperous gentleman—perhaps even as imposing as a duchess, she thought, smiling at her whimsy.

"I'm as ready as I'll ever be," she said, more to herself than to her maid. Accepting the red shawl, shot through with gold thread, she went downstairs to meet her husband.

"I didn't think it possible, but you are more beautiful than ever this evening," said Jordan when they returned home. "But then I've already told you that, haven't I?"

"Yes, but I never tire of hearing it," Nicole replied, lifting her skirt to climb the stairs.

Sitting up all night with Charles and Drew had ruined Jordan's plan to spend the previous evening with Nicole. Yesterday, in the library, she had seemed just as willing as he was to complete their reunion. He wondered whether the fire still burned within her as it did him. "It seems a shame to end such a wonderful evening."

"Umm," was her only answer.

"I don't suppose you would care to check my wound or hold my hand tonight?" he teased as they reached the upper hall.

She glanced up at him through dark lashes. "I think Willis's service will be quite adequate this evening."

"Not to hold my hand," he objected strenuously.

"Perhaps he'll give you an affectionate pat on the shoulder," she remarked, opening her door and slipping inside. His muffled laugh sounded through the door as she leaned back against it, praying for enough nerve to do what she must this evening.

Nicole removed her jewelry, giving Jordan a few minutes in his room with Willis. She moved quietly to the door that connected their rooms and turned the key, unlocking it for the first time since she had returned.

It was hard not to be buried in memories of past times when the door between their bedrooms had never been locked. But this was no time for reminiscing, thought Nicole, or the future might be lost.

Jordan had removed his coat and cravat and was in his shirt-sleeves. His glance was startled as he first caught sight of her in the shadows, then warmed as she moved farther into the light. He had planned on knocking on the connecting door himself as soon as Willis was gone, but she had beaten him to it.

"That will be all, Willis," he said without removing his gaze from Nicole. The valet nodded and left the room.

"Are you here to hold my hand?" Jordan asked, a smile tugging at the corner of his lips.

"No," she said, reaching his side.

"To see if my wound is healing properly?"

Nicole kept her gaze lowered. Why not? It would be one way to confirm her suspicions, she realized. "Yes," she said, glancing upward. "Would you remove your shirt, please?"

Jordan barely restrained his laughter at her politeness in such a situation and quickly shed his shirt.

"Come closer to the light," she said, tugging at his arm. "Now turn around."

He stood with his back to her, not knowing what to expect next. "It's my side that was hurt," he reminded her.

"Shush."

His body responded as she ran her hands over his back. His flesh burned beneath her touch, and he yearned to feel her body next to his.

"It's just as I remembered," she murmured.

"What is?" he asked, desire thickening his voice.

"Your . . . ah . . . that is . . . your wound. Yes, your wound is just as I remembered," she stammered.

"How can you tell? You haven't looked at it."

"No. I did, and it looks fine," she said, backing toward the door.

"Where are you going?" He turned, his arm snaking out to grab her wrist and pull her close.

"Ah. To my room. It's late, and we should be in bed."

"My exact thoughts," he said, his mouth crushing hers in a manner that left no doubt as to what was in his mind.

"No, I mean we should each be in our separate beds," she objected breathlessly, reluctantly pulling from his grasp.

"My God, woman, what are you doing to me?" he growled.

"Jordan, I'm sorry. I didn't mean for this to happen. Well, I did, but not now. You must understand—I don't want any doubts between us."

"There's no doubt in *my* mind," he said, advancing a step.

"And none in mine about this," she said, indicating the large bed. "But there's more to this than this," she babbled, motioning toward the inviting linens once again.

"Not right now, there isn't." He took another step.

"But you may regret this later when you hear what I have to say."

"I'll take my chances."

"I can't. I can't make love to you again, only to lose you forever. Please, try to understand," she pleaded.

"How can I when you're spouting nonsense?"

"Then be patient. Let me handle this in my own way." She moved swiftly to the door and closed it between them, turning the key in the lock.

"Nicole," she heard him roar in frustration. "Nicole, come back here."

The day had arrived and Nicole prayed for the courage to face what was to come.

Jordan was still brooding about her treatment of him the night before, but he had nevertheless agreed to accompany her to his cousin Robert's home. The ride was silent and Jordan stayed to his side of the carriage. Nicole wondered whether he would be riding home with her on the return trip.

She had sent a note to Elizabeth, asking that she, Robert, and Mrs. Worth be available to see them in private that afternoon. A return note had confirmed that the time was agreeable and that they were looking forward to the visit. Nicole had no doubt that Elizabeth would regret her words before the day was out.

Nicole sighed and stared at the passing scene without seeing it. After today, she might lose everything again. Only this time it could also include her son.

"I'll have tea brought in," said Elizabeth as soon as they had settled themselves in the drawing room.

"Perhaps you should wait," said Nicole. "This isn't entirely a social visit. I have something to say that is private."

"Wait in the hall," Robert said to Maude, who, as usual, had accompanied Mrs. Worth. They were silent until the woman closed the door behind her.

"Now what is this all about?" asked Robert, a worried frown creasing his forehead.

"I am as much in the dark as you are, cousin," said Jordan, looking toward Nicole.

"I have something to reveal today that is going to be extremely upsetting to everyone. I ask you to listen to everything I have to say before you make any judgements."

"You're frightening me," said Elizabeth.

"I don't mean to. I started out merely to discover why my marriage to Jordan was so unwelcome to his mother."

Mrs. Worth jerked upright in her chair, staring at Nicole with piercing eyes.

"I soon determined that the reason went far deeper than simple dislike."

"What is the point?" said Jordan, uncomfortable that she had brought his mother's dislike out in such an open fashion.

"There's something I must ask Mrs. Worth first," said Nicole, meeting Agatha's gaze. "I'd like you to describe the fire that killed the late Duke and Duchess of Weston and your husband."

Mrs. Worth gave a gasp and turned pale, collapsing into the chair.

"There's no need to put her through this," protested Jordan, going to Mrs. Worth's side and taking her hand.

"There's every need," declared Nicole, keeping a strong hold on her crumbling courage in face of Jordan's indignation. "I'm convinced that the reason behind our ruined marriage originated at that fire over thirty years ago. Our future, if we have one, depends on it," she stated, willing him to help her.

"Don't believe her," Mrs. Worth said weakly.

Jordan's gaze shifted back and forth between the two women who had played such a large part in his life. Once before, he had listened to his mother and had lost his wife and child for seven years. He craved a real marriage with Nicole and, if there was a reason why his mother was determined to keep them apart, then he should hear it.

Drawing a chair next to Mrs. Worth's, he spoke to her in a consoling voice. "I know it's upsetting for you to talk about the fire, but will you try?"

Mrs. Worth closed her eyes.

"Have Maude come in and see to Aunt Agatha," said Robert, sending Elizabeth scampering to the door.

Maude rushed to Mrs. Worth's side and waved a small bottle of sal volatile beneath her nose until the older woman pushed it aside.

Mrs. Worth could think of no substantial reason not to repeat the story. She had done so many times before, and to refuse might cause Jordan to wonder if she was hiding something after all.

"I will do my best, if that is what you wish," she said. Maude stood beside her, holding a glass of cool water and the sal volatile in case it was called for. Speaking slowly, Mrs. Worth began her story, halting every so often to take a sip of water.

The tale was the same that Nicole had heard before. Francis, the Duke of Weston, and his wife, Susan, the Duchess, along with his brother, Richard Worth, and Agatha had embarked on an overnight trip from the duke's country home to London. Both couples had small babes, with only a few weeks separating the two boys. They made their usual stop at the Grouse and Claret, an inn that had grown accustomed to meeting the duke's needs.

They had dinner and, anticipating an early start the next morning, retired to their rooms. Agatha had been asleep for some time when the maid had awakened her. Her son was teething and had been fretting for hours. The maid thought his mother might have a soothing effect on the baby.

Agatha joined her in the babies' room, where they stayed for approximately a half hour before they smelled the smoke. Looking into the corridor, Mrs. Worth saw flames at one end of the hall. She attempted to reach her husband, and Francis and Susan, but the way was blocked. She and the maid each grabbed a child and made their way down the smoke-filled hall until they reached the back stairs.

There were people outside from the small village and some of the other guests from the inn who had escaped, but Richard, Francis, and Susan had perished in the fire.

"I've heard nothing that bears on your marriage," said Robert to Nicole.

"Nor have I," agreed Jordan, his hope for their reconciliation dimming.

Nicole would not let the men's obvious disapproval deter her. She was determined to expose the truth. "Mrs. Worth and I both know there is more to the story, don't we?"

Mrs. Worth studied her adversary, sizing up her chances at escape without revealing the past she had taken such care to hide.

Nicole met her gaze with a confidence that sent a shiver

through the older woman. Without breaking their stare, Nicole held up a red leather book.

"If you don't believe I know, this is Susan's diary. It contains proof of what you did."

Mrs. Worth wavered; the chit could be lying. She maintained her silence, forgetting for the moment that Nicole did not need to hear her speak.

"I'm not lying," Nicole said, answering her thoughts. "You can tell this in your own way, or I'll tell it in mine."

Mrs. Worth's face twisted into a bitter mask. "I had always been jealous of Susan," she admitted. "When we were girls, she was always prettier and did everything better than I could. My dream was to best her in just one thing, but it never happened.

"We both came out in the same Season, and Susan was acclaimed a diamond of the first water. I watched the men flock around her, and I felt the old jealousy revive.

"I saw a young man," she said, her eyes taking on a far-off look. "He was everything I wanted—handsome, courtly, titled. He always had time to speak to me, and without even knowing it, he stole my heart."

She cleared her throat and took another sip of water.

"His name was Francis Worth, the future Duke of Weston." Her revelation drew astonished looks from everyone in the room except Nicole.

"Of course, he was merely being courteous. His real interest lay in Susan, and before the Season was out he made an offer which she accepted.

"With Susan affianced to Francis, Richard and I were increasingly thrown together. When Richard offered for me, I agreed. At that point, it made no difference to me whom I wed and, as Richard's wife, I would at least remain in Francis's life."

Jordan, Robert, and Elizabeth were mesmerized by Mrs. Worth's recital. Nicole was relieved that so far what she had seen had been correct.

"I was thrilled when I found I was increasing. At last, I was going to best Susan. But my euphoria was short-lived. Susan was also expecting a child, and we gave birth only weeks apart. Of course, Susan's son was heir to a dukedom, and garnered the most attention."

Mrs. Worth closed her eyes. Maude held the glass to her lips, then waved the small bottle in front of her face.

"Are you satisfied?" asked Jordan, looking at his wife. "What good has it done to drag this admission from my mother? I see no point, except to embarrass her. Can we go home now and leave her in peace?"

"This is about more than a young woman's jealousy," replied Nicole. "The story isn't finished yet, is it, Mrs. Worth?"

Mrs. Worth opened her eyes and stared at Nicole. "Why are you doing this to me? Stay with Jordan—I won't interfere again," she bargained.

Jordan was confused at her words. "What do you mean?" he asked.

Both women ignored him as if he had never said a word. There was no one in the room for them but one another. A battle of wills was being fought, and Nicole was determined to win.

Nicole's gaze never wavered from the older woman's face. "I have seen the truth with my own eyes," said Nicole.

Mrs. Worth scoffed. "More of your fortune-telling? Who will believe you?"

Nicole held up the red leather book again. "I have also read the truth, and it's here for anyone to see."

Mrs. Worth blanched.

"I'll give you one more chance to tell it your way. One chance to reveal the secret you've been guarding all these years. It was to blame for driving me away from my home and husband, it forced me to have a child alone, and it kept that child from his father for over six years.

"You conspired with Melanie Grayson, and who knows how many others, to drive me from London again to keep your secret hidden. And finally, when all else failed, you hired someone to kill me."

Nicole ignored the sounds of shock from the others. "All this for your secret, your precious secret. Has it been worth the lives ruined, the years wasted, Agatha? Only to have it come out anyway?"

Agatha remained stubbornly silent. She could not give up what she had concealed for so long.

"Tell them," demanded Nicole, her voice rising. "For the first time in your life, tell them the truth. Tell them it is Jordan, not Robert, who is the real Duke of Weston."

Her words died in an unearthly silence that fell over the room. Jordan and Robert stared at one another, too shocked to speak. Mrs. Worth looked at Nicole, thinking to deny her accusations.

"Susan wrote of her baby," Nicole said, indicating the diary. "She describes the small birthmark that is on his back. I know without a doubt that Jordan carries that mark. Unless Robert has an exact mark, there is no denying the truth any longer. You are Robert's mother, not Jordan's."

Mrs. Worth turned into an old woman before their eyes. She waved away the glass of water that her abigail offered her.

"It was after the fire," she said in a frail voice. "We had returned to London, to this house." She looked around the room, admiring it even in defeat. "I saw what Susan's baby had inherited and knew, even in death, that she had won again. It was then I realized that I had the power to right all the injustice I had felt over the years.

"The babies were nearly identical—the Worth men have always been very similar in looks. I was the only one left who could absolutely tell them apart. So I switched them."

Jordan rose and walked to the fireplace, his back to the room as he stared down into the empty grate. Robert dropped his face into his hands; Elizabeth came to his side, resting her hand on his shoulder.

Nicole wished she could comfort Jordan, but the confession was not yet over. And when it was, when she had forced all of them to face the truth, he might never want to see her, let alone feel her touch again.

"I won't apologize," said Mrs. Worth, a trace of her spirit rising to the top. "For once, Susan would not have her way. My son would be duke, not hers. My grandchildren would inherit, not Susan's."

Mrs. Worth looked at Robert. "I had planned on telling you my secret when the time was right," she said. "I could not openly claim you as my son, but we would know the truth. We would live in luxury the rest of our lives. Your children would inherit the title and wealth that should have been ours before Susan interfered."

Robert did not reply. Everyone in the room, except for Mrs. Worth, had been struck dumb.

She glanced at Jordan, whose back was still turned to the group. "It was difficult to act motherly toward Susan's child, so I left his care and upbringing to the nursemaids. He grew up with no idea that he was not in his rightful place.

"Everything went smoothly until you came into the picture," she said to Nicole. "I had known your mother, and had heard the stories about the women in her family having what they called second sight. It seemed like taradiddle to me, but I could leave nothing to chance. I did everything I could to discourage Jordan from offering for you, but he was too besotted to listen. Nothing else would do but that you should wed."

From the corner of her eye, Nicole could see that Jordan had turned and was paying close attention to Mrs. Worth once again.

"I began a campaign to turn Jordan against you," she admitted, still speaking to Nicole. "And it worked. You disappeared and, except for Jordan running all over the country searching for you, life returned to normal.

"Eventually, Jordan found someone else to take your place. I knew Melanie Grayson—she offered no threat to me. She was grateful when I arranged for her to be thrown together with Jordan so often. He was lonely, and wanted a family so badly he never suspected a thing. I knew that he still held this perfect ideal of you in his mind, but I convinced him that after seven years he could not expect you to return and that if he wanted children, he shouldn't wait."

Nicole could not look at her husband. She could not bear to see the disillusionment and betrayal he no doubt felt.

"Then you returned," Mrs. Worth spat out. "And everything I had planned was in jeopardy again. I attempted to drive you from our lives a second time, but it didn't work. You were no longer a naive young girl who would play the martyr for love. And yes, Fitzpatrick helped me arrange the attempt on your life, but to my everlasting sorrow it also failed. Now everything is ruined, all because of you." Her words drifted off and she closed her eyes.

Jordan drew close to the group again, his gaze locking with Robert's. Both were speechless at Mrs. Worth's revelation, and they were grappling with the fact that for thirty-two years they had lived lives that were not theirs.

Nicole wanted to stop. There was just so much that a person could absorb, and she felt that the people in the room had already reached that point. But the time might not come again. Mrs. Worth could rally between now and tomorrow and have the strength to deny the rest of what had happened. Nicole had to finish what she had begun.

"There is one more thing," she said softly, aware of the incredulous expressions on Jordan's and Robert's faces. "The fire was not an accident, was it?" asked Nicole. "It was deliberately set."

"You've gone too far," said Jordan, his face going as pale as Mrs. Worth's.

"It can't be," said Robert, reaching out for Elizabeth.

Mrs. Worth moaned and covered her face with her hands. Maude bent over the woman, waving the sal volatile in front of her. "No. No. I swear to you, I didn't set the fire. I was in the boys' room when it started. The inn was old," said Mrs. Worth. "It went up too fast to save anyone."

"You and the maid escaped with the babies," Nicole reminded her.

"Only because we were awake. Otherwise, we would have met the same fate."

"Think back," said Nicole, concentrating on the woman before her. "See if you can remember what happened that night."

Nicole was caught up in the events of the fire. "I can see the fire," she said. "I can smell the smoke and feel the heat of the flames. I can hear the cries for help.

"But before," she demanded of her powers. "What happened before? There's a woman," she continued after a moment. "A woman in a white night rail and cap. She's setting a candle on the floor, lighting it, piling some sort of rags, maybe handkerchiefs, around it. I smell oil. She leaves it there.

"It's later now, much later. She's running down a flight of stairs, carrying a baby. The ground is cold beneath her feet when she reaches outside. She looks back once she is safe. The inn is a giant torch against the night sky. She smiles."

"I never wore a cap. Richard didn't like them," Mrs. Worth mumbled. "I only escaped because the maid asked for my help. We were together when we smelled smoke. After we saw we couldn't help anyone, we each took a child and escaped to safety. I had no opportunity to start a fire," she protested. "Isn't that right?" she asked in a bemused fashion, turning to the woman standing by her side. "You were there, Maude. Surely you remember as well as I."

Nicole closed her eyes again for a moment. When she opened them, she shifted her gaze to Maude, who was still holding a glass of water in a steady hand.

"I was mistaken, wasn't I? It was you, not Mrs. Worth, who set the fire."

"Madam saved my life," said Maude. "She took me off the streets and gave me a chance to live a decent life. I saw how much pain Miss Susan caused her. I thought if we could be rid of her, madam would be happy."

"And you tried it a second time, didn't you? I was a threat to Mrs. Worth—she had been upset ever since I had returned. So you left a candle burning in the bedroom where you were assisting Miss Grayson. If it had worked, not only would you have done away with me, but with Jordan, and there would have been no one left to question whether Robert was the legitimate heir."

Maude's silence condemned her.

"Everything is such a mess," murmured Jordan when they were on their way home. He and Robert had agreed to meet the next day, after they had fully absorbed the changes that must inevitably take place in their lives.

"But when everything is settled, you will be where you rightfully belong. You will have your father's name and inheritance— you will be Duke of Weston, as he would have wanted."

"Is that why you did this?" Jordan demanded, anger finally breaking though his control. "For a title and a fortune? I have fortune enough as it is. There was no need to tear my family apart just to satisfy your desire to be a duchess."

"That wasn't my reason at all," she attempted to explain.

"But that will be the result," he shot back. "I hope you'll be happy, for the title will be an empty one for you. I will not give you the pleasure of having a duke by your side except when absolutely necessary."

The remainder of the ride was silent, the coach so thick with emotion that Nicole found it difficult to breathe. When they arrived home, Jordan left her immediately. She did not see him for the rest of the day.

Jordan was gone before she came downstairs the next morning and he had left no word of when he might return. Nicole had watched her marriage crumble once before. She had no need to live through the destruction of their relationship again.

Ordering Betsy to pack their trunks, Nicole sat down and wrote a letter to Jordan. She would not leave him speculating as to her destination when their son was involved. She also would not run away completely again. Everything had not changed with Mrs. Worth's confession. She still wanted Philip to grow up knowing his father. She wanted him to inherit not only the title, but the pride of his family. He couldn't achieve that living in a country village with her and Betsy.

Nicole wrote that she knew Jordan would have little time to spend with Philip over the next weeks. Therefore, she and Philip were retiring to the country estate while Jordan dealt with his affairs. Nicole decided to let Jordan decide if and when he wanted to see them again. She wrote that they would stay in the country until he requested their return.

Nicole sealed the letter, doubtful that she would ever receive such a message from him.

It was six weeks before a black traveling coach, bearing the ducal crest, arrived at Nicole's front door.

"I didn't expect to see you so soon," she said, her heart beating a little faster despite her attempt to control it.

He stood staring at her for so long, she wondered if he would ever answer. "I had to make sure you were here," he finally said.

"I told you before, I've finished with running."

"I had to see for myself. Nicole, I . . ."

Nicole interrupted him. She did not want to enter into a conversation regarding their future as soon as he arrived. She needed time to prepare herself.

"Even if I wanted to leave, I'm afraid Philip would refuse to abandon his pony."

"Does he like it then?"

"He is completely mad about the little fellow. I've hardly been able to separate them since you sent it to him."

"Just like his father," said Jordan.

"He's been asking about you."

Jordan looked pleased. "Has he?"

"He's been wanting to show you how well he rides. He'll be happy that you're here."

"I had hoped to have a private conversation with you first. There is something I must say that has already waited too long."

Nicole did not like to admit that she was a coward, but she could not bear to have Jordan condemn her as soon as he stepped through the door. She would be better prepared to hear whatever he had to say later.

"Philip is more important than we are right now. What you have to say can wait until after dinner, can't it?"

Jordan appeared disappointed, but did not insist. "It's waited this long, I suppose a few more hours won't make that much difference," he said. "Where is Philip?"

"He's in the nursery with Betsy," answered Nicole.

"I'm glad it's finally been put to use," he said, mounting the stairs two at a time.

By the time Jordan had reunited with his son and removed the dust of travel, dinner was running later than usual. Nicole was surprised at the ease with which they conversed, sharing the *on-dits* that had occurred since her departure from London.

He told her of Miss Grayson's betrothal to the Honorable William Langford, the second son of Viscount Langford. Langford could afford to keep Melanie in comfort, but Mr. Grayson would be forced to pay off his vowels without any help from his son-in-law.

Jordan related all this without any sign of distress, and Nicole began to believe that he was finally over and done with his preoccupation with Miss Grayson.

Then he disclosed the details of the agreement he and Robert had reached in returning the title and entailment to Jordan.

"I left it to Robert to decide what to do with his mother and Maude. I hope you don't disapprove," he said.

"That is something for you and Robert to deal with," she answered shortly.

"But her actions almost killed you."

"It is all over now," she replied. "I would like to forget it."

"Then we shall." He smiled and saluted her with his wineglass.

Jordan's resentment seemed to have disappeared; however, that did not insure they would resume their life as a married couple.

She should not complain, she thought. Many women lived with far less than she had. As long as Jordan took an interest in their son, she would learn to be satisfied.

Jordan joined Nicole in the drawing room after dinner. He poured himself a snifter of brandy and settled on the settee next to her. The silence had almost become awkward when he finally spoke.

"I want to apologize for what I said the last time we spoke," he said, staring into the amber liquid as he swirled it in the glass.

Nicole set her embroidery aside and gave him her full attention.

"I had just lost my mother, and my identity. It's a confusing experience to find that you're not who you thought yourself to be your entire life," he explained.

"I can only imagine how you feel."

"After I calmed down, I realized you didn't expose my mo— my aunt for your own benefit. I don't think you even did it wholly for me," he said, looking at her. "It would be impossible for you to care for a man who had such little faith in you, and who drove you from your home when you were increasing."

"You didn't know."

"I should have," he said. "That is a failure for which I'll never forgive myself."

"Jordan . . ."

"No, let me finish. I finally understood that there's only one reason you would return and do what you did. And that is for Philip. When I realized that, I was thankful. I've never questioned that Philip is my son, no matter who tried to make me think differently. I want him to have everything that is his due. Without you, that would not be."

Jordan reached for her hand and lifted it to his lips, pressing a kiss against the warmth of her skin. "Thank you for bearing my son and raising him in such a manner that makes me extremely proud."

He seemed reluctant to release her hand, and when he did, he rose and took a few paces away. Returning, he pulled her to her feet. Placing her hands flat against his chest and covering them with his own, he spoke again. "I'm deeply sorry for the way I've treated you, Nicole. God, I wish I could change it," he said, resting his forehead against hers and closing his eyes. "I can only promise," he said, opening his eyes and looking deep into hers, "that I'll never be skeptical or ridicule you again. You can live anywhere you desire, have anything you want, and if you don't wish to see me again, then I will honor that request."

Jordan's speech was almost all that Nicole could have craved, but there was one question he had not yet answered. "Do you continue to hold me in disdain because of my ability?" she asked.

"I have never done so. I've always loved you," he said. "I allowed my . . . my aunt to convince me you were playing childish games and doing our family harm, but I never stopped loving you. When you left, I thought I would go mad. Then when I couldn't find you, I felt my life was over. Even when I was with Melanie, I was merely going through the motions. I was doing what was expected of me and hoping that a family would bring me to life again, all the time realizing that no one could do that but you."

"You must realize by now that I'm not the same as I was."

"No, you are better," he said with a small smile.

She was tempted to accept him without further conversation, but it was important for both of them that he understand her position. "I won't renounce my gift, no matter how much I embarrass you."

Jordan smiled and pulled her closer. "I wouldn't have it any other way. In fact, I intend to take your businessman's advice and use it for my benefit."

"Then I shall inform my *modiste* to direct my bills to you," she teased.

"I would be extremely pleased to pay for your gowns again. But, be warned, I expect all of my investments to be successful from now on."

"You should remember, my gift isn't always accurate. I'm afraid Mr. Grenville didn't mention those instances."

He guided her arms around his neck. "Now's the devil of a time to tell me," he murmured.

"If it were in my power," he said, his voice once again serious, "I would begin our life together anew. I would not make the mistakes I did before. I would believe in you, and cherish your love as it should be cherished."

Nicole threaded her fingers into the hair at the nape of his neck, pulling his head down toward hers.

"I would also like to begin anew," she admitted.

"Do you see anything promising in our future?" he asked, placing a delicate kiss on the beauty mark at the corner of her lips.

"A long, loving life, if you are sincere in what you say."

"I am," he replied, his lips hovering over hers. "And do you see more children?"

"You are old enough to know that it takes something more substantial than a vision to make a family."

"Then shall we deal with reality tonight, my lady?"

"I would be pleased to, my lord," she managed to utter before his lips claimed hers.

If you would like to read the first of the second-sight books, ask for *A Gifted Lady*. Then follow the stories of some characters from *A Gifted Lady* into *Heart's Deceit*, both by Alana Clayton from Zebra Books.

WATCH FOR THESE REGENCY ROMANCES

ROMANCE FROM ROSANNE BITTNER

CARESS   (0-8217-3791-0, $5.99)

FULL CIRCLE   (0-8217-4711-8, $5.99)

SHAMELESS   (0-8217-4056-3, $5.99)

SIOUX SPLENDOR   (0-8217-5157-3, $4.99)

UNFORGETTABLE   (0-8217-4423-2, $5.50)

TEXAS EMBRACE   (0-8217-5625-7, $5.99)

UNTIL TOMORROW   (0-8217-5064-X, $5.99)